PENGUIN B

NANCY AS

Derek Marlowe was born in London in 1938. He was sent down from London University for a controversial article in his college magazine, and for a while took up acting. In 1960 he wrote a play, *The Seven Who Were Hanged*, which was performed at the Edinburgh Festival and then transferred to the Royal Court as *The Scarecrow* in 1961. This won the Foyle Award for the Best New Play of that year. In 1962 he adapted *Lower Depths* for the Royal Shakespeare Company. Two years later he went to Berlin on a Ford Foundation Grant and wrote two plays which were performed there and at the Questors Theatre. He also won an American 'Emmy' for the television series, *The Search for the Nile*. In 1965 he wrote *A Dandy in Aspic*, which achieved immediate success. It has been published in fifteen countries and made into a film (with Laurence Harvey and Mia Farrow) for which he wrote the screenplay. His other novels include *The Memoirs of a Venus Lackey* (1968), *A Single Summer With L.B.* (1969), *Echoes of Celandine* (1970; reissued and filmed as *The Disappearance*), *Do You Remember England?* (1972), *Somebody's Sister* (1974) and *Nightshade* (1976). His recent novel, *The Rich Boy from Chicago*, is shortly to be published in Penguins.

Nancy Astor

THE LADY FROM VIRGINIA

Derek Marlowe

Penguin Books

Penguin Books Ltd, Harmondsworth, Middlesex, England
Penguin Books, 625 Madison Avenue, New York, New York 10022, U.S.A.
Penguin Books Australia Ltd, Ringwood, Victoria, Australia
Penguin Books Canada Ltd, 2801 John Street, Markham, Ontario, Canada L3R 1B4
Penguin Books (N.Z.) Ltd, 182-190 Wairau Road, Auckland 10, New Zealand

First published 1982
Published simultaneously by Weidenfeld and Nicolson Ltd

Reproduced, printed and bound in Great Britain by
Hazell Watson & Viney Ltd, Aylesbury, Bucks

CONTENTS

AUTHOR'S NOTE

This book is not intended to be an authoritative biography of Nancy Astor. There are too many of those on the bookshelves if the reader cares to find them. Instead I have attempted to write a novel inspired by and based on a television series I wrote for the BBC. Its aim, as in the television series, is a study of the character and private life of Nancy Astor from her birth in Danville, Virginia, concentrating on her relationship with the key figures in her life: her father, Chillie Langhorne; her sisters Phyllis and Irene (known to the world as 'The Gibson Girl'); her first husband, Robert Gould Shaw; her second husband, Waldorf Astor; and four men, less familiar perhaps in the history of Nancy Astor, but no less significant: Archdeacon Frederick Neve, Lord Revelstoke, Lord Lothian and, most important of all, her eldest son, Bobbie Shaw.

Apart from the invaluable help of the Astor Archives, the biographies of John Grigg, Elizabeth Langhorne and Christopher Sykes, the memoirs of Michael Astor and Alice Winn, and many private letters and personal reminiscences, I must also acknowledge the help and encouragement of the following, all of whom contributed in giving me a fresh insight into the complex character who is the subject of this book: the Hon. David Astor, the late the Hon. Michael Astor, the Hon. Sir John Astor, Sir Edward Ford, Mrs Nancy Lancaster, Mark Bonham Carter, Reginald Winn, Alice Winn, Michael Brand, Mr and Mrs Francis Gould Shaw, Phyllis Langhorne Draper, Mrs Margaret Beamiss, Mr and Mrs Carter of Redlands, Virginia, Mr Arthur Schmidt, William Douglas-Home, Michael Holroyd, Lady Veronica Maclean, Lord and Lady Gage, the Reverend Douglas Pitt, Lady Virginia Ford, and the Valentine Museum of Richmond, Virginia.

This book is dedicated to Philip Hinchcliffe, producer of the television drama series *Nancy Astor*.

ONE

·

The Langhornes of Virginia

The parade assembled just before dawn outside the Tobacco Exchange at Shockoe Slip, the veterans from Richmond arriving first. The temperature was lower than expected as the wind changed course, bringing the cold Atlantic air into Virginia so that fires were lit on the cobblestones and the men in their grey uniforms huddled into groups, staring at the flames. By seven o'clock, as the first church bells were heard, Jahnke's Lake had begun to freeze over. By eight o'clock more wagons and horses had entered the city, bringing men from as far away as Norfolk and Lynchburg and Arlington, many wearing black armbands in memory of dead brothers, dead sons, killed on battlefields where sheep now grazed. It had been twenty-five years since the last shot had been fired in the War between the States, but the echo still lingered.

In May of this year, 1890, a monument to Robert E. Lee had been unveiled in the centre of Richmond, an equestrian statue on a granite pedestal as tall as an oak tree. Its silhouette could now be seen on the skyline, and the wagons and

1

buckboards halted as the occupants removed their hats in remembrance of the greatest Virginian of them all.

By nine o'clock the parade was ready to begin its journey. More than two hundred men, some on horseback, but the majority standing before the banners of their regiments as the crowds began to gather along the boardwalk dressed in their best clothes. At the head of the procession the military band waited silently for the signal; before them a riderless horse carried the boots of a dead soldier reversed in the stirrups. And before that, standing alone, a boy of twelve was holding the Confederate flag, the wind snapping the cloth above his head. Then a baton was raised and the first notes of the Southern anthem were heard.

The men began to move, slowly at first as they adjusted to an even pace, then faster as they lengthened their stride into a march and children moved out of the shadows to run alongside. And then, as one, the men began to sing, their voices loud and defiant, as they had sung before Gettysburg and Manassas, and before Richmond itself had been burnt to the ground. In the windows of the frame houses along the street could be seen the faces of women, watching silently for a moment before turning away, and drawing the curtains in order to weep in the privacy of darkness.

On this same Sunday morning, one mile away across the James River, families from the area around Grace Street were worshipping God, as was their custom twice a week, in the small Episcopalian church of St John. Most of the congregation knew each other; their children had grown up together and some had even linked family to family by marriage. They were respectable, devout, worked hard when work existed, and recognized that each in his own way had lost not only relatives because of the War, but also land and property and, in many cases, everything they had except their pride. They no longer lived on plantations, had servants, bred horses or raised cattle; they had surrendered that to the North during the years of Reconstruction. They had also surrendered the right to choose where they should live. Homes were abandoned, possessions sold as necessity drove them from city to city in pursuit of the privilege of earning a means to live. To the Langhornes of Danville, Virginia, it was not easily granted.

'The lesson for today is taken from Ecclesiastes, Book Twelve, Verse One. "Remember now thy Creator in the days of thy youth, while the evil days come not, nor the years draw nigh, when thou shalt say, I have no pleasure in them."'

It was said that Nanaire Langhorne, *née* Nancy Witcher Keene, had been the most beautiful child born south of the Blue Ridge Mountains. Certainly, looking at her now as she sat in the darkened church listening to the preacher, it would have been difficult to question that statement. The skin was fair, almost translucent, so that the bones of the nose and cheeks seemed almost too fragile to be touched; the hair was blonde, curled into a bun over the nape of her neck, fine hair that seemed to shiver in the light from the narrow windows. The mouth was wide, the lips full but curving downwards, suggesting a melancholy in her character that was not unattractive. But it was the eyes that enchanted; wide, deep-set, pale azure in colour, an inheritance from her Irish ancestors. In photographs they gazed at the camera with the candour of intimacy. In reality they revealed something more, a profound sadness that she could not disguise. For Nanaire Langhorne was no longer a child but a woman who married

3

at seventeen as enemy soldiers marched into Virginia, gave birth to eleven children and buried three of them before they could even walk. The memory of the dead babies haunted her constantly, and when the grief became unbearable she would return to their graves, travelling alone for days and nights to stand there amid the weeds. It was probable, as she sat with her eight surviving children, that she was thinking of them then.

'While the sun, or the light, or the moon or the stars, be not darkened, nor the clouds return after the rain.'

The aisle seat to the left of Nanaire was empty, the missal in its rack. It belonged to her husband, Chiswell Dabney Langhorne, and his absence did not go unnoticed. On her right was her youngest daughter, Nora, aged four, dressed in a sailor suit; bored by the sermon, she stared disconcertingly at an elderly spinster clutching a palm fan in her gloved hands. At a whispered word of admonition the child turned and slumped down in the pew as her eldest brother, Keene, took her hand. He winked at her, smiled and looked away. In Richmond, Keene Langhorne was already known to be wild, a loner with a touch of madness, creating fantasies for young girls. It was rumoured that he had once run away and lived with a travelling circus; it was also rumoured that he had shot a man dead, 'a nigger with the devil in him'. Both stories were never denied.

'In the day when the keepers of the house shall tremble and the strong men shall bow themselves, and the grinders cease before they are few, and those that look out of the windows be darkened.'

Next to Keene his sister Lizzie, in contrast to him, was plain, serious and utterly without charm, her sole eccentricity being her hats, extravagant cartwheels of velvet and lace under which she hid herself from the frivolities of the world. She was, at twenty-three, the eldest of the Langhorne daughters and the only one married, having decided that hats and children were all she ever wanted in life.

Understandably it was not towards her that the adoring eyes of the young men in the church turned and gazed, pink cheeks above tight white collars, defying the sanctity of the occasion in order to catch the attention of the tall girl on Lizzie's right. She was posing as if for a fashion plate, dimpled chin tilted, neck as smooth and pale as copy paper. It was not only her beauty – she had her mother's eyes, but revealing romance and passion rather than sadness; her mouth was that of a corner angel, and her hair long enough for her to lie full length upon – but the fact that the girl seemed to have a destiny that men wanted to share. She was the quintessential Southern belle, the most desired of them all. Men fell in love with her on sight and never forgot her; the beaux who courted her could not be counted on a string of pearls. In time, a few years, no more, her face, with the sleepy-lidded eyes beneath clouds of hair, would become immortal, and it seemed that the girl already knew it. She was simply biding her time being adored until it happened. Her name was Irene Langhorne but, like one of her younger sisters, her fame would be remembered by her married name. Irene, on this Sunday morning in Richmond, was just seventeen years of age.

'And the doors shall be shut in the streets, when the sound of grinding is low, and he shall rise up at the voice of the bird, and all the daughters of music shall be brought low.'

The two youngest Langhorne boys, Harry and Buck, sat side by side, bored by the service and thinking of the fish they would catch in a favourite creek. They stared around the church, seeking out distractions to pass the time, then Harry folded his arms and closed his eyes. Hidden in his pocket was a small hip flask full of bourbon.

Finally there were two more sisters, separated in age by a year and the closest of friends. The younger, Phyllis, was ten years old with soft brown hair and her father's features, a romantic dreamer who cried as easily as she giggled, every aunt's favourite niece, who was hugged and given candy and would rather die than live in a world without horses. The elder sister, at eleven, seemed at first glance to be the total opposite and in many respects that was true. Her hair was fair, not dark, and, though not as beautiful as her mother or Irene, the image lingered in the eyes and mouth, but not in the aquiline nose nor in the jaw which was too stubborn and strong. However, such details mattered little to her. She had, as yet, no vanity, considering all boys to be a bore and, being a girl amongst boys, even worse. Unconventional by nature, she had inherited her father's restlessness and 'Virginia grit' and the energy of all the Langhornes combined. She was known as 'Nannie' to her family, an affectionate corruption of the name she was christened on 19 May 1879: Nancy.

In the pulpit the preacher, his voice a hesitant drawl, continued with the sermon, but Nancy was not listening. Her attention was drawn to something else, the distant sound of drums and bugles and marching feet, indistinct at first as if it came from across the river.

'Phyll – listen.'

'What?'

'Listen!'

Slowly, as the parade drew nearer and cheering could be

heard and as the music grew louder, heads began to turn, ignoring the preacher as he struggled to attract their attention.

'D'you hear it, Phyll?' Nancy shouted, defying the glare from her mother. 'D'you hear it now?'

Phyllis nodded, smiling, tears already appearing in her eyes.

'They're playing *Dixie!*'

In a second-storey room in a hotel across the street from the church, four men were playing poker. In fact they had been playing poker for twelve hours, and were the sole survivors of a game that had begun early on Saturday night. They were now nearing a state of exhaustion, their eyes dead, tempers rising, as they sat in shirtsleeves, waistcoats unbuttoned, revealing the ponds of sweat under their arms. The blinds on the window were drawn, shutting out the daylight, and a single lamp burnt on the table amid the cigar stubs and empty bottles and cups of cold coffee. Above their heads a fan stirred lazily in the smoky, congested air.

'You win again, Chillie,' the dealer said wearily, pronouncing the name 'Shillie'.

The man he addressed made no reaction for a moment, then slowly removed a cigar from his mouth, spat a plug of tobacco accurately into a spittoon, and picked up the money, placing it on a pile next to him. He was a broad-shouldered man in his late forties, with the stocky build and ruddy skin of a farmer, but also with the alert eyes of a gambler and opportunist. He was a man who had clearly seen the worst of life and had survived, living on his wits and, if need be, his brawn. For that, at least, he was respected, and there were few men in Virginia who had failed to like him. He was considered a gentleman, despite his unorthodox ways of earning money, who welcomed anyone into his home, whether black or white except, of course, Yankees.

'Deal 'em again,' Chillie said quietly, parting his moustache with thumb and finger. 'We ain't finished yet.'

Although no one, apart from his wife, called him anything else but Chillie, his real name was Chiswell – Chiswell Dabney Langhorne.

The preacher had decided that there were times when the pride of Virginia took precedence over God, and had cut the service short as the parade approached the church. He stood now in the white wooden porch as the congregation hurried out, children scampering into the sunlight, with Nancy in the lead pulling Phyllis after her.

'Come on, Phyll, let's see who can scream loudest!'

'But, Nannie, Mama wants us to – '

'Great saints, Phyll, what's the matter with you? Come on – let 'em hear us.'

Behind them, the preacher smiled and turned towards Nanaire.

'I think the Lord will forgive Miss Nancy her enthusiasm on a day like this, Mrs Langhorne.'

'The *Lord* might, Reverend,' Nanaire replied, her face tense. She was suddenly nervous, as if hiding a guilty secret. On the steps below her she could see the upturned faces of four young men spit-licking their hair and jostling for position as from out of the church appeared Irene – white dress, white parasol, white gloves. Nanaire watched as her daughter immediately lidded her eyes, the lashes long, then

descended the steps towards her admirers, assuming that
natural ability for seeming to favour each in turn without
teasing, but simply by being herself.

'Miss Lang'n – may I call on you today?'

A brief look from Irene, neither encouraging nor dismissing, before walking on.

'Miss Langhorne?'

A second voice, more urgent. 'Miss Langhorne – do you
remember me? We met at the Richmond German.'

Irene hesitated and slowly turned her gaze full on to the
freckle-faced youth, looking directly into his eyes. 'But I
met so many people at the German,' she said, her voice soft
and lazy. 'I'd be hard put to remember them all.'

'But we *danced* together, Miss Langhorne.'

'Then I declare, you must have danced divinely,' Irene
replied, encouraging assignations before adding: 'because I
only remember those who don't.'

And then she was gone, the parasol raised, moving from
shadow into sunlight, towards yet another beau, another
heartbroken youth. From the top of a buckboard Nancy and
Phyllis, who had been watching, looked at each other, pulled
a face and then continued to yell at the parade.

Immediately their mother moved forward to reproach
them, then stopped and turned away. It didn't matter any
more. In a few hours they would be leaving Richmond.

'Good morning, Mrs Langhorne,' a neighbour said, a
spinster from Emporia. 'Chillie isn't with you, I see. Not ill,
is he?'

'No, Mrs Beaumont. Thank you kindly for your interest,
as always. But the reason Mr Langhorne is not here is because
he's working.'

'On the Lord's Day, Mrs Langhorne?'

Nanaire seized Nora by the hand and held it tight. 'Yes, Mrs Beaumont,' she said steadily. 'On the Lord's Day.'

'I'll take two.'

Chillie took the cards, glanced at them, then placed them face-down and waited. Poker was a precarious way to make a living for a man with a wife and eight children, and he knew it. Since the war he had worked as a nightwatchman, a tobacco auctioneer and a peddler of pianos, but each time employment was short-lived and Chillie was obliged to return once again to the card table. He was, however, an optimist by nature, having developed, like many Virginians, a Micawber attitude towards life. Despite everything, something was bound to turn up.

'You, Daniel?' the dealer asked, turning to the man on his left.

'One.'

A card was placed on the table.

'Andy?'

The fourth man, his face revealing defeat, sighed and stood up.

'I'm out,' he said.

Chillie narrowed his eyes and looked at him: 'Is that out for good or is that just out?'

'That's out *out*. Dammit, Chillie, I can't beat you.'

'You use the same deck as I do.'

Andy opened his mouth to reply, then turned away and slumped against the window, peering through the blinds at the street. 'I should've gone to church instead,' he murmured to no one in particular. There was a silence in the room until finally Daniel gestured to Chillie to play, but was ignored.

'Is my family out there?' Chillie asked, offering Andy a cigar.

'Well, that sure isn't *my* daughter who's doing all the hollering.'

'Chillie – are you playing poker or not?'

'Patience, Daniel.'

'What do you mean – *patience*?'

'My friend,' Chillie said, tilting his head towards the window, 'have you no respect for *Dixie*?'

'Goddammit, what do you want me to do? Stand up? I fought at Bull Run and Manassas same as you. So don't let's talk respect, let's talk poker.'

Slowly, Chillie turned and studied the player on his right, lighting a cigar, taking his time. Finally he nodded and said quietly: 'All right, Daniel. Let's talk poker. How much you got left?'

'Twenty. Twenty-two.'

'I'll raise you that.'

'All of it?'

'All of it.'

The money was dropped into the centre of the table and Daniel suddenly found himself studying his cards in a new light. Next to him the dealer surrendered, throwing in his hand.

'What's the matter, Daniel?' Chillie asked, his face impassive. 'I thought you wanted to play poker.'

At the window Andy quietly lowered the blind and watched.

'You know,' Chillie added, 'you look as happy as a dead Yankee. Now what are you going to do?'

'I'll see you.'

'I didn't hear that.'

'I said I'll see you,' Daniel shouted, his face pink.

'That's what I thought – '

'So show your cards.'

'Daniel – do you know what General Beauregarde said about you?'

'Just show me your cards.'

'He said you were hot-headed. That's what he said – '

'Will you show me your damn cards!'

'Spade flush,' Chillie said quietly, snapping the cards over one by one. 'Ace to ten.'

'Damn you!' Daniel shouted, hurling his cards at the wall.

'See what I mean?' Chillie smiled, scooping up the money. Opening the window, he breathed in the clean, fresh air and gazed down at the last of the parade. The band was playing *Ol' Virginney*. 'Sure makes a man feel he's won, don't it?' Chillie said quietly, then turned quickly away, thrusting his hat on his head. Walking towards the door, he stopped before Daniel and pushed some money into the man's pocket. 'Just don't say a thing. We've both got to eat.' And then Chillie was gone, descending the wooden stairs of the hotel, out across the lobby and into the street.

He could see the buckboard being loaded with furniture as he turned the corner into Grace Street. On the sidewalk was the rocking chair that had travelled with him from his home in Lynchburg when Virginia was at peace. Behind it, beyond the broken picket fence, his wife and children stood on the porch as the house was emptied of its contents. Reaching the buckboard, Chillie stared at a framed portrait of Thomas Jefferson, the glass cracked, then carefully picked it up, wiping the frame with his sleeve.

'Buck! Come here,' he called out to his youngest son, and

watched as the boy ran towards him from the shadow of the house.

Handing him the portrait, Chillie said: 'Take Mr Jefferson into the house. And give your mother this money.'

Buck looked at the poker winnings as Chillie began to walk away. 'Does that mean we're staying, Poppa?'

Chillie hesitated and glanced towards Nanaire. He couldn't see her face from this distance, but he knew her expression would be one of scepticism. Moreover, if she knew that the money came from gambling she would refuse it, and Chillie could never lie to her.

'Just do what I said, Buck,' he said, relighting his cigar. 'I'll be back soon.'

Virgil Smithson tipped his chair back against the wall of the tobacco warehouse and said with genuine regret: 'I can't help you, Chillie. I know you're the best auctioneer in Richmond. Maybe the best in the State of Virginia. But we can't use you.'

Before him, Chillie stopped pacing the platform and stared at the bales of tobacco waiting to be taken east to the sea and eventually to Europe. 'That don't make sense to me,' he said finally. 'If I'm the best, why don't you give me a job?'

'Because we can't afford you. You want to sweat on the money the others are getting – then you're hired.'

'That's nigger pay and you know it.'

Virgil shrugged. 'Maybe so. But I'm not the boss. I don't make the rules.'

'To hell with the rules. There's not a man south of the Mason–Dixon who doesn't know that I could double your sales in half the time. I've sold everything. You name it and I've sold it. Now don't you deny it.'

'I'm not denying anything,' Virgil replied helplessly. He had known the Langhornes since they had arrived in Richmond. His eldest son had fallen in love with Irene but only from afar. 'We've had a war, Chillie. Virginia's got a hole in its pocket now. You want to live in style, you go work for the Yankees.'

'Style!' Chillie shouted. 'Don't talk to me about style. The Dabneys and the Langhornes lived in style before your family was a speck on a mule.'

'What does that mean?'

'You know what it means. Now are you going to give me a job or aren't you?'

Virgil sat up straight, suddenly aware of the faces of Negroes looking with curiosity from the depths of the warehouse. In the distance, a string of freight wagons were being shunted into a siding.

'Well, are you?' Chillie repeated.

'I'd like to say yes. But I can't. Not on your terms. Tobacco isn't interested in bloodlines. Now you can hit me if it makes you feel better, but it won't make any difference.'

He tensed, waiting for a reaction, but Chillie merely nodded wearily, took a cigar from Virgil's pocket and patted him on the shoulder. 'Give my regards to your wife, Virgil,' he said. 'Keep her warm.'

If Chillie had conceded defeat, he didn't show it as he walked away across the empty tracks, head held high, his back straight. He held no grudge against Virgil; the man was just repeating what he already knew. If they met again, Chillie might even buy him a drink and then, perhaps, suggest a quiet game of cards.

He quickened his pace as if to banish the rejection from his mind and suddenly found his attention being drawn to the far side of the tracks. A new line was being laid and he could see the heavy wooden sleepers stacked on a wagon and then, before it, a crowd of Negroes who had stopped working and were gathered around something hidden from view. A white overseer was running anxiously towards them holding a pick handle, and then Chillie realized what was happening. It was a fight. Immediately he began to walk towards the commotion as the overseer began to strike out furiously, screaming at the Negroes, striking one of them on the shoulder. It was an action, as Chillie knew from experience, that could lead to a riot. Moving closer, he saw the fighters themselves; one of them he recognized.

'Hello there, Billy,' Chillie said calmly, pushing through the crowd and standing, thumbs in belt, as if he were just admiring the view.

The Negro hesitated in mid-punch, looked at Chillie in surprise, then grinned and said: 'Why hello, Mr Lang'n,' before being knocked to the ground by an uppercut from his opponent.

The overseer was now standing over him, the pick handle raised.

'I wouldn't do that,' Chillie said, his voice steady, stepping in front of him. 'Liable to make ol' Billy mad.'

'Who the hell are you?'

He was ignored as Chillie turned towards the Negro, offering him his hand, helping him up.

'Billy – you never did learn how to fight.'

There was a moment's hesitation as Billy looked at him, breathing hard. 'I hold no quarrel with you Mr Lang'n.'

'Well, that's good to hear. Now tell me, how many kids you got now?'

'Five, sir. One died.'

'That's too bad. But if you want to keep the others in grits, I'd go back to work. Jobs are hard to find nowadays.'

Chillie casually picked up a hammer and handed it to him. 'Go on, Billy. Show them all what you can do.'

On an embankment beside the tracks a man had dismounted from his horse and was watching Chillie intently. In appearance he looked like a city businessman, dressed in a dark suit with polished shoes and a wide-brimmed hat, his face lean and sun-tanned. He saw Billy carry the hammer along the rails, glance back, then begin hammering in spikes, followed in turn by the other Negroes until it seemed as if nothing had happened.

'One moment, sir,' he called out to Chillie, walking towards him. 'May I have a word with you?'

Chillie stopped, studying the man. He was a stranger to him but Chillie recognized the type – one of the new breed of industrialists who were taking over Virginia from the old-time carpetbaggers, but whose horizons were wider.

'My name is Colonel Douglas,' the man said, tipping his hat.

'Chiswell Dabney Langhorne.'

'Well, Mr Langhorne, I'm impressed by the way you handle niggers. What's the secret?'

'Secret? There's no secret, Colonel. If you're born on a plantation, you soon learn which ones are like Billy there and which ones are as lazy as hogs. And you treat them accordingly.'

Douglas smiled: 'That simple?'

'It's just like poker, Colonel. Takes you a minute to know how to play. A lifetime to learn.'

Thumbing his waistcoat, Chillie began to walk away.

Douglas hesitated, then caught up with him, not speaking

for a moment. Then finally he said: 'Mr Langhorne, may I ask what line of business you're in?'

'At the moment, Colonel, *you're* calling.'

'All right. Let me ask you this. What do you know about building railroads?'

'Are you offering me a job?'

'I'm asking you a question first.'

'Then I'll answer it. Not a damn thing. But I do know about managing horses and men, if that's what you mean.'

'That's exactly what I mean,' Douglas replied.

Chillie stopped and studied the Colonel. 'How much money are you offering?' he asked.

'That's up to you. This is a big country and it's going to need a lot of railroads. A man could clean up if he's smart enough. Are *you* smart enough, Mr Langhorne?'

Chillie slowly eased his mouth into a grin. 'Colonel,' he said, offering his hand, 'I think both our troubles are over.'

It was, on the surface, as simple as that. Within five minutes, on the instinctive perception of a stranger, Chillie was hired as manager with a guaranteed salary for two years and a percentage of the profits. His luck that had begun at the poker table had not failed him. By noon he was back home in Grace Street, telling them to unpack everything and put it back in the house. They were staying.

'Nan,' he said to his wife, 'you must have prayed hard in church because I promise you, we are never going to be poor again.'

It was a reckless boast perhaps, after almost half a century of disappointment and deprivation. But Chillie Langhorne was, as always, a man of his word. Within two years he had risen from manager to partner in the company, had increased the profits by forty per cent and the wages of the employees accordingly. The Douglas/Langhorne railroad soon ran from the Blue Ridge Mountains east to the sea, and there was only one thing left that Chillie wanted in life: the happiness of his family. He would begin by finding for them the most beautiful house in Virginia.

TWO

·

Mirador

The house, known as Mirador, was of Victorian red brick
with white stucco pillars, set in a valley west of Charlottes-
ville. It was a grand house which the English would describe
as a mansion, but without the formality of design implicit in
that word. Wooden sash windows looked out across acres of
grassland, small creeks that wound between copses of Virginia maple and beyond to the Blue Ridge Mountains on
the skyline. It was a house that one fell in love with immediately and vowed never to leave. It was also, in 1891,
isolated in the heartland of Albemarle County so that Chillie
Langhorne discovered it only by chance. He had been sur-
veying land in north-west Virginia, had lost track of the time
and had decided to find refuge before it grew dark. The day
had been hot, his horse was tired, and Chillie, much to his
initial annoyance, had found himself on an uncharted dirt
road skirting a field of maize. He resigned himself to a night
in the open, an experience he had endured many times in the
past, though lately, as a man of wealth if not property, he
had begun to like his comforts. Chillie led his horse towards
the shade of a stone wall, only to discover a young Negro
lying asleep, a straw hat covering his face, his bare feet in the
red dust of the road.

'Hey – you sleeping?' Chillie asked.

There was no reply for a moment, then a voice under the hat said: 'I *was*.'

'Is there a hotel in the neighbourhood?'

'I don't know the neighbourhood,' the voice replied. 'I only know where I am. And that's right here.'

'And where *is* "right here"?'

In response, an arm was raised and casually waved towards an open gate in the centre of the wall. Tying his horse to a tree, Chillie walked towards the gate, looked in and stopped. Before him was a driveway that bisected a lawn shaded by oaks and maples in which doves fluttered among the branches, and then divided into a circle, a 'bullring' for carriages to park before wide wooden steps that led up to the pillared porch. Chillie stared at the house for a long time, realizing immediately that fate once again had been kind to him.

'What do you call yourself?' he called back towards the Negro boy.

This time the hat was raised and curious eyes peered up at Chillie. 'Sam, sir.'

'Well, Sam, that's a mighty pretty house there.'

'Yes, sir. But that ain't a hotel. That's Mirador.'

'Prettiest house I ever saw.'

As he began to walk up the driveway with the confidence of someone who had already staked his claim, Chillie heard Sam running after him, calling out: 'Hey, mister, you can't go in there. That belongs to Miss Ellen Funsten.'

'Is that a fact?'

'Yes, sir.'

'Miss Ellen Funsten, you say?'

'Yes, sir.'

Chillie stopped and looked at him, then smiled. 'You work here, Sam?'

'No, sir. I don't work anywhere.'

'Is that because you can't, or because you're lazy?'

'Oh no, sir. That's because I'm particular.'

Chillie grinned, lit a cigar and stared back at the house. He was silent for a moment, then said: 'Sam – I'm particular too, and I'm going to buy that house. And when I do, I'm going to hire you as number one boy to show my gratitude.'

'Gratitude for why, sir?'

'For showing me Mirador, Sam. That's why.'

The next day Chillie returned to Richmond.

In the evening, sitting on the porch in Grace Street, a mint julep in his hand, his wife Nanaire beside him, he listened to the sound of crickets and, in the distance, the voices of Negroes by the warehouses singing *Steal Away Jesus*. He said nothing for a long time, reflecting on his decision, and glanced now and again at Nanaire, a sewing box on her lap. In the room behind him a young man in a starched collar and checked suit sat, knees together, hand within hand, and gazed at Irene as she sang a ballad of lost love, her face in profile. On the piano, a pink globe lamp had been carefully placed by the singer so that its light haloed her hair, accentuated her cheekbones and shaded her eyes in mystery, presenting a portrait for the nervous suitor that he would never forget. He felt blessed to be in the presence of the most beautiful girl in Richmond, even if she had said no more than two words to him since he had arrived, had kept him waiting for more than an hour, and then had declared that she was 'hard put to remember his name'.

'Nan,' Chillie said finally. 'You notice how the children are growing up?'

'I never stop noticing.'

'Well, do you think I brought them up right?'

Nanaire hesitated, thimble and cotton in hand, before replying. She recognized the mood of the conversation, invariably brought about by guilt on the part of Chillie after he had been unusually strict with one of the children – or, more particularly, with Nancy. It was she who defied her father, had no fear of him and provoked his anger. And it was she who was most often punished. Once Chillie had said, after underestimating the gin, 'It's because she's like me. I'm just hitting out at myself because I hate to admit to a weakness.' If it was the truth – and certainly Nancy and her father shared a common stubbornness – Chillie refused to accept the admission and show more compassion to his daughter. Earlier that very day, after catching her fighting with a boy in the street, he had taken her across his knee and whipped her. He had been proud that she had not cried.

'Are you talking about Nannie?' his wife asked, cautiously.

'All of them.'

One hour before, Chillie had left a box of candy on Nancy's bed.

'Well,' Nanaire said, 'I hope *I* had a hand in raising the children. They're mine as well.'

'Sure they are. I was just thinking about this house.'

'This *house*?'

Nanaire put the sewing box aside. The conversation was taking a different tack altogether, but familiar nevertheless.

'Wouldn't you say it was a mite small?' Chillie asked, avoiding her eye.

'Not as small as the house in Danville.'

'But it *is* small, isn't it? I mean, what did we fight for if it

22

wasn't to give our children a good home? Only last week Irene was saying that she didn't have any privacy.'

'Irene! That girl's got more privacy than anyone. She can't do wrong in your eyes. Besides, she'll be married soon.'

'What do you mean – married? She's only eighteen.'

'I was only *sixteen* when I married you.'

'That was different.'

'Why was it different?'

'There was a war on,' Chillie replied, and then realized what he had said. Beside him, Nanaire slowly stood up. Behind him, the piano was suddenly silent.

'Chillie,' Nanaire said steadily, 'is that the only reason why you married me?'

'No – '

'*Is* it?'

'No. Dammit, Nan, you're changing the subject. Now sit down and hear me out.'

'Are we still talking about Irene?'

'I was never talking about Irene. I was talking about this house. I was talking about the fact that it's too cold in the winter and too hot in the summer. Damned streetcars everywhere. Neighbours knowing everything you do. It's not a fit place to bring up a dog. *That*'s what I was talking about. And I just want you to appreciate that fact.'

Turning towards his wife for a reaction, Chillie saw her suddenly smile, reach over and take his hand. 'Dab,' Nanaire said, using her most personal name for him, Dab being short for Dabney, 'what are you *really* trying to say?'

Before Chillie could answer, a voice was heard from an upstairs window. 'Poppa?' Nancy called down to the porch. 'Are we moving again?'

Five months later, in the first week of summer, Chillie

Langhorne, his wife and family left Richmond for ever and moved into Mirador. A Confederate flag was raised above the house and Chillie fulfilled his promise by hiring Sam as butler, on the assumption that the job was 'particular enough'. On the first evening, as the fires were lit and the crates were unpacked, Chillie stood in the round hall in the centre of the house and vowed that they were never going to leave Mirador, that they would stay there until they died. Nancy was now thirteen years old.

It was the happiest of times, a period in their lives which the children in their individual ways would never forget. Although the dark years of poverty could never be erased, Mirador symbolized a turning point not only in the fortunes of the Langhornes, but also in the development of each of their characters. Dreams now became reality, even if that reality was not always fortuitous.

To Chillie, now the successful railroad contractor with his son Keene a partner, Mirador represented a challenge, a reminder to all who entered its doors of the Virginia that existed before the War. In short, Mirador meant hospitality, so that not a day passed without friends' or relatives' carriages lining the driveway from porch to gate. The house was filled with light and people and if, by chance, a chair was empty at the table, then Chillie would stand in the street and invite strangers into his home, offering them everything they desired and, if he liked them, asking them to stay a day or two. He planned to retire in ten years, since to him only 'niggers and Yankees worked after they were sixty', and devote his days to riding and hunting and his evenings to poker, bourbon and, of course, companionship. If the demands on his wife and family resulted in rows that shook the foundations, the martinet in him would suddenly become the benevolent patriarch as he organized weekends in the Blue Ridge Mountains with picnics, fishing and lazy afternoons, or holidays in White Sulphur Springs in the grandest of hotels.

Certainly Chillie's zeal for pleasure was excessive, but then, perhaps, it was no more than he deserved. He worked hard, provided for his family and denied them nothing except his attention. He was Christian but not a churchgoer, strict but generous with gifts, a man who liked to drink but who would slap a son to the ground if caught with a glass in his hand. On the surface he seemed to prefer the friendship of strangers to that of his own kin; but in truth he knew that he could not exist without his wife. He loved her more than he would admit, and had been faithful to her since the moment he first met her. He believed her to be happy in Mirador because of the simple fact that he had given her the best that the State of Virginia could provide, including himself. Indeed, Nanaire could not deny that she was privileged. She had the finest of homes, land to walk on and servants to attend to her every need, including a pipe-smoking negress, Aunt Liza, to look after the youngest children. Nevertheless she contrived to work as hard as she had always done, because it was in her nature. She equated leisure with idleness and, although she repeated that she was happy, melancholy clung to her like a mist. In contrast to Chillie, she was a recluse.

Of the children, Phyllis was the happiest in Mirador, because Mirador meant horses. On her twelfth birthday her father had presented her with a horse of her own and would watch her with pride as she practised over jumps. At local gymkhanas Phyllis would invariably win, receiving yet another rosette to decorate her bedroom wall.

'Phyllis rides a horse like an angel,' Chillie once said to Nancy, unable to resist adding: 'even better than you. You've got the courage but she's got the style.'

Nancy, resenting being upstaged in Chillie's affections by another – especially by her own sister – had said nothing, biding her time until she could take her revenge. A week later, while the two girls were riding alone to Monticello to pay homage to Thomas Jefferson, Nancy suddenly broke the silence by saying: 'Phyll – if I tell you a secret, will you promise not to split?'

The tone of voice seemed to mask the most dire of tragedies, and Phyllis had looked at her sister in dread. 'I promise,' she replied. 'What is it?'

'Cross your heart.'

'Cross my heart.'

'You're not really my sister. You were adopted.'

Phyllis immediately gasped in alarm.

'Poppa found you in a ditch,' Nancy continued, glancing around like a conspirator, 'and he kept you because he felt sorry for you.'

As her sister's eyes had filled with tears of despair, Nancy had added the *coup de grâce*: 'It's all right, Phyll. Don't cry. We all still love you just the same.'

Although Phyllis was to remember this incident all her life, Nancy dismissed it immediately, changing the subject, laughing and riding on ahead. She had reinstated her superiority and that was all that mattered. It was a trait in her character that she was never to lose. That evening, in unconscious imitation of her father, she gave Phyllis a present of a box of silk ribbons for her hair.

After two years in Mirador Nancy began to be noticed not as the stubborn, restless tomboy, but as a woman. She had assumed the fragile beauty of her mother, coupled with an independent spirit and a mischievous sense of humour, that was attracting admirers from as far away as Charlottes-ville. Naturally Nancy resented this attention, refusing to be like Irene, considering that there must be more to life than 'boys'. Her heroine was Joan of Arc and her bedside reading was the Bible, most of which she knew by heart. She would quote page after page verbatim so that her brother Harry was convinced that she would become a nun. Nancy vehe-mently denied this, saying that she couldn't think of any-thing worse than hiding from the world. She would rather lie down and die than do that.

'No fear of that, Nannie,' her mother said. 'The world's never going to show a blind eye to you. That's for sure.'

But when questioned about what role in life she wished to take, Nancy was unable to answer. She could only say that she would know when the opportunity was offered to her, and then she'd shout it from the rooftops. In March 1894, two months before her fifteenth birthday, the oppor-tunity arrived without warning.

By that year Irene's beauty had been celebrated not only in Virginia, where her photograph appeared regularly in the society columns and her beaux were numbered as sixty-four, but also across the Potomac in Washington itself. Men who had never met her proposed marriage to her; hostesses in every Southern city sought her presence at a *soirée* or ball. Her mantelpiece was white with invitations. The highest accolade, however, came from New York when Ward McAllister, the arbiter of fashion and ruler of the Social Register, invited Irene, out of all the beauties in the country, to lead the grand march at the Patriarch's Ball. It was the first time a Southern débutante had been so honoured since the War between the States and Chillie considered it a personal victory, a battle won against the Yankees. His pride was such that he even agreed to leave Virginia and travel with Nanaire and Irene to New York. They would be away for a month, leaving Mirador in the care of his eldest daughter, Lizzie Perkins.

On the platform of the local station at Greenwood, Nancy and Phyllis, wrapped in furs, watched the train, covered in flags and bunting, move slowly along the track, with Irene's face at an open window. As a military band played *Ol' Virginney* and the steam drifted to the sky, Nancy said quietly: 'I hope Irene does something silly, like fall in love.'

In the first days alone with the younger children at Mirador, Nancy amused herself by ridiculing Lizzie's attempts at authority. Once, sitting on the staircase, she watched as her elder sister, an absurd hat on her head and a basket of linen in her arms, attempted to gain the obedience of the black housekeeper.

'Aunt Liza!' she heard Lizzie shout. 'Why is all this linen still dirty?'

'Well, Miss Lizzie,' was the reply, 'I can't wash anything today.'

'Why not?'

'Because Mr Jesus told me not to.'

'Mr Jesus did?'

'Yessum. Mr Jesus, he came to me last night and he said to me: "Liza, honey, don't you go for to do any washing tomorrow. You go right to your prayers."'

'What about Anne and Molly?'

'He told them too, Miss Lizzie.'

On hearing this Nancy burst out laughing until Lizzie,

her face flushed with anger, screamed at her: 'Nannie! Didn't I give you some book learning to do?'

Nancy, whose talent for mimicry was unequalled, replied: 'Yessum. But Mr Jesus, he came to me and said: "Nannie, honey ..."' before scampering up to her room and locking the door.

But Nancy soon tired of such diversions. Without Chillie the house became unnaturally silent and Nancy became restless. She would go for walks alone, often not returning until it was dark; or spend the day with Sam and the other servants, sitting behind the ice-house, listening to stories of chain gangs and runaway slaves. She considered the Negroes her best friends, apart, of course, from Phyllis. And yet she remained restless, solitary, easily bored by distractions. She became uncharacteristically lazy, willing herself to be ill in order to justify her depression. And then, on the first Saturday in March, a stranger came to call.

THREE

·

Poor Whites

His name was Frederick Neve, and he was an archdeacon and an Englishman who had left his native country in order to serve God in the New World. At the age of thirty-three he had found himself in Albemarle County, Virginia, was horrified by the poverty of the hill farmers and had decided to stay. A makeshift mission was established in the foothills which he called 'The Sheltering Arms' and for which every penny he could raise was needed in order to educate the illiterate and house the crippled. Consequently he made a list of every wealthy family west of Charlottesville and began to walk from house to house seeking donations. It was only a matter of time before he arrived at Mirador.

Nancy was sitting alone on a swing reading a book when she saw the tall, hawk-faced man enter the driveway of the house, his black suit covered in dust. Shading her eyes from the afternoon sun, she watched as the Archdeacon Neve gazed up at the pillars of Mirador, hands behind his back; then, seeing Nancy, he removed his Lincoln hat and walked slowly towards her across the lawn.

'Good morning,' he called out. 'Fine day.'

Nancy, puzzled and intrigued by the English accent, placed a marker on the page, closed the book (*The Tragedy of Puddenhead Wilson*), and sat, hands together, looking up at him.

'Is Mr Langhorne here?'

No answer.

'This *is* Mirador?'

A word of affirmation.

'Then is Mr Langhorne here?'

'No,' Nancy replied finally. 'He's in New York. Won't be back for a week or more.'

'Oh, I see.' Then: 'Are you his daughter?'

'One of them. Who are you?'

'My name's Frederick Neve. I'm the Archdeacon at Ivy.'

'And do they all talk like you there?'

'No. I'm the only one. You might say, as an Englishman, I'm somewhat off the beaten track.'

'Why?'

'*Why?*'

'Yes, why? Why do you come all the way from England? We've got our own preachers here. We've got hundreds of them. We've got more preachers than jack rabbits.'

Neve studied Nancy, her blue eyes staring at him intently. On the porch of the house, twenty yards away, he saw a young Negro appear wearing the white jacket and waistcoat of a butler. 'Well,' he said, 'my work is slightly different. I'm more what you might call a missionary.'

Immediately he saw Nancy's expression change from suspicion to curiosity. 'You mean – like Dr Livingstone?'

'Yes ... I suppose there is a similarity – '

And then Nancy was jumping up from the swing, peering up at his face as if she had unexpectedly discovered gold and couldn't quite believe it. 'A missionary? With a real mission?'

31

'Well, yes. That's why I came to – '

'A missionary! Heavens above. Reverend – my name's Nancy Langhorne.'

'How do you do, Nancy?'

'Better at meeting you. Want some barley water?'

Later, sitting on the porch in a rocking chair, with Nancy cross-legged at his feet like a disciple, Neve said: 'You see, Nancy, these families in the mountains haven't seen civilization for centuries. And they're white people like you and I. It's as if they are on another planet and all of us don't exist. They live up there in the Blue Ridge without medicine or money, without all those things we take for granted, and no one in the world cares. Well, I think it's about time someone did.'

'*I* care, Reverend.'

'I believe that. But, unfortunately, it's not enough. The mission needs money.'

'Poppa never gives to church charities. He just plain refuses to. Says it's against his religion. But I've got some money saved up. Ain't much but – Buck! What are you doing here?'

Her attention had been distracted by the sight of her youngest brother, whose dust-smudged face had appeared between the railings of the porch and was scrutinizing Neve.

'Who's that?'

'Go away, Buck.'

'Who are you?' Buck asked Neve directly.

'My name is Neve. How do you do?'

'Are you selling something?'

'Buck – will you get out of here!'

'Do you want to see me tap dance?'

'Buck – if you don't go away, I'll whack you.'

The face disappeared instantly, its mouth a grin, then Buck was seen scurrying towards the servants' cottages to join Tom, a black orphan and his closest friend. The voice of Lizzie was heard yelling at the cook.

Standing up, Neve said: 'Well, I'd better get on my way. I have to be at the mission house before dusk.' He picked up his hat. 'Goodbye, Nancy. Thank you for the barley water.'

Nancy watched as Neve began to walk away along the driveway, towards the gates. And then suddenly she was running after him: 'Reverend Neve! Reverend Neve – can I come with you?'

Shaking his head, Neve replied: 'I'm afraid not, Nancy.'

'Why are you afraid?'

'I didn't mean it like that.'

'You want help in the mission, don't you? Well, I'm offering. And for free.'

'That's very kind of you, but . . . it's not really a place for young girls.'

'They didn't say that to Joan of Arc,' Nancy replied defiantly, jaw thrust out, hands on hips, 'or to Florence Nightingale when she went to wherever it was.'

Neve hesitated, seeing the determination in her face, and was about to reply when Sam called out from the porch: 'You'd better agree now, Reverend, because you're never goin' to win against Miss Nancy.'

Neve glanced at Sam, then at Nancy, and said quietly: 'I have a feeling he's right.'

'Reverend Neve,' Nancy replied, 'it's more than that. You don't realize it but I've been waiting for you for fifteen years. I tell you now – you've just found yourself a friend for life.'

The next day Nancy, accompanied by the Archdeacon

Neve, rode on a mule into the Blue Ridge Mountains and met 'the poor whites' for the first time. Despite everything that Neve had warned her about, she was still unprepared for what she saw: a commune of Virginians, inbred over the centuries, living in squalor, all of whom were illiterate, many of them imbeciles. They were a lost tribe, unaware that a Civil War had taken place in the country or, before that, a Revolution; even their language owed more to England under the Stuart kings than to the American South. Moreover, Nancy was as much an anachronism to them as they were to her; they treated her at first with hostility, then suspicion, then apathy; they wanted nothing from her.

After the initial despair, Nancy resolved that if she could teach just one child to read, to discover the Bible, she would feel contented. It was not exactly the role of the missionary that she had envisaged, but it was a beginning. The child she chose was a girl of eight. It took her four days to win the child's confidence, and a week to learn the girl's name, Hannah, and to see her smile for the first time. It was a breakthrough that she was eager to tell Phyllis, as she did every night, returning to Mirador in the early hours, exhausted. On this particular evening, however, she discovered that, having devoted her time to one family, she had forgotten another. On arriving at her home she saw a carriage in the driveway and voices anxiously calling her name. In the doorway was the silhouette of Chillie, a cigar in his mouth, a bamboo cane in his right hand.

'Go to your room,' was all he said, refusing to listen to the voices of supplication from his wife and children. Only Nancy remained silent, entering her room, bending over a chair, accepting the beating without tears.

Later, Phyllis entered the darkened room and put her arms around her sister. 'Are you hurt bad, Nannie?'

'I don't mind,' Nancy replied. 'After what I've seen in the Blue Ridge, it don't hurt at all.'

Lying in their respective beds, they listened to their parents quarrelling, then there was silence. Outside, they heard the creaking of a gate as it opened and closed and they knew Harry was sneaking out to the barn to get drunk.

Finally, Phyllis said: 'Nannie?'

'Yes?'

'Irene did something silly, like you said. She fell in love.'

'Again?'

'I think this is different, Nannie. She wants to marry him.'

Silence. Then: 'Who is he?'

'Irene says he's an artist. Comes from Boston.'

'A Yankee?'

'Sure made Poppa mad.'

'I never noticed Poppa was mad, Phyllis.'

Phyllis was now in tears.

'What's his name?'

'Charles Dana Gibson,' she said.

The next morning, as Nancy was getting dressed, Chillie knocked on the door, entered and closed it behind him. He stood solemnly staring around the room, avoiding her eye, making a fuss of cutting and lighting a cigar. He walked to the window and stared out at the garden, then studied a row of books on a shelf, picking up each one in turn. He never read books himself; in fact had never read one in his life. Behind him Nancy ignored him, finished dressing and left the room, abandoning him before he could speak. In the paddock, while Nancy was saddling a horse prior to running away, she heard footsteps, then someone coughing.

35

She turned to see Chillie leaning on a rail, looking at her.

'Nannie, I want to apologize for my temper.'

From the house another man appeared and stood, a few yards away, watching. It was Neve.

'Your archdeacon friend,' Chillie continued. 'Well – he's told me all about it.'

Nancy didn't reply, turning away.

'Dammit, Nannie,' she heard him say, 'I'm asking for your forgiveness. Not that I'm happy about you coming back at all hours. Did you hear what I said?'

Chillie stared at the back of Nancy's head, then sighed. 'Well, I've said my piece.'

As he began to walk away, Nancy finally spoke: 'You really want my forgiveness, Poppa?'

'I said so.'

'Then I'll give it to you on one condition.'

'Now hold on now. I didn't come out here to make a contract out of it.'

'Will you contribute towards the Reverend Neve's mission?'

'By heaven, Nannie, you've got a nerve.'

'Will you?'

'Are you blackmailing me, girl?'

'Poppa – it's not for *me*. It's for people who are starving and dying. If you saw it, you'd know what I mean.'

'I don't hold no truck with missions.'

'You can't turn your back on them. I couldn't live in a house like Mirador and just forget these people exist. We've got to help them.'

Chillie stared at her, then shook his head in bewilderment. 'Nannie – you can't save the whole world.'

'You can begin by starting with part of it.'

'Is that what the Reverend says?'

'No. *I'm* saying it. Now, do you want your forgiveness or not?'

'God in heavens, you got grit, child.'

'Is that why you whack me?'

She saw Chillie's face redden. 'All right, Nannie. I'll see what I can do. But I've got a condition, too. Until you come of age, you'll abide by *my* rules. And no one else's.'

'Does that mean I can't visit the mission?'

'That's exactly what I mean. And before you start screaming, ask yourself this: What's more important to the mission – you or my money?'

Nancy glared at Chillie, knowing he was right. 'Sometimes I wonder, Poppa, how you lost the War.'

'Then it's *my* rules until you come of age?'

'And what exactly does that mean?'

In her room, Nancy collapsed on to the bed and burst into tears.

'Did Poppa hit you again?' Phyllis asked.

'Worse. When I'm sixteen, he's going to send me away.'

'Send you away? Where?'

'Not *where*. But *why*.' Clutching her sister's arm, Nancy added in horror: 'Oh, Phyll. He's going to send me away to be a *lady*!'

The tall, broad-shouldered man with the appearance of a dandified prizefighter was clearly from the North. Stepping off the train at Greenwood Station, he was dressed for a high society salon rather than the backwoods of Virginia, and when he spoke his voice had the clipped nasal accent of Massachusetts and the refined vowels of Boston. Moreover, his luggage carried the labels of ocean liners and grand hotels, marking him out as a rich man of the world; and when he tipped the stationmaster, he paid him more than a week's wage. Therefore it was not surprising that, even before he reached Mirador, Charles Dana Gibson was unlikely ever to be forgotten in Albemarle County, especially when it was discovered that this elegant Bostonian with the face of a bruiser earned his money by drawing beautiful women in sultry poses for high-quality magazines.

As the buggy turned into the gateway of Mirador, Gibson leant forward to admire the house and saw Chillie arguing with a butcher boy. He couldn't hear what was being said, but he recognized the mood. It was not the best of omens. Stepping down from the buggy, he took a leather portfolio and his walking cane from the seat. Opening a bill-fold to pay the driver, Gibson looked up to see Chillie striding towards him, thumbs thrust in his waistcoat pocket.

'Now hold on there a minute. Let him wait, 'cos you won't be staying long. You'll be on the train back to Boston in three hours.'

'You obviously didn't get my letter, Mr Langhorne.'

'I got it and I'm telling you now, I don't want any Yankee sign painter coming down here to interfere with my daughter's life.'

Gibson didn't move, then he suddenly smiled: 'So this is what you call Southern hospitality, sir. You invite a man a thousand miles to your house, and when he arrives you tell him to hightail it out of here.'

'I didn't invite you. My wife did.'

'Then I must offer her my regrets that I must refuse her kind invitation.'

With a brief nod, Gibson began to walk towards the

house. He heard a window being raised above his head, but he didn't look up.

'Just a minute, son,' Chillie said. 'If you enter my home you enter it with me or not at all.'

Gibson stopped and waited as Chillie slowly paced around him on the gravel, taking his time, assuming command. Finally: 'Mr Gibson, you're in love with my daughter Irene.'

It was a statement, Gibson noted, not a question, but nevertheless he replied: 'Yes, sir. I am.'

'So are a hundred other men.'

'I want to marry her, sir.'

'So do they.'

'But she, I believe, wants to marry *me*.'

'She, I believe, does,' Chillie said matter-of-factly.

'But you, sir, do not approve?'

There was a long silence as Chillie seemed to stare into space as if he was suddenly alone. Out of the corner of his eye Gibson could see two children creeping along the side of the porch, looking at him in curiosity. He smiled at them.

'What you got in there?' Chillie was pointing at the portfolio.

Opening it, Gibson revealed a collection of ink drawings, faces of a woman gazing at the observer in surprise as if suddenly disturbed from a pleasant daydream.

'They all look like Irene,' Chillie said.

'Yes, sir. Even though many of them were drawn before I met her.'

'How did you manage that?'

Gibson was about to reply when something caught his attention and he glanced up to see the incarnation of his portraits looking at him from a bedroom window. Irene smiled nervously as Chillie saw the exchange of looks, then closed the portfolio.

'Mr Gibson, we seem to be on show for a buggy driver and a butcher. So if you drink bourbon and don't insult our flag, I'd be more than happy to have you sit at my table.'

'Thank you, sir.'

'Now wait a minute. That's *all* I'm offering you. Because, mister, I'm going to need a lot of convincing before I take you for my son-in-law.'

Gibson grinned and the two men shook hands.

At the window, Irene hugged Nanaire. 'Oh, Momma, for a moment there I nearly died.'

Fourteen months later, on 7 November 1895, Charles Dana Gibson married Irene Langhorne at St Paul's Church, Richmond, Virginia. The best man was Richard Harding Davies, and the maids of honour Nancy and Phyllis Langhorne. A photograph of the wedding group was taken outside the new Jefferson Hotel and circulated in the national press above the caption: 'Love Wins from Art'. All the wedding party were smiling except Nancy, standing to the left and in front of the bride. She was solemn, not because she was unhappy that Irene was married, but because of something more personal. She was now sixteen years of age and old enough to learn to be a lady.

FOUR

·

The Gibson Girl's Younger Sister

It began with farewells. Nancy realized that her childhood was over and that she was leaving Virginia for the first time in her life. And alone. She would miss her family, of course, but above all she would miss the mission. She had not saved the world or even the poor whites, but her youthful enthusiasm was not without result. She had befriended the young girl, Hannah, and had persuaded her teacher, Miss Jennie, to take her into her class; on the eve of her departure from Mirador, Nancy had returned with Neve to the Blue Ridge Mountains to say goodbye. There were tears and promises to return but, apart from Hannah's family, she was ignored. It was, she told Neve, understandable and yet to be regretted. 'My vocation is simply not here. God has willed it.'

The next day, trunks were placed on the train at Greenwood and the Langhornes said farewell, hugging her in turn, urging her to write. Phyllis was in tears. Refusing to show any emotion, Nancy strode down the platform, entered a carriage and sat alone, not looking out. She had spoken not a word to her father for a week, leaving the room if he was there, remaining in her room at mealtimes. At the station he had stood hunched up in a greatcoat, away from the others. He had not even acknowledged his daughter. And then, as the stationmaster called 'All aboard!' and the windows clouded over with steam, Chillie was standing before her.

'I'll miss you, child,' he said quickly, then turned away, hesitated, hugged her and was gone.

The blast of the engine whistle was heard and the train began to move. It was only as the familiar landscape of Albemarle County disappeared into the distance that Nancy discovered the gift that had been left by Chillie on the table before her. Opening it, she saw that it was a medal for valour bestowed on Colonel Chiswell Langhorne during the War. It was the most precious object he possessed.

Predictably, Nancy was unhappy at Mrs Brown's Academy for Young Ladies in New York. It seemed to her that being a 'young lady' was to be an insufferable snob whose way of life revolved around clothes, Daddy's money and men. If that was intolerable enough, Nancy soon discovered that these same young ladies considered the South as a country inhabited by savages and as remote to them as another planet.

On arriving at the Academy, an imposing brownstone mansion on the smart side of Manhattan, Nancy found herself being driven past dozens of girls on bicycles, all identical in appearance since they all seemed to be clothed and coiffured like her sister Irene, or, more demurely, like Irene's *alter ego*, 'the Gibson Girl'.

One of them bicycled alongside and called out in a Connecticut accent: 'What's your name?'

'Nancy.'

'No. I mean your *name*.'

'I just said it. My name's Nancy. Nancy Lang'n. Why? What's yours?'

A frown, then a giggle: 'Are you from Texas or something like that?'

'No,' replied Nancy coldly. 'I'm not from something like that. I'm from Virginia.'

'Virginia. Don't you have *slaves* there?'

Recognizing that, as a daughter of Dixie, she ought to enter the Academy with appropriate style, Nancy replied: 'But of course, honey. We skin 'em alive every mornin' and hang 'em up in a tree. Jus' can't move in Virginia without seein' dem niggers swingin' up there. Back 'n forth. Forth 'n back.' Stepping down from the cab, she added with a disarming smile: 'Sure been a pleasure talkin' to you - honey chile!'

If she was to be seen as the unsophisticated child from a briar patch, then Nancy, to whom mischief was preferable to boredom, was all too willing to play along with the game. She exaggerated her accent, wore outrageous clothes, and invented a home life that owed more to Uncle Remus than to Chillie Langhorne.

'It wouldn't be so bad,' she would say wearily as her room-mates recovered from yet another startling revelation, 'if Poppa wasn't a drunkard, always ending up in jail. And as for poor Momma - if she didn' take in washing, why, I declare, I don' know what we'd do.'

It was also part of the mischief never to reveal that she was related to the woman who had now become the adored arbiter of all that was fashionable and beautiful in society, whose portrait drawn by her husband, Dana Gibson, was everywhere, not only in magazines but also in salons and couturiers and even duplicated as wallpaper. Songs were written about the Gibson Girl, revues were staged around her, and every débutante in the Four Hundred wanted to be seen in her image. For Nancy to reveal that she was the sister of this goddess would have been to destroy all the illusions of every young lady in the Academy, and perhaps Nancy even entertained that idea for a while. But then, as she reasoned, they would probably never believe her.

But if secrets and charades passed the time for a while, ultimately Nancy was not only bored but sickened by the frivolous world that pre-débutantes inhabited.

'I hate it. I'd die if I had to stay there any longer. All they talk about is boys and dresses and dresses and boys.'

'That doesn't sound too unusual for girls of seventeen.'

Irene smiled under her parasol at Nancy as the landau made its way across Central Park. It was the morning ride when society showed itself off to society.

'But all day long, Irene. Sometimes I think it's perfectly disgusting!'

Seeing Irene laugh, that light, high, genteel arpeggio, Nancy glared at her: 'Well, it is. And you can tease me as much as you like.'

'I didn't mean to tease you, Nannie. But you can't hide yourself away in Mirador for ever.'

'I know that. But it strikes me there's more to life than just *boys*. I mean – I'm not like you.'

A rider passing by tipped his silk hat to Irene and bade her good morning. Irene acknowledged with a brief tilt of the chin, a dimpled smile.

'Do you think Poppa'd take me away,' Nancy murmured, sinking down into the seat, 'if I asked him?'

'Well, I'd wait a while. Give it a couple of months.'

Nancy pulled her mouth into a sulk, then suddenly looked up and giggled: 'You ought to see some of their boyfriends. They look as though they've got a peach stone stuck in their gullet and they can't get it out. There's one poor boy called Horace. *Frightfully, frightfully rich, my dear. Daddy owns half of Manhattan and just an itsy little bit of Maine!*'

She laughed, then was silent, her forehead tightening into a frown. Finally she said: 'Irene?'

'What?'

'Is there anything wrong with me?'

If Nancy ever thought she was abnormal in her apathy towards men, it was, at least, to the outsider, short-lived. In the summer of that same year Irene invited her to stay in the Gibson house at Bar Harbor and Nancy accepted immediately. She planned to spend her time reading, writing letters and walking on the beach, free from all the frivolous blandishments of New York.

After a week she reluctantly accompanied the Gibsons to a polo match, but the game held little fascination for her. Sitting before a marquee, refusing champagne, Nancy idly watched the players, unamused by the exhibitionist antics of a rider on a one-eyed horse. She declared loudly to her sister that she found that kind of man tiresome, the worst of his kind; he was clearly too handsome and too vain to have any strength of character and she would not be in the least surprised to learn that he had a bad reputation. He was another playboy, flirting with every silly woman in sight, and Nancy found his behaviour 'perfectly disgusting'. When he was introduced to her she nodded formally and looked away, dismissing him. She told Irene that she wanted to leave, that she had better things to do than meet people like Robert Gould Shaw the Second.

Entering the carriage she heard her name being called, and saw a boy running towards her carrying a box tied in ribbons.

'It's from Mr Shaw,' the boy said, and hurried away.

Opening it, Nancy saw that it contained a single, long-stemmed rose. There was no message.

'He must have made a mistake,' she said, throwing the rose aside.

The Independence Day Ball at Bar Harbor was more insufferable to Nancy than any event of the season. She had agreed to attend merely out of politeness to Irene and Dana Gibson, but she was already beginning to regret it. Seeking refuge on a chaise longue in the corner of the ballroom, she hid her face with her fan and stared at the dancers. Earlier that day she had written to Phyllis, envying her for being at Mirador.

'Do you believe in destiny, Miss Langhorne?'

She had also written to Archdeacon Neve.

'Do you, Miss Langhorne?'

Turning her head, Nancy saw that a pink-faced youth with sandy hair was sitting next to her. His name, she recalled, was Esmond Delafield, and his sister was at the Academy.

'I believe, Miss Langhorne, that I was destined to be born at the same time as the greatest creation that has ever been invented by mankind.'

'Is that a fact, Esmond?' Nancy said with a sigh. The band were now playing a waltz. In a far corner, behind a gold and white pillar decorated in white roses, a girl in a green dress was raising a glass of champagne to her mouth.

'I knew that as soon as I saw you that you were a kindred spirit and that you would know what I meant.'

'What *do* you mean, Esmond?'

'The automobile, Miss Langhorne.'

'The automobile?'

'Yes. The automobile, Rr-rrr-rrhhr!'

'What on earth is that?'

'That's an automobile. Rr-rrh-*rrurh*! Don't they have automobiles in Virginia?'

'Well, I'm afraid not, Esmond. You see, we're still having a mite trouble inventing the wheel.' Nancy smiled briefly and tilted her chin, anxious to escape.

'Miss Langhorne?' Another voice, another youth, his face shiny with sweat. 'I believe this dance is mine.'

A hand was pointed towards Nancy's dance card. Glancing at it in dismay, she read out: 'Henry Forbes Hunnewell?'

'The *Third*.'

'Oh! And what happened to the other two?'

'Well,' Hunnewell replied, 'Father's dancing over there, but I'm afraid Grandfather's not.'

'Why? Where's he dancing?'

'Oh, he isn't dancing anywhere, Miss Langhorne. You see, Grandfather was killed at Bull Run.'

'Oh my! Ain't that a shame?'

Dancing with Hunnewell, Nancy said nothing. She could smell cheap eau-de-cologne. In a gilt-edged mirror she saw her reflection and beyond that other dancers, and behind the dancers the door opening into the ballroom. A man had entered and was studying each guest in turn with detached indifference as if he was *en route* to better things and was merely passing the time. He was tall, lean, sun-tanned, with looks that bordered on prettiness, not unlike the heroes in Gibson's drawings that decorated the room. He was totally at ease, a cynosure to everyone in the room. The men had heard the gossip of his drinking, his gambling and his womanizing, and secretly envied him. It was said that he had made love to the most beautiful women in society and had broken their hearts. It was also said that he kept the company of whores. Nancy recognized him immediately before his image was gone, dismissed from view as Hunne-well circled her round towards the far corner.

'Good evening, Bob,' Dana Gibson said, greeting the new arrival. 'I'm surprised to see you here. I thought you were in Europe.'

'I was,' Robert Gould Shaw replied, his voice pitched low, world-weary. 'But I got bored.'

He then glanced at Gibson and winked. The two men, both from wealthy Boston families, had been childhood friends, growing up together until Gibson had left for New York and Shaw for Harvard. After that their lifestyles had changed; Gibson, the married man, was content to observe the foibles and romances of the Gilded Age; Shaw, the bachelor, was the quintessential part of it.

'This is Lucy Fisher,' Shaw said, gesturing without look-ing at a red-haired beauty with hazel eyes who clung to his arm. It was as if he had forgotten she was there. 'Lucy – this is Dana Gibson. Famous artist. Draws beautiful women. Talk to him.'

He then abandoned her, took a glass of champagne from a tray, drank it, took another and surveyed the room once again. After a third drink, he decided that there was nothing to keep him there, that he would celebrate the Fourth of

July elsewhere. It was then that he saw Nancy, returning to the chaise longue to sit alone.

'Bob – she's very young. Remember that.'

Irene was standing beside him, looking in the same direction. Shaw smiled but didn't reply, waiting until Nancy saw him before turning his back on her, engaging Irene in conversation, talking of this and that, making her laugh as if her younger sister didn't exist, that he had forgotten all about her. And then he was suddenly standing in front of Nancy just as she was about to leave and was saying: 'Good evening, Nancy. I hoped you'd be here. In fact it's the only reason I came.'

He was sitting next to her, talking to her as if she was the only person in the room. He behaved in the relaxed and intimate manner of someone who had known her for years, had shared experiences with her that only they knew, that were a secret between them. It disarmed Nancy completely. She had never met anyone like Robert Gould Shaw, had never felt what was happening to her. It frightened her. And yet, when he suggested that they go outside into the garden for some air, she agreed without hesitation. It seemed to her the most natural thing in the world.

As the orchestra played *Oh Tell Me, Pretty Maiden*, Irene saw that the chaise longue was empty and the door to the terrace and the night were open.

'They're playing croquet,' Gibson whispered to her.

'Croquet? In the *dark*?'

'In the dark.'

The croquet ball hurtled across the lawn and bounced against a tree before falling into an ornamental pond. Immediately there was a scream of laughter and Nancy shouted through

the darkness: 'I thought it was your *horse* that had one eye.
Not you!'

Shaw grinned, narrowed his eyes and looked at her: 'Well,
you just try and do better.'

'All right, you Yankee, I will. Now stand back.' Raising
a mallet, Nancy peered across the garden towards a summer-
house. 'I said stand back.'

'I *am* standing back. The hoop's only just there.'

'I know where the hoop is.', Then, 'Where is it?'

'There,' Shaw said, moving closer, sipping from a flask
and returning it to his pocket.

'Where?'

'There. Right in front of your nose.'

'I can't see it.'

'Are you teasing me, Nancy Langhorne? Now give me
your hand. I'll show you.'

A hesitation. Nancy didn't move.

'I said give me your hand.'

Taking her right hand, Shaw drew Nancy towards him,
then placed her fingers on the metal hoop at the edge of the
lawn. 'See? There it is.'

His face was very close to her. She could see his eyes
looking at her and saw him smile. From the house a voice
called out Nancy's name, and Irene's silhouette was seen
highlighted against the tall windows.

'Nannie?' Irene called again above the music. 'Are you
out there?'

'Are you going to answer?' Shaw said quietly, his hand
still resting on her hand.

Nancy didn't reply, suddenly aware that she was trembling. She felt him kiss her on the corner of the mouth.

'You smell of whisky,' she said quickly, but didn't move

away, allowing him to kiss her again, his mouth moving towards her eyes.

'I'd better go in,' she said.

'Why?'

'Because I want to. That's why.'

And then Nancy was gone, hurrying towards the house, saying to Irene that she was just taking some air.

Shaw didn't follow. Instead, he sat on a bench in the darkness and slowly finished off the flask of whisky, gazing out towards the sea. When he was as drunk as he wanted to be, he returned to his carriage, sent his driver to collect Lucy Fisher, drove her to her hotel, accompanied her to her suite and locked the door. The next morning he wrote a letter to Irene and Dana Gibson, apologizing for leaving the ball without saying goodbye. It was accompanied by a crate of champagne. No mention was made of Nancy nor was any letter written to her. All she knew was that Robert Gould Shaw had left Bar Harbor and was sailing south on his yacht towards the tropics. There seemed no reason why he should ever return.

FIVE

·

The Rich Boy from Boston

He was the son of a wealthy industrialist, Quincy Adams Shaw of Boston, who had made his fortune out of copper, had invested in art and was considered to have the finest collection of Italian and French paintings on the Eastern seaboard. He himself had been named after Robert Gould Shaw, a first cousin who had been a hero in the Civil War, the pride of the family, whose portrait hung in a place of honour; it was a daunting reputation for anyone to follow, no matter how ambitious. Shaw, however, didn't even try.

Instead, after leaving Harvard, where he excelled at fencing and sculling and won the Astor Cup for polo, he devoted himself to a life that soon outlawed him from Boston society and eventually from his own family. Some critics blamed his irrational behaviour on heredity since his mother's family, the Agassiz, was tainted by insanity – his maternal grandfather had died mad, and his mother was a recluse living in darkness. Others simply considered him the creator of his own failure, a 'black sheep', a description that amused him. But if, by his mid-twenties, he was dismissed by his own kin as an alcoholic and a lecher, Robert Gould Shaw had no regrets.

Dana Gibson walked along the swaying corridor of the Long Island train until he reached the buffet car. Sitting on one of the maroon velvet seats, he signalled to a waiter, opened a newspaper and turned to the society page.

'Dana! Dana Gibson!'

He was now the most successful commercial artist in America, whose sketches in *Life* and *The Ladies' Home Journal* not only influenced how the fashionable world lived, but also how other artists drew.

'Dana! That *is* you, isn't it?'

Moreover, he not only had the house in Bar Harbor, but a permanent suite in the Albany Hotel in London as well as apartments in the Life Building in New York. He was also married to the most beautiful woman in America who was now pregnant with her first child.

'For Godsakes, Dana – can't you *hear* me?'

Looking up, Gibson saw Robert Gould Shaw leaning over the seat, slightly drunk.

'How are you, old buddy?'

'Fine,' Gibson said, gesturing to an empty seat opposite. 'Couldn't be better.'

'That's what I like to hear. Now ask me what I'm drinking.'

'What *are* you drinking?'

'The waiter knows.' And Shaw grinned, leaning back in his seat, an unlit cigarette in his mouth. 'Just tell him – the usual.'

'You're looking well, Bob.'

'Of course I do. Bad living is good for me.' Shaw grinned again, then winked. 'How's Irene?'

'Just as beautiful.'

'That's good. You know, I wish I could find a wife like that.' After the drinks arrived, Shaw said: 'I've just been in Florida for the past month. Went down there to see what the fish were like. You ought to join me one day.'

'I'd like to, but some of us have to work.'

'The old man keeps reminding me of that fact.' He was then silent for a long time, staring out of the window at the flat landscape of potato fields and solitary clapboard houses on the horizon. Finally, he asked quietly, without looking round: 'How's that pretty sister-in-law of yours?'

'Nancy?'

'Yes. Nancy. You know, I must admit I really took a shine to her.'

'She's fine,' Gibson replied quickly, as if to change the subject.

'Is she? Well, that's good. I'm glad about that. And ... is she still at that Academy place? Whatever they call it?'

'Not any more. She persuaded her father to take her away.'

'Did she now? I admire that. That shows strength of character. And I know all about strength of character.' Shaw smiled, then suddenly turned to the waiter, holding up his glass. 'Hey, Bill - how much gin did you put in this? Can't taste a damn thing.'

'I made it the same as always, Mr Shaw.'

'Well, I suggest that you try it again.'

'Yes, Mr Shaw.'

'Bill falls for that every time,' Shaw said, leaning towards

Gibson. 'You get one and a half drinks for the price of one. You betcha.' Lighting a cigarette, he asked casually: 'Now then what were we talking about? Florida, wasn't it?'

'Yes. That's right. Florida.'

'Dana – you may be a damned fine artist but you're a poor liar. We'd finished talking about Florida. We were talking about Nancy. In fact, you were just about to tell me where I could call on her. Weren't you, old buddy?'

One week after this conversation Nancy, while staying in the Gibson apartment in New York, received an invitation to the theatre from Robert Shaw.

She accepted immediately.

'The fact that Mrs Stuyvesant Fish called you "impish", Nancy, should be taken as a compliment. She describes everyone she likes as "impish" because the poor woman thinks it the height of wit.'

It was Shaw talking, sitting in an open carriage, wearing a black suit, white stock and black top hat. Beside him was Nancy, dressed as a contrast all in white, including her parasol and jewellery. She was now seventeen years old, the age when a girl officially made her début into society. Under the aegis of Shaw Nancy had done just that, and although she was not quite the Galatea to Shaw's Pygmalion, the transformation had been a success.

'I think Mrs Stuyvesant Fish wears too many pearls.'

'That's because she'd rather someone said that she wore too many than not enough.'

'Berrymans and Vanderbilts and Astors and Rockefellers,' Nancy sighed, gazing around the park. 'Aren't there any plain folk in New York?'

Shaw smiled, and tilted his hat to a man in a passing carriage. The man, casting an admiring glance at Nancy, did the same. 'Of course there are, Nancy,' Shaw said. 'There's you and I.'

'Well, we sure aren't *behaving* like plain folk.'

'Then tell me – how *do* plain folk behave?'

Another carriage passed and another man raised his hat, but Shaw merely smiled, keeping his own hat firmly on his head. 'He must have forgotten we passed each other before,' he said.

'How do you know that?'

'Well, there's a rule of etiquette in the Park. First meeting, you raise your hat and bow. Second meeting, you simply smile.'

'And the third meeting?'

'The third meeting, you turn your head away like this.'

Slowly, Shaw leaned closer to Nancy, taking her hand. 'Of course,' he added, his voice a whisper, 'since we're plain folk, we change the rules.'

'How?' She was now nervous but she didn't move.

Removing his hat, Shaw kissed her. 'Like that,' he answered.

The two youngest Langhornes, Nora and Buck, leaned over the banisters at Mirador and stared down at Phyllis. Their sister was half-kneeling before the closed door of the draw-ing-room.

'What's happening, Phyll?' Nora called out.

A hand was raised semaphoring silence as Harry appeared in the hallway, followed by two dogs. 'How long has Nan-nie been in there?' he asked.

'Ages.'

Harry gave a low whistle, then grinned. 'New York sure turns their heads, don't it?'

'Shut up, Harry.'

'Your turn next, Phyll.'

'Just shut up, Harry.'

Hands in pockets, Harry strolled past Phyllis, stopped and looked back. 'I bet I know one thing. Poppa's sure going to think twice before he sends *you* away to be a lady.'

In the drawing-room Chillie, a cigar in his mouth, stood full-square before the hearth beneath a portrait of himself as a younger and more tolerant man. 'I blame myself. If I hadn't sent you North, this wouldn't have happened.'

On the window seat, Nancy gazed out at the lawns, at the swing tied to the tree, and didn't answer. She had arrived at Mirador earlier that day, unannounced. Her luggage was still unpacked.

'It isn't a crime to fall in love,' she heard her mother, the only other occupant of the room, say. Nancy had written to Phyllis from New York telling her about Shaw, saying how much she was in love with him. Predictably, on seeing her, Phyllis had hugged her and burst into tears.

'It *is* a crime when it concerns a Yankee,' Chillie said.

Sighing, Nancy turned away from the window: 'Poppa – the War's been over for thirty years.'

'No, it hasn't. We just don't use bullets any more. Saying the War's over is saying the South has lost and dammit, that ain't so. Never will be.'

'Chillie, will you quit fighting the War? We're talking about Nannie's future. Besides, we can't ask for a better son-in-law than Dana.'

'Dana behaved like a gentleman. He came down here and talked to me man to man.'

'Bob will too,' Nancy said, standing up and facing her father. 'I know that. I just wanted to talk to you first.'

'Well, you're changing your spots mighty rapidly, Nancy Langhorne. Who was that smart-ass girl who was going to slam the door every time a beau came to call? Seems to me she went to New York 'n never came back.'

'She came back all right and she's talking to you now. But she's beginning to regret it.'

'Is that another one of those things they taught you at that Academy? Deny your own kin and run after the first rich boy who comes along?'

'You ought to know, Poppa. You're the one who chose the Academy – '

'Don't turn that on me – '

'Now, Chillie!' Nanaire interrupted, attempting to temper the mood. 'Stop being a hypocrite. Ever since the girls were born, you've been enticing every millionaire's son from here to Jamestown.'

'Well, at least I know who they are! I don't know a damn thing about this Shaw feller. What's he do to keep his head up high?'

'Nannie told you. He breeds horses. He's got land. And his father's head of Calumet and Hecia. That's copper '

'Dammit, I know what that is. We use it enough on our railroads.'

'The Shaws are a fine family, Chillie,' Nanaire said, glancing at Nancy and gesturing to her to calm down. 'They're always in the society columns.'

Chillie glowered at her, removing his cigar and throwing

it into the fire, followed by a jet of tobacco juice. 'Society columns. I wouldn't wipe my backside with 'em.'

'No need to cuss, Chillie. You talk about being a gentleman and you behave like an animal.'

'Well, I've got a right to. Seems I can't even blow my nose in my own house without someone criticizing.'

'Now that ain't fair – '

In a mixture of frustration and rage Nancy was screaming at them, regretting that she had ever come home; wishing that she had eloped and be done with it. 'I'm not surprised that Keene hardly steps foot in this house. Everyone hollerin' at each other.'

'Don't you sass me, girl.'

'I'll sass you if I want to.'

'Now, Nannie, you cut that out.'

'But, Momma – '

'I said cut it out, you hear? And you too, Chillie. The three of us fighting like roosters when it's Nannie's happiness we should be talking about.'

There was a silence as Chillie glared at his wife and then at Nancy, then finally sat in a chair staring into space. He suddenly looked very old. 'Seventeen,' he said quietly, almost as a lament.

In the hall Phyllis found she was holding her breath, straining to hear what was said.

'Seventeen,' Chillie repeated. 'Seems it was only the other day I saw you being born. There are some things you never get used to.'

Kneeling beside him, Nancy said: 'I'll always be your daughter, Poppa. You know that.'

'I know, Nannie.' Turning towards her he studied her face, and was about to reach out to touch her. Then suddenly he stood up and left the room, oblivious of Phyllis as she fell to the floor.

'Leave him, Nannie,' her mother said. 'It's hard on any man when he sees his favourite daughter grow up and give herself to someone else. Let him be awhile.'

'Momma, I *never* was his favourite daughter. And you know that.'

On the back porch Chillie stood alone and gazed out across his land, past the paddock and the ice-house and the stables towards the mountains. He remained there for over an hour. As it grew dark, he walked through the house, through Mirador, stopping before a moose head in the hall on which hung his Confederate hat. He picked it up, held it in his hands, then put it back.

Entering Nancy's room, he said: 'Are you serious about this boy?'

'I love him, Poppa.'

'Well, child, if you love him, then I reckon we'd better have a look at him. Show him our home.'

Nancy's first mistake was to arrive at Shaw's apartment in New York without warning. It was not surprising, therefore, that she was kept waiting in the hall by his manservant until Shaw, his face flustered, emerged finally from the bedroom, closed the door and ushered Nancy quickly into the study. She was so puzzled by his behaviour and his lack of any enthusiastic greeting that she didn't notice him discreetly hiding a long silk glove, abandoned on a chair, in his pocket; nor that he filled a glass to the brim with bourbon and gulped it, with his back to her, as he studied a shelf of sporting trophies.

Her second mistake, far graver, was to have made the

assumption that Shaw wished to marry her. He had never even hinted at the idea; in truth, it was the last thing on his mind. Consequently she had only herself to blame when she told him the true purpose of her visit to Mirador.

'Engaged!' Shaw shouted in amazement, turning to confront her. 'But, Nancy, you didn't have to tell them we were *engaged*.'

'But why not?' Nancy replied innocently. 'We are, aren't we?'

Such was her naivety. Refilling his glass, Shaw walked slowly around the room, avoiding her eye, staring out of the window at Fifth Avenue as he tried to resolve the matter in his mind. Nancy watched him, standing in the centre of the carpet, hand clenched within hand.

'Nancy,' Shaw said finally, speaking slowly. 'It just isn't as simple as that. There are a lot of things to consider – '

'I've considered them.'

Shaw hesitated, and studied her. She was beautiful and, in his way, he loved her more than any other woman he had met. To be honest, she was *different* from any other woman he had ever met. But marriage was another matter. 'Nancy – listen to me. You're only seventeen and we haven't known each other long. Let's not rush into things.'

'Why not?'

'Well, because – '

'Because what?'

'Because – '

'Bob Shaw, are you telling me that we're *not* engaged? Are you saying that?'

'No, Nancy, not exactly, but – '

'You kissed me, didn't you? You said you loved me.'

'Yes, but – '

'Are you denying it?'

'No, I'm not denying it. I said "Yes". But, Nancy, every-thing's moving so fast. Maybe that's the way they do things in Virginia – '

'It seems to me that's the way they do things *every-where*. If folk love each other, they get married. Don't they?'

'Well . . .'

'*Don't* they?'

Shaw looked at her, then smiled and held her hand. 'Yes, Nancy,' he answered quietly. 'They do.'

Hugging him, she said: 'And I love you, Bob. I really do. I want to be your wife and that's all that matters to me. You *will* marry me, won't you?'

The following evening Robert Shaw invited his father, Quincy, to dinner at Delmonico's, the most fashionable restaurant in New York. A table for three had been reserved in a corner and when Quincy arrived he discovered his son sitting alone in the booth, a half-empty bottle of champagne beside him.

'Good evening, Dad,' Shaw said, standing up. 'Glad you could make it.'

'Does that mean I'm paying?'

'Of course not. Sit down.'

'Just like to be sure before we start. I don't hold any stock with Delmonico's.'

Unsmiling, Quincy sat in the centre of the booth between Shaw and an empty chair. He removed his watch, checked it against the restaurant clock, then replaced it and folded his arms.

'How are you?' Shaw asked.

His father didn't reply, but glanced once again at the empty chair.

'So where is the young lady I'm supposed to meet?'

'She'll be along. The truth is I asked you here early so I could talk to you. Champagne?'

'No, thank you.' Then: 'Your first bottle tonight?'

'Oh come on, Dad,' Shaw sighed. 'Let's not get into that.'

'All right. So what do you want to talk about?'

'Well ... it's kind of difficult.'

'You're never usually at a loss for words.'

'Maybe it's because you're making me nervous. Why don't you relax? Have some wine. I hate drinking alone.'

'It's never bothered you before.'

'Now, Dad, *please*. I'm tired of your lectures. Let me just be myself for a moment. All right?'

At a neighbouring table a woman in a green silk dress leaned on her gloved hand, looked at Shaw and mouthed 'Hello'. Shaw ignored her.

'Is it the absent young lady you want to talk about?' Quincy asked, handing a cigar to a waiter to be cut.

'Yes.'

'No trouble, is there?'

'No.'

'That's a change.'

'Did you *have* to say that?'

'Then tell me – what's so unique about this young lady?'

'I want to marry her.'

Slowly Quincy turned and looked at his son.

'I want to marry her, Dad,' Shaw repeated, as if he was startled by what he had said the first time.

'She's not pregnant, is she?'

'No!' Shaw shouted, oblivious of the sudden silence in the restaurant. 'God almighty, can't you see anything good in me?'

'I'm sorry,' Quincy said finally. 'You just didn't sound very convincing.'

'What did you want me to do? Rehearse the conversation? I want to marry her.'

'And I assume the mysterious young lady is – '

'Yes.'

'And her name is Langhorne. Am I right?'

'How did you know that?'

'Because I received a letter from a Mr Chiswell Langhorne of Virginia asking to meet me. Now I know why.'

'Oh. . . .'

'Oh indeed. No doubt he'll want to know whether I'd recommend you as a son-in-law. Whether you're an honest, upstanding young man of clean habits. What do you suggest I tell him? I never was very good at lying.'

Pushing aside his glass, Shaw leaned forward, his voice steady: 'I want to marry her, Dad. I love her. Whatever you think of me is all in the past.'

'Is it?'

'*Yes*. She's not like any other girl. When you meet her, you'll see for yourself.'

'It's not her I'm worried about,' Quincy replied. 'It's you. You're Robert Gould Shaw. Every move you make reflects on our family. People may tolerate your indiscretions as a bachelor, but not as a married man. Have you thought about that?'

'Of course I have.'

'Robert, your mother and I have prayed for the day when you'd marry and settle down. But even so, I'm asking you to think hard about it. Are you *really* convinced you want to marry this girl?'

Shaw hesitated, his eyes suddenly nervous. Then a voice behind him said: 'Am I late?'

Looking up, he saw Nancy. Turning towards his father, he stood up and said: 'Dad, I want you to meet Nancy Langhorne. The lady who is going to be my wife.'

SIX

·

Farewell Lucy Fisher

Robert Shaw was drunk when the train finally arrived in Albemarle County two hours late. It was his first visit to Virginia and, like Dana Gibson before him, he was there to win the approval of Chillie Langhorne. It was an encounter he dreaded and consequently, since Washington, as the sky suddenly darkened and rain began to fall, he had proceeded to get drunk. At Greenwood Station only the solitary figure of Nancy, standing on the wet platform holding an umbrella, waited to meet him.

'You look beautiful,' he said. 'That makes me even more nervous.'

'Don't worry. Poppa's bark is worse than his bite.'

As they walked towards a buggy Nancy reached in her purse and handed him a sweet: 'Here. Better chew on this.'

'Why? What is it?'

'Peppermint. Wouldn't do for you to meet Poppa with whisky on your breath.'

At Mirador he was introduced to each of the Langhornes in turn, was polite and charming – a natural gift that had saved him on the worst of occasions – flattered Nanaire and praised the house.

Phyllis adored him. 'You're so lucky,' she told Nancy in private.

Chillie, however, said nothing, studying Shaw with the suspicion of a father towards his daughter's suitor. He refused to make a hasty judgment but would treat Shaw as just another guest at dinner. And then he would observe.

At table, Shaw was placed on Nanaire's right in the chair usually occupied by Keene. He had changed into an evening suit, had privately consumed a small flask of whisky and was feeling at ease, enjoying the hospitality. To Nancy, sitting beside Chillie, he looked the most handsome man she had ever seen; and yet there was an air of sophistication about him, in the very way he moved and talked, looking at the listener directly in the eye, that unnerved her. There were times when his very physical presence frightened her and she didn't know why. He could be just lighting a cigarette or entering a room unexpectedly and she felt afraid.

'So I grew up surrounded by all these beautiful paintings, but they meant nothing to me ... Not that I didn't appreciate them, ma'am,' Shaw continued, addressing Nanaire. 'It was just that they were always there. I mean – there were more pictures than wall space. And if someone had told me then that just one of them was worth, say, ten thousand dollars, I'd have thought they were crazy.'

'I *still* think they're crazy,' Buck murmured, his mouth full of chicken pie.

'You haven't seen them, Buck,' Chillie said. 'Bob's father showed me them. They're Italian, I believe. Ain't that right, Bob?'

'Yes, sir. Most of them.'

Behind him, Sam leaned over with a decanter. 'More wine, sir?'

Shaw glanced up and was about to accept when he saw Nancy discreetly shake her head. 'No, thank you, Sam,' he said.

To his surprise, he saw Chillie stare at him in puzzlement, then look away.

'Nancy tells me that one of the Shaws was a hero,' he heard Nanaire ask.

'Yes, ma'am. My first cousin. That's why I was named after him.'

'Why was he a hero?'

'Fighting in the War against . . .' He hesitated as all eyes turned towards him, '. . . against the South.'

'Did he die?' someone asked.

'Yes. He was killed at Fort Wagner.'

He gazed down at his plate, attempting to think of another subject to change the conversation. But it was not to be.

'Hell of a fight, that,' Chillie remarked, leaning back in his chair. 'Almost as bad as Gettysburg. That's where *I* fought.'

'Poppa,' Nancy warned, conscious of the embarrassment at the table. 'Don't let's talk war.'

'Why not? Bob brought it up.'

'He did not.'

'Bob,' Chillie asked, over-riding her, 'what regiment was your cousin in?'

'The 54th Massachusetts, sir.'

'The 54th Massachusetts? I can't say I've heard of that one.'

'Chillie – Bob wasn't born then.'

'Makes no difference. A family remembers things like that.'

Raising his head, Shaw looked steadily along the table

towards Chillie and said: 'The 54th was a Negro regiment, sir. My cousin asked to be put in command of it.'

'A *Negro* regiment? You mean, they were all niggers?'

'Yes, sir,' Shaw replied, his voice steady. 'They were.'

'Are you saying your cousin was an abolitionist?'

'Yes, sir. I'm saying that.'

And then, to Shaw's surprise, Chillie suddenly laughed: 'Bob, I like a man who stands up to me.'

'I was just saying the truth, sir.'

'And the truth is – your cousin would have been welcome here in the old Dominion. Why, Virginia's been wanting to abolish slavery since before the Revolution. We was even fighting the *British* about it.'

'I . . . didn't know that, sir.'

'No reason why you should. I've heard that Yankee propaganda just like you have. But let me tell you something. Virginia ain't the South and the South ain't Virginia. There are things that happen in Georgia and Alabama that make a man feel ashamed to be alive. And believe me, you'll find no burning crosses and hooded bigots in this State. But Virginia ain't the North either. Up there they treat folk like Sam and Aunt Liza worse than anyone.'

'Poppa – let's stop this.'

'It's all right. Just wanted to make things clear for our guest. Besides, I think it's time Bob and I left you ladies alone for a while. We've got some drinking to do. You *do* drink, don't you, Bob – and I'm talking about liquor?'

Shaw hesitated, then smiled. 'Yes, sir. A little.'

Chillie studied him, then stood up and walked to the door. 'We'll see you all later.'

Placing a cigar in his mouth, he ushered Shaw out and closed the door, leaving the room in silence.

Finally Nancy asked: 'Do you think Poppa approves?'
No one answered.

If Robert Shaw believed he had scored a success with
Nancy's father, he soon realized he had underestimated the
man. As a gambler, Chillie Langhorne was without peer,
not only because he knew the rules of the game, but also
because he took the trouble to learn the mind of his fellow
players. Alone with Shaw in the drawing-room, his attitude
suddenly changed to what was the heart of the matter:
Shaw's suitability as a son-in-law.

'Now then,' he said, handing him a drink. 'Let's talk
straight out and get it over with. I talked to your father and
now I want to hear it from you. All this talk that's about. Is
it true?'

Startled, Shaw took the whisky but didn't drink.

'Talk, sir?'

'You heard me.'

'What kind of talk?'

'I'm not going to spell it out unless I have to.'

'I'm sorry, sir. But I don't understand.'

'Is that a fact? Then answer me this: are you a womanizer?'

Shaw immediately laughed, nervously. 'No, sir. . . .'

'No?'

'No, sir.'

Chillie narrowed his eyes, looking Shaw up and down.
'Do you like spreading a few wild oats around?'

'No, sir.'

'Why not? You're a handsome boy. Plenty of charm.
Plenty of money. I'm sure you could take your pick.'

'I did, sir. I chose your daughter.'

'That's a slick answer.'

Silence. Shaw realized he was sweating and sipped at the whisky. Before the hearth, a dog rolled over in his sleep.

'Sir,' he said finally, 'I love Nancy and I want to marry her. With your permission, of course.'

'Damn right, with *my* permission,' Chillie replied, his voice hard. 'But before I give it, I want to say one thing, first and last and never again. I believe that you love my daughter and I know she loves you. And to me that's enough. But if you marry her and step out of line just once – I'll cut your heart out. Do you hear me right?'

'Yes, sir.'

'Without hesitation or fear of the Lord, I'll cut your Yankee heart out.'

Robert Shaw returned to Boston haunted by these words. If his own father, in attempting to reform Shaw's way of life, had talked of honour and the family name, Chillie, knowing his man, had instilled fear. There was no going back now. He was committed. On arriving in Boston Shaw immediately went to an apartment house in the downtown area of the city, made sure he was unobserved and walked up darkened stairs to a back room. After knocking twice, the door was opened by the red-haired Lucy Fisher, dressed only in a peignoir. She welcomed him in immediately, removing clothes from the bed.

'I can't stay long,' Shaw said nervously, remaining near the door.

'Why? What's the matter?'

'You got any whisky?'

'You know I have. Now let me take your coat.'

'No.'

Lucy frowned, pushing her hair away from her forehead. Then she smiled and walked towards him. 'Don't be silly, Booboo. Take off your coat.'

'I said no. Now listen to me, Lucy. I can't visit you any more. I mean ever.'

'What do you mean – *ever*?'

'What I said.'

'But why?'

Opening a cupboard, Shaw took a bottle of whisky and filled the glasses. 'I'm getting married, Lucy,' he said, without looking at her.

There was a shriek of laughter. 'You're *what*? Oh, Bob, stop teasing me.'

'I mean it. I'm getting married. The announcement's going to be in all the papers tomorrow, so I'm telling you now. I'm getting married and that's it.'

'You're serious?'

'Yes.'

'You're *really serious*!'

'It's what I want and it's got to work.'

Walking across the room from shadow into light, Lucy moved closer to him. 'Bob, you are a fool because it won't make any difference.'

'What do you mean?'

'Just because you're getting married doesn't mean we can't still see each other.'

'No, we can't.'

'Of course we can. Just like always.'

Pushing her aside, Shaw opened the door. 'I said we can't. Now get that into your head.'

He turned back to see that Lucy was smiling. 'I know you better than you think, Bob Shaw. You're not going to

72

change. I'll give you six months and then you'll be back, knocking on my door.'

As Shaw hurried down the stairs, he turned to see Lucy, her robe loose, her hair tinged scarlet from the light of a gas lamp.

'Knocking on my door . . .' She tapped the wood with her fingernails, '. . . just like this.'

And then Shaw was gone, stumbling out into the street as he heard her laughter.

In October 1897, at Mirador, before seventy witnesses, Robert Gould Shaw the Second and Nancy Witcher Langhorne were married.

It was arranged that they would honeymoon at the winter resort of Hot Springs in the Appalachian Mountains. Nancy had often visited the town with her family and consequently she saw the honeymoon as just another holiday in a familiar place. It was probable that she would meet friends there and go for long walks in the mountains as she had done before. In the evenings they would meet in the Homestead Hotel and gossip before the fire, sipping mulled wine. In other words, Nancy considered this visit as no different from those in the past, and that was the madness of it. She was, of course, a virgin, not only in body but also in mind. She knew nothing about sex; it had never been explained to her and what little she had learnt confused and horrified her. Strange, then, that she should be so eager to marry at such a young age; even stranger that she should choose as a husband one of the most notorious and experienced lovers on the Eastern seaboard. But that was the way it was; and in that lay the tragedy.

Shaw and Nancy arrived at the Homestead Hotel just

after eight o'clock in the evening. The manager welcomed them personally, fussing over them and presenting Nancy with a bouquet of rare flowers. When he addressed her as 'Mrs Shaw' she became nervous for the first time. On being shown into the bridal suite, that nervousness became fear. She stood in the centre of the bedroom, clutching the flowers, unable to move. The room seemed to be dominated by the bed, pillow next to pillow, sheets turned down at each corner. A maid had unpacked her luggage and placed her nightdress on the silk coverlet next to Shaw's mono-grammed dressing-gown. Her dressing-room was adjacent to his; her clothes and his clothes hung in identical mahogany wardrobes. As Shaw, her husband, removed his jacket, she suddenly realized that she was alone in a bedroom with a man without the slightest knowledge of what to do next. She was terrified, she wanted to run away but couldn't move. The very atmosphere seemed to suffocate her; every action he made was heightened – the crackle of a starched collar, the rattle of cufflinks being dropped in a glass dish. If Shaw, however, was experienced, he was also understanding; nor was he blind to Nancy's predicament.

'You're not little Miss Langhorne any more,' he said to her quietly. 'You're Mrs Shaw.'

Still she didn't react, but remained staring ahead of her. When he reached forward to undo the clasp of her pearl necklace, she gripped his hand, her knuckles white.

'I'll leave you alone for a while,' he said, replacing his jacket.

He remained in the hotel bar for an hour, aware of side-long glances and mischievous smiles, then returned to the suite to find the door locked. When Nancy finally let him in, he saw that she had placed a pillow and some blankets on a chaise longue in the sitting-room of the suite. Without a word she entered the bedroom and locked the door. Thus bride and groom slept apart on the wedding night.

The next morning Shaw woke to discover that Nancy was dressed, smiling at him, pulling on her gloves as if nothing had happened. It was daylight, the sun was shining and there was nothing to fear.

'Good morning, Bob. Now don't you worry about breakfast because I've already ordered it for both of us. Omelettes and French toast. Muffins. Or maybe you'd prefer griddle cakes?'

Sitting up on the chaise longue, Shaw didn't answer.

'But I'm not so sure about the griddle cakes,' Nancy continued, adjusting her hat in a mirror. 'I'll have to ask what receipt they use.'

'Nancy?' Shaw said, attempting to attract her attention.

'I thought we'd eat in the dining-room at nine. And then, as it's such a *divine* day, I'll show you all the places I knew as a child.'

'Nancy – '

'I was going to order a buggy and then I thought no, Nannie, that's just plain laziness, and Aunt Liza would be ashamed. Bob and I will walk – '

'Nancy – don't you think we ought to *talk* instead?'

Looking at him, Nancy tilted her head and smiled. 'But of course, you ol' jackass. Ain't that the silliest of questions?'

And then she was gone, sashaying out of the suite and closing the door without looking back.

After three days, Shaw's patience began to crumble. He could endure Nancy's reluctance to share the same bed, but her alternate behaviour of teasing and flippancy was becoming unbearable. She had adopted the role of a child, treating Shaw as just another guest at the hotel whom she had happened to meet by chance and had consented to pass the time of day with as a favour.

'And did I tell you that it was here, at the Springs, that my sister Phyllis and I first learnt to ride?'

A routine had now been established, a morning promenade in the mountain air. It was the fourth day of the honeymoon and Shaw had decided to abandon the chaise longue once and for all.

'Poppa gave us some money and said that we could spend it on fishing or swimming or riding. Well, I was just mad about all three. And I never could make up my mind which to do most.'

'Nancy – can we please talk about something more important?'

'More important? But I declare, Bob Shaw, you don't realize that to a child there's *nothing* more important than riding.'

'I'm talking about us. About last night and the night before that.'

Nancy suddenly stopped and looked at Shaw with curiosity as if she hadn't the faintest idea what he was talking about. Then she was looking past and waving to a fellow guest, a man walking a labrador. 'Good morning, Mr Reid. My, you look as elegant as ever. Quite the dandy.'

The man smiled and raised his hat and walked on.

'Isn't that a surprise?' Nancy laughed, twirling her parasol.

'Nancy – let us talk as man and wife, shall we?'

'You know that he was the first boy that I ever fell in love with?'

'I don't care – '

'I was only eleven. He came here with his father because his mother had just died and the thing I remember most about him – '

'Nancy, I said – '

' – were his shoes. He always used to wear the most divine shoes – '

'*Damn* his shoes!'

For a brief moment Nancy stopped, looking around startled as Shaw guided her away from the promenade towards an avenue of pines.

'Nancy,' he said, his temper simmering, 'will you listen to *me* for a moment?'

'But of course, Bob.' A pout, a frown of concentration.

'We'll forget about last night if you like. But we are here on our honeymoon, not on a nostalgic tour of your past. You're my wife now.'

'Yes?'

'My *wife*.'

'Yes?'

'Do you understand what that means?'

Silence. Then: 'Oh, Bob, I must tell you about this wonderful man who came here once. He used to run a leper colony – '

'Nancy, will you please stop this?'

'But he was a perfect angel. He used to talk to Phyllis and I about the lepers – '

'I said stop it.'

' – and the way he talked about them, you just knew – '

It was then that Shaw hit her, striking her across the face in full view of everyone. He regretted it immediately, but it was too late.

'Take me home,' Nancy screamed, her eyes blazing with

anger. 'Take me home *now*. If you don't, I'll go anyway. *Walk* if I have to.'

The honeymoon was over. In the early hours of the following morning Shaw and Nancy arrived back at Mirador, having spoken not a word since leaving the hotel. Shaw watched as she ran into the house, heard the front door slam and saw the lights go on in each window. He didn't move; he had nowhere to go. He just felt numb, helpless, sitting alone in the carriage listening to the night creatures. And then, as it grew colder and he pulled a fur blanket around him, he heard voices raised in the house, heard shouting. A woman was crying and dogs began to bark.

Finally, the front door was thrown open and the broad shape of Chillie loomed into sight and stared down the path at Shaw, his face grim. Slowly he began to walk towards the carriage, hands clenched by his side. Shaw was suddenly nervous. Chillie was now opening the carriage door and looking up at him, breathing hard. He said nothing for a full minute. When he finally spoke his voice was quiet: 'Come on in, Bob. Come on, son. I reckon this might take some time.'

The house was now silent as the two men sat in their respective chairs before the drawing-room fire, a glass of brandy in their hand. The only sound was the ticking of the clock and a log settling itself into the hearth.

'I'm sorry, sir,' Shaw said after a while.

'Don't say a thing. I know my daughter better than you do. And for sure, she can't lie to *me*. She thinks marriage is easy. Well, do you think we survived thirty years and three babies dead without suffering?'

'I shouldn't have hit her.'

'Bob – the only thing that surprises me is that you took four days to do it. A wife beds with her husband and if she doesn't know how she has to learn. You did nothing to be ashamed of, son. Now have some more brandy. It's going to be a long night.'

Nanaire sat next to her daughter and placed a silver-framed photograph in her hand. It was a small, oval portrait of a six-month-old girl gazing at the camera with wide-eyed curiosity. 'You know who that is, don't you?' she asked quietly, her fingers caressing the glass.

Nancy didn't reply, but she knew. She had seen the photograph before. Her mother would take it with her when she visited the graves in Danville.

'I don't know whether it pained me more to give birth to her or to see her die. When she was born, I'm not sure which one of us screamed loudest. But that's why I married. To have a family. And I finally succeeded.'

'It's not children I'm scared of. . . .'

'I know that, honey, and I blame myself for not talking to you like this before. It's the most natural thing in the world and yet I couldn't find the words to describe it.' She suddenly smiled: 'Before I was wed, my own mother said "Nanaire, you put a silver shoe under your pillow and next morning there'll be a baby."'

'I wish your mother had been right.'

Nanaire held her daughter's hand tightly. 'It's going to hurt at first. I can't hide that fact from you. But, you know, it could turn out to be fun.'

'I don't believe it could ever be fun. Behaving like animals – '

'Nannie – you're a grown woman now. A grown woman and a *bride*.'

Nancy looked at her mother, then at the photograph of the dead child. 'She sure was beautiful, wasn't she?'

'Yes. If she had lived, she'd have been the most beautiful of them all.' Taking the photograph, she held it close to her heart, then, uncontrollably, burst into tears.

The next morning, as the mists lay on the frosted ground, Nancy walked across the paddock where Shaw was standing alone, smoking a cigarette, a fur coat over his shoulders. She stopped ten yards away from him, but if he knew she was there, he made no reaction.

'If you still want me,' Nancy said, 'I'll try to be a wife to you.'

Shaw neither looked at her nor replied.

'Well, do you or don't you?'

A silence, then Shaw threw the cigarette away. 'I reckon I do, Mrs Shaw.'

Neither of them moved for a long while, then Shaw walked away and returned to the house.

SEVEN

·

Mr and Mrs Shaw

They lived at Prides Crossing, a thousand-acre farm west of Boston. The house was colonial in design, furnished with antiques from Europe and Russia, and the walls were hung with paintings, many of them gifts from Quincy Adams Shaw. Nancy, as wife to Robert Shaw and a member of the Massachusetts élite, had everything a woman could desire; and if she didn't it was given to her, generously and without question. Her husband, above all, wanted her to be happy. That she wasn't was inevitable; she had ceased to be happy on the day she took her wedding vows.

For two years her life revolved around the tedious routine of dinner parties and charity bazaars and committees, the daily *ennui* of the society calendar, but she couldn't disguise the fact that she was bored. However, she refused to complain, especially to her parents, for to do that would be to admit that she had failed. She had promised them that she would be a dutiful wife; her natural pride and Taurean stubbornness refused to reveal otherwise. She even submitted to Shaw's sexual desires, without passion, hating the act and thanking God when her husband was too drunk, as he increasingly became, to do anything more than collapse into a stupor. In time Shaw made love to Nancy less and less, whether drunk or sober; her revulsion towards sex increased, and she refused even to be seen naked. It was a sickness for which she refused a cure. But if this 'sickness' angered and frustrated Shaw, he was never unfaithful to her, although the opportunities were there. He had promised not only his father but also himself; his life may have been wretched but he would be above reproach. Both husband and wife knew, however, that a marriage on these terms could not last for ever. It would have to change or it would have to end.

In the summer of 1899 Nancy invited her sister Irene to Prides Crossing. In the letter to her she said that all was well, that she was happy and without any regrets. The truth was that in the twenty months since the wedding Nancy had become a recluse suffering from hallucinations, and often had to be chloroformed if her husband wanted to make love to her; while Shaw himself was now an incurable alcoholic.

Shaw arrived late at his club – a euphemism for a downtown cabaret – after a quarrel with Nancy regarding Irene's visit. It was not that he resented seeing Nancy's sister; he simply resented being seen. It made him aware of the degradation in his character. Consequently he was in no mood for the usual *bonhomie*, and just wanted to get drunk. For an hour he sat at the long bar alone, pushing aside the few friends that remained, listening to a female singer who stood on a stage in a smoky red spotlight. He smoked cigarettes and drank brandy and champagne, waiting for the black dog of depression to slink away. It was then, in the mirror, that he saw a woman standing near him, looking as if she were waiting for a companion who was late. She was not the usual kind of woman one saw in the club and it was this fact that intrigued Shaw. He studied her, unobserved: the dark hair, elegant profile, sad eyes. Shaw liked what he saw immediately. He also recognized her.

'Mrs Convers?'

The woman turned in surprise. She was in her early twenties and her eyes looked even sadder. They were the eyes of a widow. 'Yes?'

'My name is Bob Gould Shaw. I knew your husband.'

'Did you?'

She stared at him as if studying each pore, each gradient in his face. And then she smiled. 'Oh yes. Perhaps he did talk about you.'

'I didn't know him very well but . . . I'm sorry about what happened. He was admired. I know that doesn't sound very much, said like that, but, well, he was.'

'Thank you.'

Her voice was soft so that one had to lean close to hear the words. And when one did, one could feel the warmth within her. She was a woman of confidence and sexuality that didn't inhibit a man; she was also maternal.

'How did you know I was his wife?' she asked.

'Well, forgive me but I saw you at the funeral.'

'Oh, I see.'

'I don't mean to get morbid – '

'That's all right.'

'It's just that that's where I saw you.'

'I understand.'

Shaw glanced around, gesturing into the crowd, faces in darkness. 'Are you – '

'Waiting for someone? No. I came here with some friends.'

'And do you like it here?'

'Not really. But I'm curious enough to stay.' A smile. Then: 'Mr Shaw, would it be impertinent if I asked for a drink?'

'No, of course not. What would you like? Champagne. Or there's champagne. On the other hand, there's champagne. . . .'

'Are you married, Mr Shaw?'

'Yes. Yes, I am.'

'I think champagne would be fine.'

It was in such a manner that Robert Shaw met the widow Mrs Mary Convers. The meeting was to change the lives of both Shaw and Nancy more dramatically than anyone could ever imagine.

At this same hour, in the drawing-room of Prides Crossing, Nancy sat on a sofa next to Irene, a photograph album on her lap. No mention had been made of her unhappiness with Shaw; the subject had been avoided like the plague. Instead she had attempted to feign contentment, retreating into echoes of the past.

'And that's a photograph of Bob and I in Chicago. We'd just been out on the lake and I thought I was going to die of cold. I had goose bumps the size of butter beans.'

Another page was turned over. Another photograph.

'And that's Bob's grandmother, Mrs Agassiz. She's an amazing woman. Why, the things that she's done in her life. For a woman, I mean. She's perfectly amazing. And that's Bob again, of course – and look, Irene, see that one of Poppa. Doesn't he look grand? Doesn't he now? Ain't he the best – '

Irene was about to agree when she saw Nancy suddenly gasp, closing her eyes tight as if in agony. 'Nannie, what's the matter? What's the matter, honey?'

She saw Nancy shudder, then relax, opening her eyes

wide, almost in fear. 'Oh, Irene, for a moment I suddenly wished I was dead. I don't know why. I just did.'

'But, Nannie, why would you – '

Nancy stopped her with a touch on her arm, and stared into space as if witnessing a premonition of doom. Her whole body seemed to be racked with pain until she suddenly screamed, willing herself to relax, her skin moist with sweat. And then she was still and there was silence.

'I'm sorry …,' she murmured helplessly, attempting to smile. 'Oh, if Aunt Liza could see me now she'd whack my backside. Wouldn't she now? Whack it hard.'

'Nannie – what's wrong? Tell me.'

'I can't.'

'Tell me.'

'I said I can't.'

'Tell me, Nannie. I'm not made of stone.'

'No. But maybe *I* am.'

'Why do you say that?'

'Because. Because. *Because!*' A hand fumbled towards the photographs: 'And this is Bob and his father … and his father at – ' The album was hurled aside. 'Because I won't *bed* with him when he wants. That's why!'

Shaw grinned, a lock of hair falling over his forehead, and refilled Mrs Convers' glass. The orchestra was now playing *A Bird in a Gilded Cage*, quiet beneath the laughter.

'Four. Two brothers. Two sisters. All older than me.'

'So you're the baby? The spoilt little baby.'

'More like the black sheep, I'd say. You see, Dad made his money out of copper, smart man. He knew Edison would come along and make his fortune for him. That's how smart he is. You betcha!'

'And what does he think of *you*?' Mrs Convers asked, chin resting on her gloved hand. 'Does he think *you're* smart?'

'The old man? Do you really want to know what the old man, old Quincy, thinks is the smartest thing I ever did?'

'What?'

'Do you?'

'Yes.'

'Then I'll tell you... You're not drinking your champagne.'

'Tell me.'

'Getting married. Would you believe it? You ask Freddie over there. You ask Walter Duke. Getting married.'

Shaw laughed, spilling his drink as he attempted to light a cigarette.

'I don't see anything wrong in that,' Mrs Convers said quietly, placing a match to Shaw's cigarette.

'You don't? Oh, I forgot. You're married too. At least, you *were*. Apologies. Bad taste.'

'Is your wife at home now?'

'Probably. Well, no, that's not "probably". That's definitely. She's got her sister there. I bet they're sitting right now fighting the Civil War all over again and wondering why they damn well lost.' Taking Mrs Convers' hand, he added: 'You're not Southern, are you?'

Withdrawing her hand, she replied: 'No. And I think you'd better go home now.'

'Go home! Is that a joke? Do you want me to laugh?'

'Goodnight, Bob. It was a pleasure to meet you. I mean that.'

'Hey, wait a minute. You can't go like this.'

'I'm not your wife, Bob. But from what you tell me – you obviously love her very much.'

'Are you serious?'

'Goodnight. I hope one day we'll meet each other again.'

And standing up, Mrs Mary Convers smiled and walked away until she was lost in the darkness. Shaw shouted after her, began to follow, then collapsed on to the floor.

'Leave me alone,' he screamed as waiters rushed towards him. 'Just damn well leave me alone.'

In the early hours he returned to Prides Crossing, found Nancy's bedroom door bolted and threatened to break it down. Finally, incapable of doing anything, he sat like a child in the corridor, suddenly aware of Irene watching him.

'You know something, Irene?' he murmured. 'I once said to Dana that I'd married the best of the Langhornes. Well, I don't think that's so any more.'

But Irene didn't answer. She simply watched as Shaw, the former idol of Harvard, lay down on his stomach outside his wife's room and sobbed like a baby.

For three months after this event Nancy remained in her room, confined to her bed. She refused to see any visitors, including her own family, and in time none came to call. Her only contact with Mirador was through the letters she received from Phyllis – now engaged to yet another rich Northerner, Reggie Brooks. It was not surprising, therefore, that when an 'old friend from Virginia' came to Prides Crossing to pay his respects Nancy declined to meet him, remaining in her room. It was only when it was revealed who it was that she finally left her bed, running down the stairs like a child to greet the tall Englishman.

'Reverend Neve! Oh, Reverend Neve – I didn't know it

was you. I can't believe it. This is the nicest thing that has happened for months!'

If Neve noticed the change in Nancy's appearance – she had the body of an anorexic, and her wrists were thin enough to be snapped like breadsticks – he made no comment, and was delighted to be hugged and kissed by the young girl from Mirador.

'You look just like the child I first saw,' he said. 'The one who wanted to be a missionary.'

'All children have dreams, Reverend. Now, what are you doing here? There are no poor whites in Boston. Least, not the ones on display.'

'Well, I was on my way back from Canada and I thought I'd make a detour to visit an old friend.'

'Is she pretty?'

'Pretty as ever.'

'Why, you flirt! Don't deny it. You're just a flirt.'

Moving away from her, Neve blushed and glanced around the room. A portrait of Shaw hung over the mantel, a portrait painted before the wedding when he looked young, supremely handsome and immortal. 'How is he?' Neve asked cautiously. 'Is he here?'

'No.' The answer was immediate and dismissive. 'He had to go to a horse sale upstate. He'll be back this evening.'

Nothing more was said as Nancy hurried out of the room to return dressed and wearing a coat and hat. 'Let's go for a walk,' she said. 'Let's get some air.'

They walked along the bank of a stream that bordered the Shaw land, the clear water shaded by willow trees. A blue kingfisher could be seen among the reeds.

'Your maid said you'd been ill.'

'Stuff! I wasn't being ill. I was just being lazy.'

'I can't imagine you ever being lazy, Nancy. You've got more energy than anyone I know.'

Nancy didn't reply but stared at two boys fishing on the far bank. The last time she had been here there had been snow on the ground.

'Phyllis tells me you've taken up golf,' Neve said, and heard Nancy suddenly laugh.

'Isn't that something? Golf! And I'm good, too.'

'I believe it.'

'I'd like to show them mules at the Country Club. But they won't let me in 'cos I'm a woman. Isn't that the silliest thing you ever heard? Your country's ruled by a woman. They build statues to her. They stand up and implore God to save her. But I bet they wouldn't let her play golf in a country club. Not in Boston anyhow.'

Neve smiled and looked at her, eyes in shadow. 'Seems to me you don't like Boston too much.'

'It's not just Boston, Reverend. I can't see any purpose in my life any more. I don't want to be just another wife, just another old biddy watching the world go by. It's so easy when you've got money to forget what's happening out there. But I thank God that I've seen what it's like to be poor, watching my mother trying to stretch one dollar to ten and no one giving a tinker's cuss. I want to work, Reverend. I just don't want to sign charity cheques and think that's it. Bye-bye. Problem's over. Well, it's not. I don't want to sound righteous, but there isn't a so-called lady I know who's prepared to get her nose dirty for something she cares about.'

'So what's stopping *you*?'

Nancy turned away, a flicker of guilt in her eyes, then replied quietly: 'I'm *not* the same little girl you first met,

Reverend. I'm Mrs Shaw now. I've got to learn to be that first. Isn't that how things have to be? Till death us do part. . . .'

When they returned to the house it was dark. Fires had been lit and a meal had been prepared. Three places were set at the table, but there was no sign of Shaw nor any message from him.

'He'll be back,' Nancy said without conviction. 'He's just been delayed.'

Realizing that his luck had changed for the worse, Shaw stood up from the roulette table, threw a chip to the croupier and walked across the salon, a glass of champagne in his hand.

'Ask a cab driver to meet me outside,' he said to a waiter, picking up a telephone and asking for a number in Newton, Massachusetts. When the call was answered he was told that Mrs Convers was not at home and that she would not be returning for two days. Slamming down the receiver, Shaw poured another glass and told the waiter to send the driver away since he wouldn't be needing him. After finishing another bottle of champagne, Shaw slumped deeper in the armchair and stared at the blurred elegance around him. He suddenly felt very alone, almost suicidally depressed. He thought of the happiness that once was; of a past he believed he could never recapture. He needed, more than anything, to be comforted; just for the night. Leaving the salon, he took a cab and paid a visit to Miss Lucy Fisher.

The Reverend Neve left Prides Crossing at midnight, regretting that he couldn't stay any longer and that he had to take the early train from Boston.

'I'll write to you, Nancy. As soon as I'm home.'

'I'm sorry you couldn't meet Bob. . . .'

There was a silence. A carriage was already waiting, the lanterns lit.

'Nancy,' Neve said, taking a parcel from his pocket, 'I've saved this moment for the last. It's a present.'

'You don't have to give me presents.'

'It's not from me. It's from Hannah.'

'Hannah?'

'Don't tell me you've forgotten the girl from the mission?'

'Of course not.'

Opening the parcel, Nancy discovered a Bible, decorated with seashells by Hannah herself. Inside, the once illiterate 'poor white' had written: 'To Miss Nancy. Thank you. Hannah.'

Bursting into tears, Nancy clutched the Bible in her hands. 'Oh, Reverend Neve. There's nothing in the whole world better than this, is there? Nothing at all.'

At this same hour, in a rooming-house in North Boston, Nancy's husband was being beaten to a bloodied pulp by a client of Lucy Fisher's. Shaw had arrived at her room and had demanded to be let in, only to encounter another man sharing her bed. As Lucy watched with a smile of revenge, the man had taken Shaw into the corridor, punched him until he was almost unconscious, removed his wallet and then thrown him out into the gutter. It was the final indignity.

In the early hours of the morning Nancy was woken from her sleep by knocking on the main door of the house. Sending the butler back to his room, she opened the door herself, a robe over her nightgown, to discover Shaw, his face bruised, his clothes torn, leaning on the wheel of a cab.

'Morning, Nancy. Someone took my money. All my money. Took it away.' He attempted to smile, then stumbled into the mud. 'Pay the man. He's a good man. Pay him.'

Walking past her, Shaw entered the drawing-room and reached immediately for the whisky decanter. He heard Nancy slam the front door and the cab being driven away.

'You're drunk,' Nancy said, standing at the doorway, her voice cold with suppressed anger.

'Of course I'm drunk. I've been drinking. What *else* do I do each night?'

Shaw turned and looked at her, supporting himself against a table. He suddenly thought that she looked very beautiful and very young. He wanted to kiss her.

'What happened?' she asked.

'I told you. Someone took all my money.'

'Where?'

'What does it matter?'

'Where did it happen?'

'In Boston.'

'*Where* in Boston?' Her voice was now more incisive, cutting through him. 'Where?' she repeated. '*Where?*'

'Some madman picked a fight on me, so what the hell does it matter where? Haven't you got any sympathy?'

'Not an ounce.'

'Thanks. Thanks a damn lot.' Refilling his glass, he said: 'What are you looking at me like that for?'

'Because I haven't seen anything so disgusting in all my life.'

'Don't talk to me like that – '

'Why? Are you going to hit me? Am I more your size?'

'Don't provoke me, Nancy. I've had my bellyful tonight.'

'I know. I can smell it.'

It was then, for the second time in their marriage, that Shaw hit her, striking her hard across the face.

'You asked for that.'

'Where were you tonight?'

Shaw looked at her, startled as she remained staring at him, unflinching, standing her ground. 'Are you sure you really want to know?'

'Yes.'

'Really sure?'

'Yes.'

'No, I don't think you are – '

'*Where?*'

Silence. Then: 'I went visiting.'

No reaction.

'Did you hear what I said? Or maybe you don't know what I mean.'

'I know exactly what you mean.'

Turning, Nancy walked towards the door as Shaw seized her arm: 'Don't you walk out on me. I haven't finished yet.'

'Yes, you have.'

'Not until I get some reaction from you. Come on now. You've got flesh and blood like everyone else. I didn't plan to get married to a block of ice. Now say something, dammit. Or do I have to hit you again?'

'You're drunk. You've been drunk ever since I met you.'

'That's right. That's right, I have been. And do you know why? Because if I drink enough of this, I can forget what I'm missing. That's why. You make me feel guilty every time I touch you. My own wife.'

'And so you choose to go "visiting" instead?'

'Yes. But shall I tell you something funny? I haven't been unfaithful to you once. Not even tonight.'

'I don't believe you.'

'I know you don't. You'd like to think I'm bedding everyone in sight, wouldn't you? It'd make you feel easier. Make you feel pious. Give you a *cause* to lock your door!'

'I still don't believe you – '

'The truth is that you don't *want* to believe me. What do you want me to do? Swear on the Bible?'.

Hannah's Bible was now in Shaw's hand, and he was holding it up mockingly over his head. 'This is what you're married to, isn't it?'

'Give me that – '

'Why?'

'I said give me that.'

Shaw suddenly grinned, seeing her tremble, reaching for the Bible. 'All right, Saint Nancy. You can have the damn book. Take it!'

Stepping back, Shaw hurled the Bible at a case of sporting trophies, watching it split open, the seashells breaking into pieces on the wall, the book falling to the floor. He saw Nancy run towards it horrified, saw her double up in pain, gasping, clutching the pages of the Bible in her hands.

'I should never have taken you back,' Shaw said, picking up the decanter and walking out of the room. 'It was the biggest mistake I ever made.'

When Nancy finally returned to her bedroom her body was shaking and she believed she was dying. She prayed to God, holding the remains of Hannah's Bible in her hand. When Shaw ripped off her clothes and made love to her she offered no resistance but simply lay back with her tears. Six weeks later, after being continually raped and beaten by her husband, she ran away, leaving Prides Crossing for ever.

EIGHT

·

Welcome to the Twentieth Century, Ladies and Gentlemen

The massive marble and granite waiting-hall of Washington Station appeared empty, except for a black porter, as Irene entered from the street. It was only as she hurried from bench to bench, her footsteps echoing on the stone floor, that she saw Nancy sitting huddled in a corner, a suitcase at her feet. She was staring into space, almost catatonic, unaware of anything, the light gone out of her eyes.

'Nannie!'

Nancy didn't react. A train was heard shunting into a siding and the porter lit a pipe and watched.

'Nannie – it's Irene.'

Sitting next to her, she took Nancy's hand, felt the cold skin and pressed it against her face. She saw her sister tremble, then suddenly shake her head as if wondering where she was. And then she heard Nancy speak, the voice barely audible.

'I'm sorry I did this to you. But you're the only one I could call.'

'Don't be a fool. I'm glad you did. But what are you doing *here*?'

'I just didn't know what to do or where to go. But I just couldn't stay there any longer.'

'You don't have to explain.'

'Oh, Irene, it isn't all his fault. You mustn't think that. I'm not the kind of woman he wanted and I never can be. But it isn't all his fault. I'm just bad for him.'

'Now don't talk like that.'

'It's true. I make him do things he doesn't mean.'

'Nannie – you stop chiding yourself. I've seen Bob Shaw and I know what he's like. He's a drunk and a bully. Best thing you ever did was leave him. Why, it's perfectly clear to everyone that you should never have married him in the first place.'

'Perfectly clear!' Nancy cried, rising to the defence. 'Now you hold on now, Irene Gibson. I'm not going to sit here and listen to you being holier than thou!'

Irene was startled but not surprised by Nancy's outburst. She knew that, like Chillie, her sister reacted violently to personal criticism – that pride of Taurus yet again – although she was never shy to reverse the attack. 'Just because you married a saint and I married a sinner – '

'Nancy, I didn't intend – '

' – don't mean you can put on your righteous ways with me. I've seen the way you treat men. There are sixty-four of them down in Virginia who'd bear me out. Cast them aside like bad apples.'

'No, I did not.'

'Yes, you did. Used to keep their presents, too.'

'Now that's not fair.'

'Certainly isn't. Back in Mirador there's a whole cupboardful.'

Nancy glared at Irene as the black porter shuffled nearer, listening intently.

'Nannie,' Irene said finally, 'what are we quarrelling about?'

A hesitation, then Nancy suddenly hugged her. 'Oh I never felt so wretched in all my life.'

'I know. I feel so helpless, but things will change for the better. You'll see.'

'It's too late.'

'No, it's not. You don't have to see him again.'

'That's not what I mean.'

'And you can be sure that Bob Shaw won't follow you to Virginia. He'd be too scared that Poppa would boil him alive.'

'I said that's not what I mean.'

'Then what is it?'

Nancy hesitated as the porter moved closer and said, grinning: 'You two ladies waiting for a train? 'Cos they don't stop in *here*.'

'I'm pregnant, Irene.'

'Whatsat, ma'am?'

'I'm carrying Bob's child.'

The baby was born in 1898. It was a boy. During the months of her pregnancy Nancy received no news from Robert Shaw nor did she know where he was. There were rumours that he was in Mexico or sailing the Atlantic. One report was that he had been seen in Paris.

After her son was born Nancy remained in hospital for a

week, since the birth had been 'difficult' and there was concern about the child's health. She lay resting in a private room filled with flowers, being visited hourly by friends and family bringing her books and presents. She was photographed for the Richmond press, reclining on pillows, her blonde hair loose. It was noted that she looked happier and more beautiful than anyone could remember.

On the eve of her departure from the hospital a man was seen watching the building from a doorway across the street. He was well-dressed but unshaven. Later he appeared at the desk, his manner nervous and furtive. When the night nurse inquired if he needed help, the man replied that he had come to visit Mrs Shaw.

'Are you family?' the nurse asked suspiciously. She noticed that the man was agitated, as if he feared he was being watched. She also noticed that his hands shook and that he had the manner of someone who was attempting to control an addiction.

'Yes,' Shaw replied. 'I'm . . . I'm a member of the family.'

'She seems to have an awful lot of family. Follow me.'

Walking down the corridor, Shaw suddenly stopped and asked: 'Nurse? . . . Are there . . . is there anyone else with Mrs Shaw now?'

'Not at the moment. Why?'

'Nothing.'

Opening the door of the room, the nurse announced: 'More family for you, Mrs Shaw,' and left Nancy alone facing her husband.

'Hello, Nancy,' was all he could say, staring self-consciously at the bed, holding his hat tightly in his hand.

Slowly, without reaction, her face impassive, Nancy put

aside a book she was reading and pulled a shawl around her shoulders. 'Who told you where to find me?'

'Walter Duke.'

'Well, I didn't think it was my father.'

She studied him. He looked like a tired, soulless middle-aged man, even though he was still in his twenties. Despite herself, she felt pity for him. 'Last I heard you were in Florida. Or was it California?'

'Both for a while. And other places. . . .'

'Can't say it's done you any good. You look as though you're fit to die.'

Shaw smiled nervously and looked away, aware of the fan stirring on the ceiling. Outside the window, some children were playing softball in a park. 'I meant to write you,' he said, 'but I didn't know where you were.'

'That was the idea.'

'I wanted to tell you . . . that I'm not drinking any more. I haven't done for three or four months now.'

Nancy said nothing but stared at him, unimpressed.

'Nancy – I'm sorry I . . .'

He began to move closer to the bed.

'Stay where you are. I don't want you near me.'

'Do you hate me that much?'

'I don't hate you, Bob Shaw. I never have and I never will. I just don't find it in my heart to love you.'

Shaw turned away, controlling his tears, knowing that he had lost her. 'I don't blame you, Nancy. We didn't get married, did we? We just decided to have our own private Civil War. Only this time, the South won.'

'Is that something you rehearsed?'

'I'm afraid so.' Then: 'You look beautiful, Nancy.'

There was a silence and then a noise was heard, a sigh of

a baby turning over in its sleep. It was then that Shaw became aware of the cot in the corner, white, decorated with broderie anglaise. The occupant was hidden by a net curtain. Shaw turned towards the cot but didn't move, as if he was incapable of it.

'Don't you want to see him?' Nancy asked.

'Him?'

'Blue ribbons usually mean a boy.'

Shaw hesitated, was about to walk forward, then stopped and closed his eyes. 'No. I couldn't see him. Not that I don't want to. . . . It's just that I'd rather not see him at all than see him only once.'

Nancy felt herself weakening and turned away, hiding her face in the pillows.

'Goodbye, Nancy,' Shaw said quietly. 'Try and forgive me.'

The door was opened and closed.

'Goodbye,' Nancy said, but her husband had gone.

In the corridor Shaw said goodnight to the nurse, then stopped and asked: 'Nurse? What did Mrs Shaw call her baby?'

'Mrs Shaw? Let me see.'

Checking through a file of papers, she replied: 'She called him Robert Gould Shaw the Third. After his father, I suppose.'

Shaw turned and walked slowly away. Reaching the end of the corridor he suddenly broke down as the tension finally snapped, and hugged the wall for support. '*The son was called Robert Gould Shaw the Third. After his father, I suppose.*' That night, Shaw was found drunk and unconscious in a waterfront alley. He had been beaten up and robbed.

Go tell Aunt Nancy,
Go tell Aunt Nancy,
Go tell Aunt Nancy,
The old grey goose is dead.

The Langhornes had decided to celebrate the last day of the century at the Gibson mansion at Bar Harbor. There were now new additions to the family: Keene had married a shy, coquettish Virginian called Sadie, while Harry had wed a childhood sweetheart, Genevieve. Phyllis, married to Reggie Brooks, had given birth to a son, Peter, and was pregnant with another, while Irene had produced a daughter named, characteristically, after herself. Buck was as yet too young to wed, while Nora, now fifteen, was already pursued by more beaux than she could ditch. And of course Nancy had her own son, Bobbie Shaw, now almost two years old. As for Bobbie's father, he had disappeared. It was known only that he was somewhere in South Dakota. And that he was accompanied everywhere by a mysterious woman.

As Irene finished singing on the stage of the Gibson ballroom, Dana Gibson stepped forward, holding up his hands for silence.

'And now a song from another Southern belle. Ladies and gentlemen, before we say goodbye to 1899, here is my beautiful sister-in-law, Phyllis.'

'Oh no, Dana, I couldn't.'

Phyllis was now twenty years old. She would never be the most beautiful of the Langhorne sisters, but unquestionably she would be the most loved. No unkind word was ever said about her; she had acquired, from her mother, that rare quality of selflessness and compassion. Moreover whereas her sister and closest friend, Nancy, was renowned for her wit – or, as others might say, her *tongue* – Phyllis was recognized for her humour, a far more precious gift.

'Come on, Phyllis. Sing the old year out.'

Phyllis gazed around the ballroom, then turned shyly to the orchestra leader.

'*Ol' Virginney.*'

As the poignant ballad began, Nancy became aware of the Gibson butler pushing his way anxiously through the guests towards Irene. She saw Irene frown, then discreetly gesture to her and point to the door. Leaving Bobbie in the care of Chillie, Nancy hurried around the room until she reached her elder sister.

'What is it?'

'It's Bob Shaw. He's on the telephone.'

'Are you sure? Oh, my God. . . .'

'I'll tell him you're not here.'

'No. I'd better speak to him. I can't avoid him for ever.' And then: 'Has he been drinking?'

But she didn't wait for a reply and hurried out into the hallway, with the voice of Phyllis receding into the distance.

'Hello, Nancy! Happy New Year.' The voice on the telephone was slurred and indistinct but recognizable as belonging to Shaw. 'Can you hear me, Nancy?'

'I can hear you. Where are you? Not in Boston, I hope.'

'What?'

'Not in *Boston*?'

'No. I'm in – just a minute.'

She could hear him shouting to someone, then the voice returned.

'It's called Sioux Falls. Hell of a place. Well, aren't you going to wish me Happy New Year?'

'Is that all you called about after all this time?'

There was a long silence and Nancy was about to put down the receiver when Shaw said: 'I want a divorce, Nancy. I want a *divorce*.'

In the ballroom, Nancy could hear applause as Phyllis finished singing.

'Nancy – I know you're listening. I'm telling you now so we can get this thing straightened out – once and for all. I want a divorce. I'm talking to my lawyers next week. Do you understand what I'm saying?'

Harry, a little drunk and wearing a paper crown, put his arms around Nancy's waist and whispered: 'Come back to the party, little sister.'

'In a minute,' Nancy replied, gesturing to him to leave.

'Nancy!' Shaw's voice was more urgent. 'It's the sensible thing. We haven't got a marriage any more. We haven't had for two years. I want to be free, so don't fight me. You won't, will you? Look, I'll handle all the legal details. And don't worry – I'll be generous. So what do you say?'

'Bob Shaw, I don't know whether you're drunk or sober – but whatever you are, the answer is no. No divorce *ever*. Do you hear me?'

'But, Nancy – you've got to – '

'I said no. And that's final.'

'Nancy!' The voice was a scream of despair.

'Happy New Year, Bob,' Nancy said quietly, replacing the telephone and returning to the ballroom, just as Gibson announced:

'Ladies and gentlemen, welcome to the twentieth century!'

In the hotel in Sioux Falls, South Dakota, surrounded by snow, some of it eight feet deep, Robert Shaw walked across the lobby like a doomed prisoner. As he reached the stairs, the desk clerk called out to him: 'Oh, Mr Shaw? Mr Shaw!'

'Yes?'

'Your wife just left a message saying that she is now in the dining-room.'

'Thank you.'

As if in a trance, Shaw returned across the lobby, past the partygoers, past a barbershop quartet singing *Auld Lang Syne*, and entered the dining-room. Mrs Convers was sitting at a corner table by the window, gazing out at the snow. Shaw sat down next to her and lit a cigarette.

'Is everything all right?' Mrs Convers asked, although that was no longer her name.

'Yes, of course. Nancy sent her congratulations.'

Mary Convers put her arm around him. 'And are you still glad you married me?' she asked. 'No regrets?'

Shaw was silent for a moment. Then: 'No. No regrets – Mrs Shaw.'

The question of Shaw's bigamy was not revealed to Nancy for more than a year. Only Shaw himself knew the truth, even withholding it from his second and illegal wife. Why he had chosen to marry Mary Convers in such a manner remains a mystery. In all probability he had gambled on the fact that Nancy would grant him a divorce on the grounds of separation; but as always he had underestimated her wilful nature, her religious upbringing, and as always, being a rash gambler, he had lost. Consequently he was obliged to remain in hiding, not only from Chillie and the press but also, more dramatically, from the police. Eventually common sense prevailed and he wrote to his father, telling him what he had done. Although stunned by the revelation and vowing to disown his youngest son, Quincy Shaw left immediately for Mirador, accompanied by his lawyer, after first sending a telegram to Nancy. On opening it, Nancy's initial reaction was laughter:

'Can't stand *one* wife, so he marries *two*!'

But the laughter was short-lived. She had married, defying all opposition, and she had failed. Worse – her husband had shown, in the most audacious way, that he preferred someone else and was even prepared to defy the law because of it. To Nancy's pride, that was the unkindest cut of all.

'You must agree to a divorce now, Mrs Shaw,' Shaw's lawyer, Simmons, told her as soon as he arrived at Mirador. 'My client could go to prison. And I'm sure that the last thing you would want is a scandal – '

'Scandal! You obviously don't know the Langhornes very well. We *thrive* on scandals. Why, we couldn't get through the week without one.'

But it was a hollow cry of defiance and she knew it. That Shaw could go to prison for bigamy was one thing; but that Bobbie could be branded for life as the son of a criminal was, in Nancy's eyes, unthinkable. In private, in the drawing-room, she asked Quincy Shaw if her husband had committed bigamy deliberately in order to blackmail her.

'I don't know,' Quincy replied. 'Of course he said he didn't, that he was convinced you'd give him a divorce before anyone found out, but I really don't know. That's the truth.'

Nancy stared at him, then turned away, unable to speak. Finally she said: 'What's she like? His new wife.'

'A widow. Comes from near Boston. That's all I know.'

'Is she pretty?'

'Not like you, Nancy.'

'But does he love her?'

'Remember the day that he first showed you off to me?'

'Yes.'

'I don't think he'll ever love anyone that much again.'

'Nor will I.' Then: 'I hate the idea of a divorce, but I wouldn't want Bob to go to jail. Even if it's just for young Bobbie's sake. What grounds have the lawyers cooked up?'

'Incompatibility.'

'They like those long words, don't they? Well, you can tell Simmons that he's won. Bob can have his divorce – but on *my* terms. I abide by the Bible and nothing else. The grounds are to be adultery on the part of Robert Gould Shaw and that woman of his. I aim to come out of this clean. It's adultery or nothing.'

On 3 February 1903 the divorce was concluded in Charlottesville, Virginia. Neither of the parties was present nor were they ever to see each other again. Nancy was given custody of Bobbie Shaw and both mother and son were granted a financial settlement that would enable them to be millionaires for life. On the very next day after the divorce Robert Shaw legally wed Mary Convers. The marriage, to everyone's surprise, was a success, both husband and wife being blissfully happy until the day they died. Robert Shaw ceased to be an alcoholic, became once again a respected member of Massachusetts society as well as a successful breeder of horses, and was never once unfaithful to his second wife. His only regret was that he was never allowed to see his son, who had inherited not only his good looks but also, as future tragic events were to prove, his youthful character.

'Ain't she a beauty, Miss Nancy? Looks like she could win every prize in the show.'

Nancy leaned over the rail and studied the mare that the black groom was exercising. Its name was Queen Bee and it had been a present from Chillie to Nancy after the divorce. Horses, he told her, were better than husbands. Not only did they stay sober but they could also jump higher. It was the only comment he ever made regarding the failure of Nancy's marriage; he refused to utter a single word of recrimination or even talk about the matter. It was as if it had never happened. He simply put his arms around Nancy and told her, for the first time in years, that he loved her.

'Sure *is* a beauty, Tom,' Nancy said, running her hand along the mare's neck. 'And I promise you, she's going to beat them all.'

Walking back to the house, she saw that the carriage was already waiting to take her to the station. From there she would take the train to the horse show in Lynchburg. Queen Bee would travel in a boxcar later in the day.

'Are you nervous, honey?' her mother said as she entered the dining-room where her parents were finishing breakfast.

Nancy shook her head, smiled, and snatched a slice of smoked ham from Chillie's plate.

'Sit down if you're going to eat.'

'I'm not hungry, Poppa. Just greedy.'

'Nanaire's got a headache.'

'No, I haven't, Chillie. I wish I'd never mentioned it.'

Nancy looked at her and suddenly hugged her. 'Well, I'd better be on my way. Wish me luck.'

Nanaire kissed her and Nancy hurried to the door. As she opened it, she heard her father say: 'You know, Mrs Langhorne, you're looking very beautiful today.'

At Lynchburg Nancy competed in two events, and was waiting for the third when she suddenly left the arena unexpectedly, without a word to anyone. She said later that she felt a sudden and overwhelming sense of foreboding. When she returned to Mirador the house was in darkness. Hurrying up the staircase, she saw a light in the main bedroom and entered it to discover Chillie sitting by the bed, his face buried in the arms of his dead wife. Nanaire had collapsed while Nancy was in Lynchburg and had died within the hour. The loss to Nancy was immeasurable.

By this darkest summer of 1903 Nancy had married, given birth to a son, divorced and seen the death of her mother. At this moment she believed she could never be happy again. She was still only twenty-four years of age.

NINE

·

Alone

After Nanaire's funeral the mourners returned to Mirador and seemed to occupy every inch of space. Even at the happiest of times the house had never received so many occupants, young and old. The driveway and the road were crowded with carriages and buggies and even one or two automobiles. And then, quite suddenly, they were all gone, leaving Chillie alone, sitting silently on the porch, staring out at the last of the summer light.

'Don't you worry, Poppa,' Nancy said, kneeling beside him. '*I'll* look after you now.'

It was a decision she had taken while watching Nanaire's coffin being lowered into the grave. With no future but only a past, Nancy resolved to take over her mother's duties, to be the new mistress of Mirador. One of the last of the mourners to leave was Chillie's sister, known affectionately as Aunt Lewis, a no-nonsense spinster from Danville. She had watched Nancy coping with the hordes of children, hungry after the funeral, watched her take charge without fuss, disguising her own grief as she tended to the sorrows of others. It was a role that Nancy unselfishly assumed with ease, tireless and uncomplaining, bringing comfort and humour when it was needed most. It was a role, though she did not yet realize it, that would be a key to her life.

'Don't take no sass from Chillie now,' Aunt Lewis said, confronting Nancy as she was stripping the beds. 'I've known my brother longer than you and I know what he's like.'

'He's taken it bad, Aunt Lewis.'

'I know that, child. Because he's just thinking about himself as always. Now answer me this: do you know how old I am?'

'No.'

'Well, I won't tell you. That's not because I'm vain. It's more because I'm ashamed. I've seen this country split in two by war. I've seen presidents come and go spoutin' them long words like freedom 'n liberty 'n emancipation. And they still keep saying it and they still keep getting elected. Emancipation? For *whom*? For your own mother? She lived and died without a penny of her own. Couldn't even buy a dress without begging for it 'n feeling guilty every time she wore it. She worked for nothing night and day, every day of the year, worked harder than any nigger, but no one went to war for her or any other woman like her.'

'Aunt Lewis – '

'Now don't stop me, child. I'm just getting into my stride. We just buried your mother. I'm getting sick of wearing weeds and I want to make a speech 'cos I'm feeling mad at the world. Now – I said I was ashamed, and I'll tell you why. I was born before Nanaire and I'm goin' to die after her and in all that time nothing has changed. I hear tell it's the twentieth century, but to me it's still the Dark Ages. I just pray that if you ever get to my age that emancipation will mean the emancipation of women. And if there has to be another civil war over it, get in the front line. Don't hesitate a tick. Jus' get in there. Well, that's the end of what I've got to say so I'll go home now.'

Startled, Nancy watched as Aunt Lewis, thrusting a jewelled pin through her hat, opened the door with a flourish and disappeared, only to return immediately and add as an encore: 'Don't hang up all your clothes, child. You're too young to be Chillie's lackey for ever.'

'He needs me, Aunt Lewis.'

'I declare, you didn't hear a word I said, did you?'

'I heard you.'

The old woman suddenly smiled and kissed Nancy on the cheek: 'You're the best of the Langhornes. You're going to be fine because you've got guts, child. And remember – this doesn't have to be a man's world. We've got every right to it, too. God bless you, honey.'

Aunt Lewis then left without another word and returned to Danville. It was the first time Nancy had ever met her. It was also the last. Aunt Lewis died three months later with a request in her will that she should be buried without any mourners. Her money was bequeathed to women's suffrage.

'Nannie!'

No answer.

'Nannie – where are you?'

Chillie hurried down the stairs at Mirador, his face scarlet with anger. Below, Nancy appeared carrying a bowl of flowers and, even to the casual observer, she suddenly looked far older than her years. Her hair was unkempt, her body thinner than ever, and a weary melancholy hovered around her like a shroud.

'What is it now?' she asked.

'What's the meaning of this letter from Luke Harris? Says he's not going to deliver any more.'

'That's right.'

'Why in tarnation is that?'

'Because I told him we can't pay his prices, that's why.'

Footsteps were heard on the porch steps, followed by a knocking on the door.

'What do you mean – we *can't*?' Chillie thundered.

'Housekeeping allowance don't stretch to it. Sam! Door!'

'Your mother never complained.'

'She *thought* it. I'm *saying* it. Sam! Poppa – you want your bourbon regular, you give me more money.'

Hurrying from the kitchen, Sam crossed the hallway towards the door, stepping aside as Chillie pushed past him.

'By heavens, Nannie, you're richer than *I* am now.'

'That's not for your liquor or anyone else's. Who is it, Sam?'

At the door a teenage boy in a new suit, a straw hat on his head, blinked self-consciously, clutching a bouquet of flowers. 'Is th-this Miss Nora Langhorne's place?' he stammered.

'Sure is,' Nancy replied. 'But she's in boarding school.'

'Oh, but she said – '

Ignoring him, Chillie held up another invoice: 'Then what's this seventy-five dollars for? Answer me that!'

'That's your contribution to the mission.' Turning back to the young beau, she said: 'She won't be back from Baltimore for a month or more.'

'But it used to be *fifty*!' Chillie raged.

'Saving souls is more expensive today.'

A sudden strangled cry broke from the boy: 'But we're engaged to be married!'

There was a sudden silence as both Chillie and Nancy

slowly turned and looked at the pink-faced youth, the flowers already wilting in his hand.

'Engaged to my Nora?' Chillie asked in amazement.

'Yes, sir.'

'But you don't look like the boy in the photograph she
sent.'

'What boy?'

'Harry Miller.'

'But my name's Lloyd Stevens. Who's Harry Miller?'

Later, at supper, sitting beside Nanaire's empty chair and
opposite Chillie, Nancy said: 'Someone ought to say something to Nora. That's the third boy she's chucked this winter.'

Chillie didn't reply, his face contorted in mock disgust as
he attempted to swallow a mouthful of food. Finally, spit-
ting it out, he looked up at Sam: 'Is Anne ill, Sam?'

'Poppa – you're perfectly disgusting.'

'I'm talking to Sam. Is she?'

'No, sir.'

'Well, this turkey hash certainly is.'

'I think it's divine, Sam.' Nancy said. 'You tell Anne that,
y' hear?'

'Yes, Miss Nancy.'

Sam bowed, glanced nervously at Chillie and hurried out
of the room.

'Best thing I ever did was hire that nigger.'

'Then why don't you *tell* him that. Maybe he'd like to
hear it.'

'He don't need to. He knows he's appreciated.'

'Good! Because I'm raising his wages.'

'You're what?'

'I'm raising his wages. Molly too.'

'Molly! Now listen to me, woman – '

'Don't call me "woman".'

'I'm your father and I'll call you what I like.'

'You may be my father, but I'm the one who's keeping house here. And I'm saying that the servants need a decent wage. Lizzie spends more on a hat than they get in a month.'

'You been listening to that Reverend Neve again?'

'I listen to everybody, but I make up my own mind. Now the servants are going to get a raise, 'n that's final. Even if I have to pay it myself.'

'Now hold on – I'm letting no woman pay my share.'

'Then you'd better agree to the wages.'

'I'll think about it.'

'Think about it! By heaven, Poppa, I thank God every day that I'm not married to you.'

'So do I!'

For seven months this was the pattern of life in Mirador, a continual battle between father and daughter whose bullish pride allowed no favours. It was as inevitable as the dawn that one of them would finally crack, yielding out of sheer exhaustion. While tending her mother's grave in pouring rain, Nancy suddenly collapsed and lay on the wet earth for an hour before she was found. She remained in bed with a fever, hallucinating, screaming out in the night for her mother. Her son, Bobbie, now six years old, was brought to her bedside but she didn't recognize him and thought he was one of Lizzie's children. When the fever finally broke she found Chillie sitting next to the bed, studying her with a mixture of relief and guilt. She did not know it, but her father had attended her for thirty-six hours without sleep. At one point he thought she had died, and had crouched on his knees, praying to a God he hardly knew. When Nancy finally opened her eyes, puzzled by where she was, her attention was focused on Chillie.

'Hello, Poppa. You been ill or something? You look wretched. You really do.'

'I'm fine. How are *you* feeling, girl?'

'Me? Can't be anything wrong with me, can there? Where's Bobbie?'

'He's playing with the Perkins boys.'

'Oh, my God. What's he done to deserve that?'

Chillie stared self-consciously at his daughter for a long while. Then, as if coming to a decision: 'Nannie – I been thinking. Well, I've been doing more than that. I've arranged for you to take a holiday – '

'Holiday? In November? I can't – '

'Yes, you can. Lizzie can keep house.'

'Lizzie! No, Poppa – '

'Hear me out.'

'She couldn't look after a dog – '

'Will you listen to me. Now then. I've arranged for you to stay in England for a while – '

'England!'

'Stop repeating me.'

'England – '

'Now shut up for a minute and let me speak.'

Chillie glared at her, then relaxed, concentrating on lighting a cigar. 'Now, I want to say that I haven't been the best of people to look after, but I appreciate what you've done. You kept me sane, Nannie. I mean that. And I've been blind to the fact that you're still just a young woman. This is no place for you. That's why I've taken the liberty for you to go to England. I've discussed it with Irene and Dana and they've arranged everything. Where to go, who you're going to see – oh, dammit, I can't smoke this.' Hurling the cigar aside, he added: 'So what do you say?'

'But Momma – '

'Don't worry, your mother would have approved. It's my thank-you to you, Nannie. That's what it is. Besides, Nanaire always wanted you to visit the old country. She often talked about it.'

There was no reaction from Nancy. She merely lay in the bed staring at Chillie in bewilderment.

'Well,' he said, standing up, 'I'd better go and see how Lizzie's spending my money. And ... well, I had a look through Sears' catalogue and ... I reckon this might buy you a dress. Something to go away with. Something pretty.' A bundle of notes was placed on the bedside table. 'I hope it's enough.'

As he was leaving the room, Nancy suddenly seemed to come alive, jumping out of bed, seizing the money. 'Poppa – take it back. You know I can't go and leave you.'

'I wouldn't tell your companion about that. Her bags are already packed.'

'Companion? What companion?'

Opening the door wider, Chillie stepped aside with a flourish to reveal Phyllis.

'Hello, Nannie,' Phyllis smiled, then hurried into the room and hugged her sister. 'Seems like Virginia is about to invade England.'

It was arranged that Bobbie should travel with them, accompanied by a nurse, as well as Phyllis's two sons, Peter and David, the latter known as Winkie, who were now almost strangers to their father. It was clear that, like Nancy's before her, Phyllis's marriage to the rich Northerner Reggie Brooks was proving to be a mistake.

'Is it over, Phyll?' Nancy asked as she packed a trunk, one of several.

'I don't know,' Phyllis replied. She was standing before the bedroom fire, the placket of her skirt unbuttoned as she warmed her bottom. 'I saw what you went through and I don't want to go through it myself.'

'We sure splintered the Langhorne family tree, didn't we?'

'Seems like it.'

Phyllis smiled shyly, watching Nancy place her riding gear in the trunk. Their visit to England was planned to coincide with the start of the hunting season. Moreover, the Gibson connections in England were impeccable; he had been unofficial court artist to Queen Victoria as well as sketching the wedding of her son Edward, now the King, and Alexandra.

'Nannie?'

'Yes.'

'Do you remember when we were kids, you said I was adopted?'

'Did I?'

'Yes you did, and you know it. Well, I believed you. I was sick for days.'

'Were you?'

Nancy smiled, then suddenly giggled, the laughter infectious.

'You said I was found in a ditch.'

'Did I say that?'

'You said Poppa found me in a ditch. Like an old shoe or something.'

The two sisters were now holding each other for support,

shaking with laughter. Then Phyllis suddenly said: 'I wasn't, was I?'

'Course not, Phyll. It was in a rain tub that you was found.'

Lying on her stomach on the bed, dressed in her underclothes and eating candy, Nancy sorted through the invitations and letters recommended by the Gibsons.

'Irene sure has become a snob. Almost every introduction here is to a Lord or a Lady or an Honourable.'

'Got one there for King Edward?'

'Phyll! You don't get given introductions to the King. You have to be *presented* to him.'

'That's not what I heard,' Phyllis said with a mischievous giggle.

'Now cut that out. We are two respectable ladies.'

'Course we are, Nannie. *You* just happen to be *divorced*. And I just happen to be – well, I don't know what *I* am. But we're sure respectable.'

Eight days later, in November 1904, Mrs Nancy Shaw, her sister Mrs Phyllis Brooks and their respective children set sail from New York for England. They were not to know it, but for all of them their life, not only in Virginia but in America itself, was almost over.

TEN

·

Affairs of Love

On arriving in England, the Shaws and the Brookses stayed first in London at Fleming's Hotel in Half Moon Street while they studied the lie of the land. They soon discovered, from their invitations, that the land in fact lay further north in the hunting country surrounding Market Harborough.

Unable to resist the combination of the English country-side and horses, the two women took a hunting lodge called Highfield House and set out to meet 'society'. As young, beautiful and seemingly unattached ladies they were accepted with affection; as Americans, whose accents were unusual to say the least, they were viewed with curiosity and awe, as well as a hint of suspicion. Rich American women had begun to set their sights on the British aristocracy and even to marry one or two of them – a Vanderbilt had become Duchess of Marlborough, a Zimmerman was now Duchess of Manchester and a Thaw from Pittsburgh was Countess of Yarmouth – but, as yet, the results were not disastrous. However, Nancy made it clear that she was in England to hunt the fox not the men, and hunt she did. She also made it clear that she was not a nanny-coddled, frail young thing like many of her contemporaries; once, when

General Tom Holland offered to help her remount after a fall, Nancy snapped back: 'Do you think I would be such an ass as to come out hunting if I couldn't mount from the ground!'

After demonstrating not only that she could, but was also undaunted by all the other fences and ditches of social life, she and Phyllis were soon adopted by Holland and the Cunards – Gordon and Edith – and displayed like jewellery at *soirées*, *thés dansants* and, more pertinently, hunt balls.

It was at one such ball that Nancy met the notorious roué Harry Cust, who was reputed to have sired single-handed, if that is the word, the next generation of the aristocracy, although nemesis had decreed that he himself was officially childless. He liked the two sisters from Virginia immediately and he was not shy to tell them why.

'And where exactly is your husband, Mrs Brooks?' he asked Phyllis while he partnered her during a waltz.

'In America.'

'How considerate of him. And are you and your sister here for the whole of the season?'

'We haven't decided yet, Mr Cust.'

'Ah, but I am sure you will by the end of the evening.'

Nancy was also to meet a woman who was to become a lifelong, if brittle, friend, a woman with the face of Punch and a demonic wit, a political hostess with a tantalizing past and with a future as wife to a prime minister. Now in her forties, her name was Margot Asquith, and she sat on a chaise longue beside Edith Cunard and surveyed the seasonal frolic like an empress at an arena.

'Is that one of those Americans dancing with Harry?' Edith asked, peering through a lorgnette.

'My dear Edith,' Margot replied, her voice reminiscent of

a nasal yawn, 'it can *only* be one of those Americans dancing with Harry. It was bad enough when they came over singly, rattling their jewellery and practising their curtsies, hell-bent for Blenheim. But now they are arriving in *droves*, darling.'

It was then that Margot became aware of Nancy, standing before her and being introduced by General Holland.

'Mrs Asquith – may I present Mrs Robert Shaw?'

'I'm from America too, Mrs Asquith,' Nancy announced steadily. 'From Virginia. That's in the South.'

'How noble of you. And are you visiting or immigrating?'

'Why, Mrs Asquith, you ought to know better than that. I'm just over here to see what my great-grandaddy fought you for.'

'And while you're doing that, I suppose you'll also try and steal one of our husbands.'

'Mrs Asquith – if you knew the trouble I had getting rid of mine, you'd know I don't want *yours*.'

There was an immediate roar of laughter from Margot as she seized Nancy's hand. 'Mrs Shaw, thank goodness you are here.'

Later it was Nancy's turn to dance with Harry Cust.

'And where exactly is your husband, Mrs Shaw?'

'I haven't got a husband any more.'

'Oh – I'm sorry to hear it.'

'*You* may be, Mr Cust, but I'm not.'

It was then that Nancy met the third person that evening who would become an integral part of her life in England. Only this time the relationship would be far different from the platonic friendship of Cust, who had rapidly accepted that the Virginia sisters were not to be conquests, and the amicable rivalry of Margot Asquith. She had noticed a man watching her across the ballroom since the beginning of the evening. He was a tall, balding dandy with thin, arrogant features who rarely smiled but whose eyes studied everything she did. She was to learn that he was a bachelor, which was to his credit; that he was sober by nature, serious in thought and head of a merchant bank – which, of course, was also to his credit. Moreover she was to learn that he was a peer of the realm, a respected member of society, the brother of the writer Maurice Baring, and a gourmet whose cook was the legendary Rosa Lewis. It was Cust, a close friend, who made the introductions, leading her across the floor as heads turned in interest.

'His name is John Baring,' Cust whispered to her. 'Once you know him, you need know no other. Doors will open everywhere.'

'As long as they stay open. I have no intention of being closed in with anyone.'

'Don't be hasty, Mrs Shaw.'

'I have no intention to, Mr Cust.'

As Nancy passed Phyllis, cornered by a ruby-faced bore, she winked and then found herself before her admirer.

'Lord Revelstoke,' Cust said, 'may I present Mrs Shaw. Mrs Shaw is a divorcee.'

'Delighted to make your acquaintance, Mrs Shaw. Perhaps I may be your partner for the next dance.'

'I'm sorry, but I promised General Holland.'

'And then – '

'And then Gordon Cunard.'

Nancy then smiled politely and walked away, aware of Revelstoke watching her as well as the attention of the two social observers on the chaise longue.

'I do believe our friend Mrs Shaw has made a conquest, Margot.'

'Nonsense, my dear. It's *far* too early in the season.'

Early or not, Nancy *had* made a conquest. And much to her surprise she was not displeased. All resolutions were suddenly abandoned. She wanted to meet John Revelstoke again, but she would bide her time. At the age of twenty-five she had learnt from bitter experience. Revelstoke might well be the opposite in character to Robert Gould Shaw, but her initial emotions were not.

The 'season' in England was an insular affair, constant and inflexible. The same faces appeared at the same occasions with unfailing regularity so that it was impossible for Nancy not to meet Revelstoke again. Indeed Revelstoke arranged his diary deliberately to coincide with Nancy's chosen routine. He pursued her with relentless ardour; letters declaring his love were sent, flowers were delivered to wherever she stayed. At first Nancy resisted; she was flattered, but she refused all invitations for a private rendezvous. As she told Phyllis: 'I don't intend to be winter sport for the peerage. At least, not just yet.'

She was also, it must be admitted, afraid; not because she was clearly falling in love with John Revelstoke but because she found herself *physically* attracted to him. It unnerved her to experience sexual desire; the very act still revolted her and always would, and yet the very presence of Revelstoke excited her. Once, at a weekend spent at Taplow Court, the home of Ettie Grenfell – later to be Lady Desborough – she saw Revelstoke walking alone with Ettie and was immediately jealous. The intensity of the emotion startled her; she convinced herself that it was irrational and foolish, that she was transforming an innocent promenade between two people into an affair. Paradoxically, though Nancy did not know it, she was right. Revelstoke had been one of Ettie Grenfell's loves for many years – another was Evan Charteris, a third the woman's own husband – but considered it to be the best-kept secret in England. Besides, Revelstoke was seeking a wife as well as a mistress. And, having secured the latter, he had now set his sights on the former. He had chosen Nancy and could see no reason why she should refuse him.

Early in the New Year of 1905 Nancy finally accepted a personal invitation from Revelstoke, to attend a preview of *Major Barbara* at the Royal Court Theatre. Although he was not interested in the arts himself, he believed Nancy was; she wasn't, but she agreed to be his guest in his private box anyway. Both were bored by the play but not by each other, and whispered throughout. At one point, Revelstoke held her hand.

'I do hope we will see each other again, Mrs Shaw.'

'Yes.'

'Do you like the opera?'

'I'm afraid not.'

'Then perhaps a concert?'

'No.'

'Nothing musical?'

'Nothing musical. But do you play golf?'

'Not out of season.'

'Pity.'

'But I'm motoring to the West Country. Perhaps?'

'Perfect.'

'You are angelic, Mrs Shaw. Angelic and golden.'

They left the theatre during the interval.

The following week Nancy travelled in the Revelstoke Rolls-Royce to his estate in Dorset. She was now completely in love with the humourless merchant banker who had wooed her so successfully, despite the fact that he was both Jewish and a snob – two factors which Nancy would normally have considered unsatisfactory in a man. However, regarding the question of marriage she did not yet know her own mind. But she did know his.

'I'm frightened to speak to you, Nancy,' Revelstoke said as the car travelled past the winter fields of Hampshire. They both sat side by side at the rear of the Rolls, sharing a fur blanket against the cold. 'I am not an articulate man, as you know. My brother Maurice tells me I have no sense of humour and he's right. I spend my days talking money with other bankers. I could tell you the history of Baring Brothers right down to the final comma, the last full stop. But ask me to tell you how I feel and I'm speechless.'

'I don't mind silence,' Nancy said, smiling. 'I seem to have spent most of my life listening to people hollering at each other. Say it right out and be done with it.'

'And what would you say about me?'

'You mean like the truth game? Truth, promise or dare?'

'In a way.'

'Well, I'm flattered that you tried to impress me, but when you get to know me better you'll realize it doesn't.'

'Forgive me, I didn't mean to sound – '

'You don't have to apologize. I've got no regrets about accepting your invitation. I've wanted to see you again ever since Market Harborough, but you sure took a long time getting round to it. I was beginning to think that your heart was set on someone else.'

'No one else, Nancy. No one in the world.'

Revelstoke had lied without even faltering. That he should have done so, seeking marriage from Nancy, while continuing his liaison with Ettie Grenfell, revealed an arrogant self-righteousness in his character that was to be his downfall. And yet his feelings towards Nancy were genuine; he loved her and he wanted her to become Lady Revelstoke, an enviable role for any ambitious woman. And still he lied.

'No one in the world, Nancy. It's just that I've been a bachelor for so long that when I meet someone like you I want to write you sonnets. Take you around the world. Cover you with diamonds – '

'Don't be shy about the diamonds.'

'I love you, Nancy. That's my truth.'

Calmly, Nancy turned towards him and said quietly: 'Would your driver be shocked if you kissed me?'

That evening, John Revelstoke formally asked Nancy to be his wife. She replied that she was flattered and would consider it seriously and would give him her answer before the season was over. Secretly, she had already decided that she would accept his proposal; only propriety prevented her from answering yes immediately – as well as the lingering fear of marriage itself.

'I thought I loved Bob Shaw,' she told Revelstoke, 'and that the marriage would last for ever. Instead he betrayed me and I couldn't bear for that to happen again.'

'*I'd* never betray you.'

'I want to believe that. That's why I need to go away to think it over.'

'But where will you go?'

'Phyllis and I are planning to motor across France to Monte Carlo.'

'To Monte? When will you be there?'

'April.'

'Then let me meet you. I have to be in Paris for a conference. It's a wrench missing part of the season, but since I *have* to be there I could take a few days off, travel south and meet you. That is – if you think you would have an answer by then?'

'I know I will.'

Later, while playing backgammon after supper, Revelstoke said: 'Of course you would have to meet kings and queens and entertain ambassadors, but I'm sure you could do that, couldn't you?'

'These kings and queens and ambassadors seem awfully important to you.'

'They are part of my life. And they would be part of yours.'

'My son, Bobbie, is part of my life. And you would have to be a father to him. I'm sure you could do that, couldn't you?'

'But of course, Nancy. He'd have everything he ever wanted. There's nothing in the world that would be denied him. . . . Have I said anything wrong?'

Nancy was silent, and slid a counter into the corner of the board. 'I'll give you my answer in Monte Carlo.'

Society, it is said, is like the air; necessary to breathe but insufficient to live on. The same could be said about gossip, the oxygen of society. John Baring, Lord Revelstoke, should have realized this more than anyone. Gossip soon spread that he had proposed marriage to Nancy Shaw. His first mistake (as he waited for Nancy's answer) was to deny it. His second mistake was to deny it to Alastair Mackenzie, the society columnist of the *Daily Mail* which then, as now, paid more than a passing interest in the peccadilloes of the social world. The peer and the reporter met on the steps of Revelstoke's club, and the encounter was far from amicable.

'Lord Revelstoke,' Mackenzie asked immediately, resisting any opening pleasantries, 'is it true that you are about to announce your engagement to an American divorcee called Mrs Shaw?'

'No, it is *not* true. And if you print a word of it in your rag, I will deny it.'

'Then I will report it simply as rumour, sir.'

'You will report nothing. Because if you do, I will personally ask Northcliffe to drum you out of every newspaper office in the country.'

It was a threat that Mackenzie accepted as if it were a gauntlet thrown at his feet. 'May I ask, Lord Revelstoke, what exactly *do* you have to hide? Could it be that you do not wish your relationship with Mrs Shaw to reach the ears of a certain – married lady?'

Revelstoke's reply was his final mistake: 'From this moment, Mr Mackenzie, you may consider yourself one of the unemployed. Join the scum where you belong.'

The next morning the *Daily Mail* published a news item which, though discreetly within the law of libel, hinted at a relationship between Mrs Ettie Grenfell of Taplow Court and Lord Revelstoke of Baring Brothers. The story was soon elaborated as it spread from salon to salon so that it was not surprising, therefore, that when John Revelstoke arrived in Monte Carlo, still blindly expecting an affirmative answer from Nancy, he soon discovered that Nancy was no longer there. She had left, with her sister and the children, to return prematurely to Virginia. Only a sealed letter was left to welcome Revelstoke's arrival.

My dearest John,

I know I am a coward in not waiting to see you. But I cannot endure the thought that you may have betrayed me. Jealousy is evil and so is gossip. But even if the stories that there is another woman in your life, and has been for many years, are untrue, I would find it impossible to forget they exist.

Forgive me if I misjudge you, but I cannot live through my past again. I am too vulnerable. I will never forget the happiness of these past months. That would be impossible.

I am going back to Virginia which now seems a million miles away. Try to understand me, and pray that we will each find our happiness in our own way.

    Yours in love,
    Nancy

Revelstoke left Monte Carlo immediately and returned to England where he went directly to Taplow Court to seek consolation with Mrs Ettie Grenfell. His aspirations towards Nancy, moreover, were far from dimmed. He still believed that she would one day be his wife. It was possible, despite what had happened, that this might well occur. She was still in love with Revelstoke and unhappy without him. However, an unexpected encounter was to take place before the year was out that neither of them could foresee, an encounter that was to change both their lives for ever. Ironically Revelstoke, by altering Nancy's plans, was unwittingly responsible for his own personal tragedy.

ELEVEN

·

The Passenger on the Ocean Liner

To Nancy, Mirador now seemed a house of ghosts. Heart-broken after the affair with Revelstoke, she nevertheless could not forget him and even replied to his letters, though her tone was cold and uncommitted. She became depressed, her health suffered and she retreated to her room. Finally she realized that there was only one course of action; she would return to England and re-evaluate her emotions once and for all. As if seeking reassurance, she asked not only Phyllis to accompany her once more but also her father; Chillie, who had still not recovered from the death of his wife, agreed instantly. Consequently in December 1905 the family sailed east once again, only this time the voyage was to be more than memorable. It began, as the ocean liner ploughed through the icy waves of the Atlantic, with sea-sickness. Nancy, a poor sailor, was ill from the moment the ship left New York.

'Retribution! Retribution!' she cried as she hurled herself once again across the deck towards the rail.

'Retribution for what?' a voice asked behind her.

Feeling as if she was near to death, Nancy refused to turn round to acknowledge the owner of the voice, but if she had she would have seen a tall, handsome man of twenty-five with deep brown eyes, a dark moustache and black curly hair. Being shy, he would probably not have introduced himself immediately but would have smiled and walked on to wait for a more opportune moment. Nancy would then have discovered that the stranger on the deck was the heir to one of the greatest fortunes in the world, and that his name was Waldorf Astor.

The opportune moment came the following evening when Chillie and his two daughters were invited to the captain's table. Though still feeling ill, Nancy, who was placed on the right of the captain, was not unaware of the attentions of the man sitting diagonally across the table nor was she unimpressed when she learnt that he was a member of the Astor family. But if wealth alone was a powerful aphrodisiac, Nancy did not respond. She saw Waldorf simply as an intelligent and charming man and nothing more. She was therefore indifferent to his gaze and listened politely to the conversation at the table. The subject, inevitably, was politics.

'I cannot accept your view, sir,' she heard the captain say to a man on her right, 'that Balfour resigned out of cowardice.'

'Then what would you call it?'

'The chance to fight again.'

'If the Liberals will let him.'

'Well, I think the rule that one should never discuss politics or religion ought to be observed. Wouldn't you agree, Mr Astor?'

'It depends on the alternative,' Waldorf replied. 'If it is a matter of a superb dinner like this, then I'm quite content to eat in silence.'

He smiled and looked around the table until his eyes rested once again on Nancy. She ignored him, having no intention to show any favour towards yet another millionaire. Two in her short life were enough.

But, unknown to Nancy, Waldorf Astor was not just another millionaire, and very unlike both Robert Gould Shaw and Lord Revelstoke. The Astors, originally from Germany – though some reports claim that they were descended from the Astorgas, Sephardic Jews from Spain – were adventurers. John Jacob the First was a fur trapper in Colonial America whose skill, not only with a gun but also in the marketplace, enabled him to found both the American Fur Company and the Pacific Fur Company. The profits he invested in land; and the land was called Manhattan, so that by the end of the nineteenth century, the Astors not only loved New York, they also owned it. To Waldorf's father, William Waldorf, however, such wealth was not enough. He wanted to be respected; he saw himself as a Renaissance prince and even wrote an unreadable history of the Borgias. Resenting America for worshipping Mammon, he returned to Europe to establish the Astor dynasty in England, became a British subject and, in order to live like the lord he intended to be, bought two magnificent mansions – Hever Castle in Kent and Cliveden in Buckinghamshire – as well as various other properties scattered here and there.

But if William Astor was an eccentric with dreams of becoming an aristocrat, his son Waldorf was quite the reverse. As the first true English Astor he went to Eton, where he was Captain of the Boats and Treasurer of Pop, and then to Oxford where he excelled as a sportsman until his health,

or rather the lack of it, denied him these activities. Consequently he became serious in character, methodical, shunning the blandishments of the *jeunesse dorée*. Far from being
an intellectual, he chose to live the life of a gentleman,
breeding horses that he was no longer allowed to ride and
caring about those less fortunate than himself. Without having found a personal purpose in life, he devoted his time to
benefiting the lives of others. As such, he was not unlike
Nancy. Like her also, he neither smoked nor drank alcohol.
But perhaps the most fascinating similarity was that, by
bizarre coincidence, they were both exactly the same age,
having been born on the identical day, month and year: 19
May 1879. Even the stars, it seemed, had decreed that they
were destined for each other. Certainly Waldorf himself
would have agreed – he fell in love with Nancy the first
moment he saw her on the ocean liner. Nancy, however,
believed she loved someone else. Destiny and Waldorf Astor
would have to wait.

'Then I assume, Mr Astor,' the captain said, 'that you are
a Liberal? An anti-Balfour?'

'Quite the reverse, captain. I admire Balfour, but he relied
on the vote of the middle classes. The Tories have always
ignored the working man, and as a result they are out of
office.'

'Those are hardly the words I expect to hear from a
millionaire,' someone said.

'What, may I ask, is a millionaire expected to say?'

'Just that you seem to champion the working man.'

'Perhaps, unlike the middle classes, it's because we both
inherited our way of life. We had no choice.'

'But you are rich and they claim to be poor.'

'They *are* poor, sir. There is no need to claim it.'

Nancy slowly turned and looked directly at Waldorf for the first time: 'Perhaps, Mr Astor, you are considering giving all your money away? To narrow the gap?'

'I am not a philanthropist, Mrs Shaw. Nor do I wish to be. I myself would prefer to use money for the benefit of others. Though I don't pretend to be St Francis.'

'You talk like a politician.'

'Well, since I am *not* a politician, I will accept that as a compliment.'

'Yes, Mr Astor.'

Waldorf stared at Nancy, was about to speak, then suddenly looked away and was silent. Opposite him Chillie, ignoring protocol, lit a cigar and studied him with approval. Later, after the meal was over and the other guests had departed, he made a point of asking Waldorf to share a pot of coffee with him in the saloon. If Nancy did not know which cards to play, Chillie Langhorne certainly did.

'Mr Astor – I'm from Virginia and I've met many a rich man in my life though none, of course, as rich as you – '

'That's the penalty of being an Astor, Mr Langhorne. People see dollar signs before they even notice the colour of your necktie.'

'I wasn't seeing dollar signs. Because if I was, I'd suggest a quiet game of stud poker.'

'I think I can afford to resist that, sir.'

'Yes, Mr Astor, I believe you can.'

Chillie grinned and stared towards a chaise longue where Nancy and Phyllis sat side by side. He did this deliberately, moving round in his chair, and noticed with satisfaction that Waldorf did the same. Keeping his gaze on Nancy, Chillie asked casually: 'Are you married, Mr Astor?'

'No, sir. I am not.'

'I'm surprised. A man of your qualities needs a wife. Someone to share his life.'

'Well ... yes. I agree but – '

'You haven't found her yet?'

Waldorf was silent.

Chillie smiled and sipped his brandy. 'My daughter Nancy is a fine woman. When she chooses to marry again, her husband will be very privileged. Take my word for it.'

'I believe you, sir.'

'You know, Mr Astor, I think you and I share the same ideals in life. And if we ever did play that game of poker, I'd be hard put to know who'd win.'

On the chaise longue, out of earshot of the two men, Phyllis said: 'Do you realize he's one of the richest men in the whole world?'

'Who?'

'Who do you think? And he's not married.'

'Well, thank heavens Nora's not on board.'

'Oh, he wouldn't go for someone flighty like Nora. He's a serious man.'

'And rich.'

'And intelligent.'

'And rich.'

'Nannie – even if I were free it wouldn't be because he's *rich* that I'd favour him.'

Nancy immediately roared with laughter: 'Don't be a jackass, Phyll. Trying to see an Astor without seeing money is like trying to ignore the Grand Canyon. Can't be done.'

She then turned and looked at her sister and winked just as Waldorf appeared before them, stopped and bowed. 'Well, goodnight, Mrs Brooks. Mrs Shaw.'

'Goodnight,' Phyllis replied immediately, smiling, but Waldorf was looking at Nancy.

'Are you sure you're all right now? Not sea-sick?'

'No, I'm not all right. But I'll survive.'

'I sincerely hope so.' And then: 'I'm sure we'll see each other again.'

Nancy said nothing as Waldorf walked away, then heard Phyllis giggling. 'Stop that, Phyll. I've got enough trouble as it is without falling in love with someone else.'

Four days later the ship docked at Southampton and Nancy travelled north to Market Harborough to discover that John Revelstoke was already there, awaiting the opportunity to meet her again.

TWELVE

·

Rivals

The two Langhorne sisters, after spending the day hunting with the Ferne, had returned to Highfield House as it was growing dark. Both women were hungry and tired and didn't notice the car parked discreetly at the end of the driveway. It was only as they reached the paddock that they realized that a visitor had come to call, a visitor who had presented Bobbie with a Shetland pony. When asked who the benefactor was, Bobbie replied simply:

'The bald man.'

Entering the drawing-room, Nancy came face to face with Revelstoke for the first time in eight months. He was standing squarely before the fire and had obviously been talking to Chillie who immediately left the room, without comment, leaving Nancy and Revelstoke alone.

'Good afternoon, Nancy. I was on my way to Chatsworth when I heard that you were here.'

She didn't love him any more. She knew that immediately. It was a stranger talking to her, someone from the village who was just paying a courtesy visit. She wondered why this man was smiling at her with such intimacy and had the effrontery to address her by her first name.

'Your father and I were talking,' Revelstoke continued, his right hand constantly toying with his watch. 'I was telling him about banking. Advising him how to invest his money. . . .'

But Nancy was not listening. She suddenly seemed detached from everything that was happening and was peering at her reflection in the window, looking at herself standing in a mud-stained riding habit before a tall, bald-headed, pompous fop.

'Lord Revelstoke,' she said finally, 'forgive me but I cannot think of a single word to say to you.'

And then she left the room and hurried to the stairs. She could hear him running after her, calling out her name. She saw Chillie watching quietly, a cigar in his mouth. On the landing she stopped and looked down towards the hall.

'Just answer me this, Lord Revelstoke. Did you give a pony to Ettie Grenfell's boy as well?'

The words were said without her realizing it. It seemed the most outrageous thing to ask. And yet Revelstoke didn't reply. He merely turned away, his face scarlet, and left Highfield House.

At her bedroom window she watched his car drive fast along the road until it could no longer be seen, lost in the fading light. That evening she remained in her room, saying that she had no appetite. After supper, Chillie entered and sat silently by her bed, holding her hand. It was as if they were back in Mirador and she was just a child being comforted by her father. She listened to him talk about his younger days, his voice quiet and sad, reminiscing of a life that would never return. He talked of his dead wife, how he had met her and how much he had loved her. He showed Nancy a portrait of Nanaire in a locket as if she never knew who the woman was, and held in the palm of his hand a lock of her blonde hair. He kissed it and then wept openly without embarrassment.

'Kindness. Laughter. Love,' he said. 'A marriage is nothing without those. One can survive without money. One can survive deaths and sorrows. But one must have kindness. Laughter. And love.'

Not once did Chillie mention or allude to Revelstoke, nor even reveal what he felt about the man. He simply sat by her bedside until the fire died in the hearth and the room grew cold. As he covered her with blankets, he seemed to Nancy to be the loneliest man she had ever seen. He left England a month later and returned to Virginia. It was the only place in the world where he wanted to be.

In February, Harry Cust invited Nancy to a reception in London for the German ambassador. On the telephone he told her that the season had been fearfully dull and that it needed a firework or two.

'And I suppose *I'm* to be the firework?'

'But of course.'

'Why this sudden invitation, Mr Cust? Am I to be your guest?'

'Definitely not. I would not dare harm your reputation. You will be accompanied by my wife.'

On any other occasion Nancy would have been suspicious of Cust's motives, but she had been lonely in England, refusing invitations, so that they were no longer sent. She was tired of hunting, tired of the horse-and-hounds clique of Market Harborough, and London suddenly appealed to her.

'Then I accept, Mr Cust,' she said. It was to be an eventful occasion.

The ball, at the German Embassy, naturally attracted the cream of society, the women anxious to display their jewellery and the men their charms. Among the first to arrive were Margot Asquith and Harry Cust, positioning themselves by the door so that they could witness who arrived with whom and who intended to leave with whom. Margot and Cust, however, were not alone in their curious sport; they were also accompanied by two other friends of Cust, invited by him personally and both unaware of who else might arrive.

'It will be a fascinating game,' Cust had said. 'We will see what particular tune the season is playing. For one and all.'

The two friends were Mrs Ettie Grenfell and John Revelstoke.

'Lord and Lady Elcho!' the footman announced.

'Ah,' Cust smiled. 'That means poor Balfour should not be far behind.'

'Harry, my dear,' Margot purred. 'You are quite impossible. You always voice what other people think.'

'While you, of course, write it all down for the servants to read.'

'The Honourable Mr Evan Charteris!'

Heads turned and there were sidelong glances as Ettie's other suitor was presented to the German ambassador. But Charteris, as a true gentleman, dampened the rumours by walking directly to Ettie, kissing her hand and walking away. Not to be outdone, Cust turned the subject of conversation to one nearer Ettie's heart: her social status, now that her husband – shooting buffalo in Canada – had been granted a peerage.

'Ettie – now that your husband has made a name for himself, has he decided what it is going to be?'

'I still think "St Just" is perfect,' Revelstoke interrupted. 'Lord St Just.'

'John – we've discussed that – '

'Wasn't there a St Just who was hanged?' Margot inquired.

'Guillotined,' Cust said. 'The poor fellow was French.'

'Nevertheless, I still think "St Just" – '

'Willy doesn't *like* the name, John.'

'So what *is* it to be?'

'Desborough.'

'Desborough!' Margot exclaimed.

'Desborough.'

'But it sounds like a suburb!'

It was at this moment that the footman announced: 'Mrs Robert Shaw!'

The effect on Revelstoke was startling as Nancy entered and saw him standing next to Ettie, his face scarlet. Hesitating only for a moment, Nancy walked towards the group, her face impassive, and studied each one in turn.

'Good evening, Margot. I hear tell Henry's in Downing Street now.'

'Only at Number Eleven, darling.'

'Well, I'm sure he'll move next door in time. Good evening, Lord Revelstoke.'

No answer.

Nancy moved her attention to Ettie. 'Good evening – Mrs Grenfell.'

'Ettie is a Lady now,' Cust smiled.

'I would never have known.'

Immediately Nancy turned away, walking back towards the door.

'Damn you, Harry!' Revelstoke snapped and, had it been

another century, would probably have challenged him to a duel. He saw Nancy falter, as if she was about to faint, pushing past guests, stumbling out of the ballroom as her composure snapped.

'Why are you waiting, John?' Ettie asked coldly before abandoning him for Charteris. 'Comfort the woman.'

Revelstoke found Nancy in the main hall, leaning against a pillar, gasping for air.

'Nancy – '

'Leave me alone.'

'But, Nancy, let me explain – '

'You can't, because you don't know what there is to explain.' Turning towards him, she said: 'It isn't Ettie or anything like that. That's only part of it. It isn't even because you lied to me. It's something I've known all along. But I loved you and tried to put it aside.'

'I don't know what you mean – '

'I know you don't. That's why I'll tell you. The only thing that matters to you is what's happening around us now. The people in there. That small world that goes from season to season doing exactly the same thing. Year after year. They plan their future by how many invitations are handed through the door. That's how you've always lived, John, and you're not going to change now. When I arrived here, you were more scared that I'd make a scandal and a few doors would close on you.'

'That isn't true, Nancy.'

'Then answer me this. What exactly are you planning to achieve in your life that I might share? With all your money and status, what grand design do you have?'

Revelstoke didn't and couldn't answer. He merely stared at Nancy, knowing finally that he had lost her.

'Goodbye, Nancy,' he said and turned and walked back to the reception without looking back. For a long time Nancy didn't move; she found herself trembling and, sitting on a chair in the deserted hall, closed her eyes. She felt an indescribable sadness.

'Still sea-sick?'

The voice seemed unreal, as if it was part of a dream. And then she became aware of a man standing before her as she opened her eyes and looked up to see the man smiling at her.

'We met on the ship. Remember?' he said. 'My name's Waldorf Astor.'

Two months later, Nancy wrote to Chillie to tell him that she was engaged to be married. She had no doubts that he would approve of her choice of husband, although she made no mention that she actually *loved* Waldorf. In truth, she probably did, but in a far different way from that in which she had loved Shaw or Revelstoke, or even from the way Waldorf loved her. She simply knew that she was happy, that Bobbie would have an ideal stepfather and she would have a husband who was loyal, temperate and, of course, very rich. The wedding took place at All Souls Church, Langham Place, on 3 May 1906, five months after the bride and groom had first met on the ocean liner. The honeymoon took place in Switzerland. John Revelstoke, the rejected suitor, remained a bachelor for the rest of his life.

THIRTEEN

·

A House in Buckinghamshire

Although neither father was able to attend the wedding, it was clear that the marriage gained not only the approval of Chillie but also, more surprisingly, that of the anglophile William Waldorf Astor. If he had hoped that his son would marry into the English aristocracy, he didn't reveal it. Instead he presented Waldorf with Cliveden, the house in Buckinghamshire, as a wedding gift; and to Nancy he gave the famous Sanci diamond that once belonged to the Stuart kings of England. After this extravagant gesture William Waldorf retreated to Hever Castle, vowing never to set foot in Cliveden again. It was perhaps a fortuitous decision on his part, since his new daughter-in-law intended, as soon as she returned from her honeymoon, to redesign the interior of Cliveden from roof to cellar.

It was the third house to stand on this promontory above the Thames near Maidenhead. The first had belonged to George Villiers, Second Duke of Buckingham; three hundred years later it had been redesigned by Sir Charles Barry for the Duke of Westminster – transformed into a solid Victorian mansion, unfussy in aspect, unromantic in character. But if it was grand and majestic enough for William Waldorf Astor when he bought it, it still lacked his own personal fantasy, the minor details worthy of a Renaissance prince.

Consequently shiploads of stonework were removed from the Villa Borghese in Rome, and balustrades, statues, fountains and urns were transplanted below the southern face of the building between terrace and parterre. Sarcophagi of Theseus and Endymion and the gods of love lined the main driveway until Cliveden took on the appearance of a mausoleum rather than a home. Not surprisingly Nancy described its interior as 'gloom, gloom, splendid gloom'; she immediately replaced the tapestries with chintz curtains and preferred flowers in the rooms to sightless busts of Roman emperors. The entire Italian mosaic floor of the hall was ripped out and replaced by parquet; while a ceiling of romping satyrs and naked nymphs was clearly not in keeping with Nancy's puritanical mind:

'Enjoy yourself while you can,' she announced to the painted orgy above her head, 'because it's your turn next.'

If the final result was a curious Virginia prissiness more in keeping with a country cottage, the house at least had light and colour within its grey austerity and was comfortable enough to be considered a home. After a whirlwind of activity Nancy could finally consider herself mistress of Cliveden as well as its one hundred and fifty servants.

By a strange irony that was not entirely appreciated by Nancy the neighbouring house, if Cliveden with all its land could possibly claim to *have* a neighbour, was none other than Taplow Court, the home of Ettie Grenfell, Lady Desborough, where she no doubt dined with John Revelstoke as Nancy dined with Waldorf. In fact it was Bobbie Shaw, now seven years old, who first made contact between the two houses after meeting one of Ettie's sons, Billy, in the grounds of Cliveden. Although both boys were to remain friends for the remainder of their lives, the initial encounter was not a happy one since Bobbie was accused of being a trespasser, despite his denials.

'Then you must be a servant boy. Only the Astors live here.'

The fact that Billy Grenfell was himself an intruder seemed irrelevant to him.

'I am not. I am not a servant boy.'

'Perhaps not. But you're not an Astor either.'

It was the first time that Bobbie was aware that he was an outsider at Cliveden, at least by name. In time, as his half-brothers and sisters were born, as Astor followed Astor, he would find it impossible to forget it.

Finding her son brooding in his room long after the supper bell had been rung, Nancy learned the truth about the meeting with the son of a past rival. The spectre of Ettie Desborough was not yet vanquished.

'Now, Bobbie, listen to me. Just because you're called Shaw and I'm now called Astor doesn't mean we're no longer mother and son. Nothing's changed except a silly old name. Why, you know Waldorf loves you like you were his own. So don't you take any nonsense from these people at Taplow. They're just being sassy because they're Lord and Lady Desborough now.'

To Bobbie, however, it was not the vicissitudes of Nancy's past that concerned him, but his own: 'Momma – I *like* being called Bobbie Shaw. That's my daddy's name and I'm proud of it.'

A second spectre was not yet vanquished either.

'Sure you are, Bobbie. And I'll tell you something else. We're better than Grenfells and Cecils and Astors and anyone you can name. You know why?'

'No.'

'Because we're *Virginians*, that's why. And there's no one in the world better than a Virginian.'

But she could see that Bobbie was not impressed by such an argument. How could he be? By his features alone he was more a son of Boston than of Virginia. And in that lay the heart of the matter. Accepting that he was not an Astor growing up in a house of Astors was one thing; but being aware that not only the presence but also the very mention of his father was unwelcome by Nancy was quite another.

But in 1906 the concerns of a child seemed unimportant to the new Mrs Astor. What mattered more, now that the house was in order, was the future career of the master of that house. Waldorf, however, was not yet thinking of a profession. He was now supremely happy, devoted to his wife whom he adored, and proud of Cliveden. He had enough money to do nothing until eternity, but he was never an idle man by choice. He had already enlarged his stud farm, had bred champions and was making a serious study of the breeding of horses until he was knowledgeable enough to discuss even the most revolutionary theories with experts. He was also arranging to buy a second house in London, in St James's Square, a third at Rest Harrow in Kent and perhaps a fourth, one day, on the island of Jura in Scotland. Although all this was in the future, it occupied his mind and perhaps distracted him from the only true disappointment in his life; the fact that, physically, he was not in the best of health. His heart condition limited not only his energy, in contrast to Nancy's tireless dynamism, but also his choice of profession. Already, at Cliveden, he had had one minor heart attack which he had kept secret from Nancy, refusing to accept that he was ill, even to his own doctor.

'I'm twenty-eight, not *sixty*-eight,' he had shouted at him in despair, 'and you want me to live a life consisting of sanatoriums and spas and cachets of calomel?'

'I don't *want* that, Waldorf. I'm advising it.'

'No. I refuse to be idle, doctor. I've given up everything that I enjoyed. Polo, rowing, hunting. All I can do now is shout from the terraces and cheer from the banks. I breed horses that I'll never be able to ride. I own mountains that I'll never be able to walk on. But I'm not going to be idle. The fat country squire is not the life I want.'

'You have a heart condition, Waldorf. For God's sake, recognize that.'

'How can I fail to? Look at this diet that you have given me.' Waldorf had then suddenly laughed and waved the diet sheet above his head as he lay on the pillows. 'I have a dozen people in the kitchen,' he said finally, unable to disguise the irony, 'all hand-picked by my wife. A dozen in the kitchen and another thirty in the garden. Acres and acres of vegetables. Tree after tree of fruit. Dozens and dozens of greenhouses. And now – you give me *this*.'

But if Waldorf had his own troubles that he refused to reveal, so indeed did Nancy, and they were not totally dissimilar. After the initial months of activity organizing Cliveden she had succumbed once again to depression, that depression that seemed to lie constantly in the shadows waiting to suffocate her when she least expected it. Like many people who hate to be inactive, she soon grew bored of each endeavour and the boredom produced a restlessness, a search

for other channels for her energy. And if none was immediately at hand, depression took over. Aware of this private
despair and hating it, Nancy would retreat into herself,
become a physical and emotional recluse. Seeking an answer
and finding none, she would become ill, often remaining in
her room, even in her bed for days. It was a *malaise* that she
believed could never be cured.

It was during one such bout of depression that Phyllis
visited Cliveden. The house was silent and the rooms in
darkness and Phyllis was about to go, having left a message
in the main hall, when she saw a light in Nancy's boudoir
on the ground floor. Entering, she discovered her sister
sitting alone staring into the remains of the fire. Turning,
Nancy saw the darkened figure in the doorway and said:

'Momma?'

'No, Nannie. It's Phyllis.'

There was a long silence, then Nancy said finally: 'I'm
tired.'

Phyllis sat next to her and the lamps were lit. The bell was
rung for Parr, the butler, to bring in tea. 'Tired. That's all it
is. And when I'm tired, I see ghosts.'

'I'm not surprised,' Phyllis replied gently, 'after all you've
done.'

'Oh, no. I'm tired because of what I *haven't* done. Anyone
can redesign a house. Anyone can have babies – '

'You mean you're pregnant?'

Nancy didn't answer. Then, with a shrug: 'Anyway Waldorf isn't Bob Shaw, thank God. He prefers to *read* in bed.
And if he doesn't, then I just lie back 'n chew on an apple –
so don't let's go into that.'

The subject was dropped. The tea was served.

'Phyll,' Nancy said, as if to justify her mood. 'I was

thinking about Momma because I suddenly thought I was becoming like her.'

'You've got over a hundred servants – how could you be like her?'

'I didn't mean that way. I'm not ungrateful. I know I'm privileged, so maybe I'm just being sorry for myself for no good reason. I admit I've been spoilt. It's difficult to deny it. Look around.'

'Then what is it?'

'I don't know. Maybe it's *because* I just have to ring the bell to get something done, I feel so inactive. I want to do something myself. Something worthwhile.'

'Then get off your backside and do it.'

'It's not as simple as that. Waldorf must come first. His future's more important.'

Phyllis sighed: 'Nannie – I'm trying to understand. But one thing's for sure – you'll never change. You always wanted to lead other people's lives.'

'What's wrong in that?'

'Because you'll never be satisfied until you lead your own.'

Nancy stood up and stared around the boudoir. On a table was a photograph of Bobbie as a baby. Beside it stood a framed portrait of Waldorf, looking solemn and shy.

'You don't regret getting married to Waldorf, do you?' Phyllis asked cautiously.

'Do you mean – instead of John Revelstoke?'

'That wasn't what I meant.'

'Yes it was, Phyll. And you know it. And I'm not going to satisfy you by giving an answer. But I *am* married to Waldorf and I aim to prove that it's the best thing I ever done. Even if it kills me.'

It was a challenge to herself, and if Waldorf was unaware of Nancy's decision to guide his life he was soon to learn it. She was unsure which path it would take, but she knew the role she wanted him to play. The depression lifted and two days later, while walking with Waldorf on the parterre, she began, obliquely at first, to put her plan into action.

'I received a letter from my father today,' she mentioned casually as they strolled side by side above the river bank.

'How is he?'

'None better. He asked about you as always. "How's that politician of yours?" he said. He seems to have got it into his head that that's what you're going to be.'

A glance at Waldorf. No reaction. The line was pursued.

'I must admit I thought the same.'

'The same about what?'

'About you being a politician. Ever since I heard you talking on the ship – '

'Talking about politics is not exactly being a politician. I was just making conversation. Nothing more.'

'Oh, I see. Well, you sure fooled Poppa and me. Still, if you just want to idle your life away like your father, no one can stop you. Seems to me that the only Astor who did anything worthwhile was the one who shot skunks!'

Without waiting for a response, Nancy allowed the remark to settle in and crossed the parterre towards Camm, the head gardener, leaving Waldorf alone.

'Mr Camm, I want to talk to you.'

She could sense Waldorf watching, but deliberately ignored him.

'Mr Camm – would you please tell me how you get the orange trees from here to St James's Square without the oranges falling off? I declare I've been fretting about that for weeks.'

'Well, madam, I shouldn't tell you this. But I take the fruit off here, then wire them on again when the tree gets to London.'

Nancy immediately roared with laughter and saw, with satisfaction, that Waldorf was walking towards her. She continued to ignore him.

'My, Mr Camm, and I thought we Virginians knew all about them tricks.'

Waldorf was now at her side, drawing her away. 'Nancy – '

'Did you hear about the oranges?'

'Nancy – I have no intention of wasting my life. You had no right to say that.'

'Just takes them off here and wires them on up there,' Nancy smiled and then added, without looking at her husband, 'It's surprising how if you want to get something done – there's always a way.'

'Nancy – a man can't just knock on the door at Westminster and ask to be let in.'

'Why should he want to do that? I swear, Waldorf, sometimes I don't know what you're talking about. I was talking about oranges.'

But, unlike oranges, the journey from Cliveden to Westminster could not be arranged so simply. Nancy had learned that Waldorf was not averse to a political career, even if he lacked the confidence to admit it openly. She herself, however, had no such reservations. All it needed was time and influence. Later that day she drew up a list of guests to invite to Cliveden. It was time, she thought, to broaden the range of people at dinner – the right people.

FOURTEEN

·

The Unsafe Seat

The guests, from the world of politics of course, were unaware that their invitations were not just for dinner at Cliveden. They were about to play a part not only in Waldorf's future but, unknown to Nancy, in her own life as well. After assembling for drinks in the main hall – although Nancy hated alcohol, she was never ungenerous enough to deny the 'poison' to others – the guests moved into the Louis XV dining-room, presided over by a bust of Madame de Pompadour. It was a silent but not unfitting addition to the party.

On this particular evening those at table consisted of Margot Asquith, now the wife of the Chancellor of the Exchequer; Arthur Balfour, a past Prime Minister; Gordon Cunard; Lady Essex; and Viscount Curzon, the ex-Viceroy of India. It was, as Nancy was the first to admit, an impressive list. It was also Nancy's true début as a hostess at Cliveden and she relished every moment of it, sitting with Curzon and Balfour on each side of her and opposite Waldorf who was unaware that his destiny was about to be decided.

'Nancy?' It was Margot who first voiced her curiosity regarding the assembled guests, having discovered that

Nancy's actions were rarely without motive. 'Nancy – when you said there'd be a *pot-pourri* at table, I wasn't sure, my dear, whether we were supposed to talk to it or eat it. Now that I realize you meant this *mélange* of Liberals and Tories – '

'You *eat* it, Margot.'

'You took the words right out of my mouth.'

Balfour smiled: 'And is the food from Virginia, Mrs Astor?'

'It began in Virginia but something went wrong between the kitchen and here.'

'Nevertheless it is delicious, Mrs Astor.'

'No need to be polite, Arthur. Call me Nancy and we'll invite you again. Especially when you get back in office.'

'Darling,' Margot bellowed across the table, 'poor AJB will *starve* waiting until then.'

'Why? Have you already chosen the curtains for Number Ten?'

'Darling, I'll be hanging them before the year is out.'

'Where?' It was Curzon who was now speaking. He had no affection for Margot; indeed for any woman who didn't consider him the exceptional man he believed he was. 'Where will you be hanging them? Tyburn Hill?'

'George,' Margot replied, with a thin smile, 'still living your Indian summer? I'm surprised you didn't insist on curry. At least you can eat it with one hand and save the other one for your neighbour's knee.'

'I thought you'd never notice, Margot,' Nancy murmured, and winked at her husband as Curzon's hands reappeared in view.

Throughout this Waldorf had hardly spoken at all, partly through shyness and partly because he was attempting to disguise the fact that his diet denied nearly everything placed before him. However, attempting to be polite, he turned towards Margot: 'What makes you so certain that Henry will be PM?'

'Campbell–Bannerman is not exactly Peter Pan. One year at the most and we'll be living where *he* is. Pretty little house too – Mr Parr! Could you possibly remove these flowers? I refuse to spend the evening talking to a gardenia.'

'Leave them, Parr,' Nancy said. 'They're fine just as they are. Mrs Asquith will be wanting to sit *here* next. Now, Arthur, tell me this: what did you do wrong in your last election?'

'Well . . . all I can say is that it wasn't the 401 Liberal votes that worried me. It's those 29 from Labour. Without those, we'd still be in power.'

'I beg to differ – ' Waldorf began.

'My dear Arthur, your party would never be in power. It fell at Mafeking. All your Chinese coolies – '

'Margot, Waldorf was talking.'

'Of course he wasn't. You resigned, Arthur, because you're extinct. Just like the dodo – '

'Margot, shut up! Leave the speeches to your husband. Waldorf was talking and I want to hear him.'

Attention was now focused on Waldorf and he suddenly felt nervous. This was not just casual chatter at a captain's table and he was aware of it. He saw faces turning towards him. 'Well . . . I just wanted to say . . . that I disagree with what Arthur said. Though that doesn't make me a Liberal.'

There was silence and he could see Balfour look away and stare at his plate. Next to him Nancy nodded in encouragement and mouthed: 'Go on.'

'You see . . . we talk about politics but no one takes the trouble to understand what the word "politics" means. It has nothing to do with what party you belong to, but the cause you want to fight for. Nor is it hanging up curtains in Downing Street nor blaming a defeat on a handful of votes that should have been foreseen twenty years ago. There are still children suffocating sweeping chimneys and there are still women dragging trucks in coal mines. *They* should be privileged. Not us.'

The silence continued, broken only by the voice of Margot: 'Does that mean, my dear, that you are going to give them all little Clivedens to live in? And have little *pot-pourris* like tonight?'

'Margot,' Waldorf replied steadily, 'unlike your husband, I'm only Chancellor of the Exchequer to my own estate. Not to the whole country.'

The reaction was immediate. Waldorf heard Curzon laugh and saw Nancy smile at him with a pride he had never seen before. He felt a sudden sense of achievement, but couldn't explain exactly what it was. Later, alone, Nancy put her arms around him, held him tight and said: 'I love you, Waldorf.'

The next morning, without announcing her intentions, Nancy played golf with Curzon. Neither sport nor exercise was the object; it was something more personal.

'There must be room somewhere in Westminster for a man like Waldorf,' she said as they walked along the fairway.

'Well, I'm sure a safe seat can be found for him in the shires. He's inexperienced, of course, but one can't deny he's got resources. Eton, Oxford and money. Not a bad recommendation.'

'He can offer more than that.'

'I'll see what can be done ... I still have a few friends.'

'You'll have another one for life. How soon can you find out?'

'Nancy, by-elections don't exactly happen every day. We might have to wait until Asquith throws his hat on to the bed.'

'Another phrase would be more suitable, George. In the circumstances.'

Returning in the Curzon limousine, they passed a group of women carrying banners.

'Damned suffragettes!' Curzon snapped, but Nancy didn't hear. She was staring at the faces of the women, at the words on the banners, smeared by rain. She suddenly thought of Aunt Lewis after her mother's funeral: 'Get in the front line, child.' And then the women were gone and the street was empty.

On 13 August 1907 Nancy gave birth to her first child by Waldorf Astor. He was christened William Waldorf, in deference to his grandfather, but was known from the day he was born as Bill. On his first birthday, not only the son but also the father was presented with a gift – in the latter case, through the influence of Curzon and his friends, a safe Tory seat was found for Waldorf. It seemed to Nancy as if his political career was about to commence. But she had underestimated her husband. Unlike Shaw, Waldorf was a man of principle and honour as well as an almost saintly humility; these qualities, which Nancy too often failed to recognize, were the ones that set him apart from any other man in her life. Nancy had once told Phyllis that she didn't understand men – only people. It was one of the few areas where she differed in character from Chillie. For Chillie, at least, would have anticipated Waldorf's reaction to Curzon's offer of a safe seat.

'Don't you realize what a fool I felt having Curzon talk to me as if I were a child who needs to be spoon-fed?'

'I was only doing what I thought was best,' Nancy countered, startled by the outburst. 'Seems to me you're a mite short of gratitude – '

'Gratitude? Nancy – couldn't you have consulted me *first*? Or do you think I'm incapable of doing something on my own?'

'I'm your wife. Comes to the same thing.'

'No, it does not! I'm tired of people treating me like a cripple, doing everything for me. You may have meant well, Nancy, but I want to make my own decisions. Win or lose. I want to retain my self-respect. It seems the most natural thing in the world. . . .'

'Maybe, but you've been pondering a political career for two years now. I can't see any harm in speeding things up a little.'

'Not the way Curzon spelt it out. I don't want to enter Parliament through the back door, and that's what it would be. No fight, no policy. Just stand on that solid Tory platform and be wheeled in. Well, I'm not interested in being another puppet for the middle classes. If I'm going to enter the arena and *win*, then I win on my own merits.'

'Are you saying that you don't need *me*?'

'Nancy, for God's sake, that is not the *point*.' . . . And then, later, finding her in tears, he said quietly: 'Of course I need you, Nancy. More than ever.'

It was true. Waldorf not only needed Nancy as a wife and a companion, but her misguided efforts regarding his career had not been totally in vain. If he had been lethargic about his future, he was now charged with a desire to succeed. He had been shown where his true ambitions lay; he needed only to find the constituency that needed *him*. After four months working day and night, sometimes sleeping on a camp bed at Tory Central Office, he believed he was almost ready to fight for the rights of the underprivileged citizen. And he found those citizens in the Devon port of Plymouth.

FIFTEEN

Vote for Astor

The Rolls-Royce cruised silently along the wet cobbled streets of Plymouth, past tenements deprived of water and heat, past crumbling walls and curtainless windows, past workhouses and communal baths, a Dickensian landscape of squalor and poverty. On each corner, huddled groups of people stared at the shiny black vehicle as if it were an extra-terrestrial spacecraft. It held no meaning in their lives whatsoever.

'My God,' Waldorf gasped as he gazed out of the window of the car, 'if I can't help these people, I don't deserve to help anybody. What must they think of us, sitting in this damn car? Staring at them as if they were in a zoo?'

'Next time, we walk.'

A boy suddenly rushed across the street, jumped on the running-board and screamed in despair before jumping off as the Rolls moved on.

'I don't blame him,' Nancy said. 'I'd do the same. Oh God, stop the car. Just stop the car.'

'What are you doing?'

'*We're* the ones in the zoo. Not them.'

Hurrying out of the Rolls, Nancy walked towards a

group of women and children standing on the steps of a mission hall. As they saw her approach they began to back away, startled by this apparition of an elegant woman in pearls and fur. Without faltering, Nancy approached them, smiling.

'My name is Nancy Astor. Inside that ridiculous vehicle over there is my husband, Waldorf Astor. Now don't be fooled by appearances, because I assure you, *I'm* not. We're going to come back here in a year or so and ask your husbands to vote for us. I know how you're feeling. What do people like us know about folk like you? Well, we aim to find out and do something about it. God bless you.'

As she re-entered the car, Waldorf asked: 'What did you say to them?'

'Just that we'd be back. And when we do, we've got to convince those people out there to vote for you.'

'It's not going to be easy to make them trust someone like me. I can't patronize and I can't buy them. I can only convince them that I care about them more than anyone else.'

'Well, you wanted an *unsafe* seat, Waldorf. This is it.'

Waldorf's confidence that he would win the seat in Plymouth was so resolute that, even before the election campaign began, he bought a house on the Hoe at 3 Elliott Terrace. As Mirador was to Chillie, this house facing the English Channel, where Drake, another man of Plymouth, had once challenged the Spanish Armada, was where the Astors belonged. Waldorf was waiting to face his own personal challenge, and in January 1910 it began.

It was customary at this time for many constituencies to return two members in each respective party, and Waldorf found himself standing with Sir Mortimer Durand as his Conservative partner, a man more than twice his age and whose spirit for campaigning had long since died. Ordinarily, this could have proved a disadvantage to the young tyro, since he would be overshadowed by the staid, traditional views of the older and more familiar candidate. But Waldorf not only had his own policies and was determined to voice them; he also had a wife whose approach towards campaigning might have been considered unorthodox but was, in practice, very simple and direct. Nancy abandoned the platform and the formal debate and went into the streets and tenements themselves, knocking on doors and inviting herself in with a disarming smile and the words: 'My name is Nancy Astor. My husband is standing for Parliament and I want you to vote for him.'

She would bring pots of tea and hot soup, would remember the names of everyone she met, would begin at dawn and continue tirelessly until it was dark, and in all weathers; it must be admitted that she enjoyed every minute of it. It was as if she was back in Virginia visiting the 'poor whites'; it was her new-found mission in life and although some residents disagreed with the Conservative candidate's views, they could not ignore the Conservative candidate's wife.

'But I'm a Liberal,' one might protest. 'Always have been.'

'Then if this is what the Liberals have done for you,' Nancy would counter, gesturing to the squalor around her, 'you'd better invite me in.'

As election day grew nearer, the optimism of the Astors increased. They were being talked about, they were occupying the front pages of the newspapers, and the initial prejudice towards those 'millionaires from London' had been reduced to catcalls from the Opposition. And then, quite suddenly, the unexpected happened. While addressing a packed hall of supporters, Waldorf was seen to falter and gasp for breath before collapsing to the stage. His defiance of his doctor's advice had rebounded at the worst possible moment; he had suffered a heart attack three days before the election. The campaign was over. Although he recovered, it was too late. He had lost. He could only return to Cliveden with the realization that the prize had been in his grasp and, at the last moment, had cruelly been taken away.

'We could have won,' he lamented bitterly. 'I let them down.'

'Don't say that,' Nancy replied immediately. 'You proved you could win and you will.'

'No, Nancy. Who wants to vote for a – '

'I said cut that out. One day there'll be another election and we're going to go back to Plymouth and fight it over again. We promised those people and we're not going to let them down.'

'You mean – even if it kills me?'

'You talk like that and you might as well dig your grave now. You and I were born on the same day and we're going to die on the same day. And I intend to live till I'm eighty.'

'Take up thy bed and walk?'

'By heaven, no one else is going to do it for you. Now listen to me. Next time, we *will* win. And if we don't, we'll keep coming back until we do.'

After the initial days of remorse and self-pity, Waldorf knew that Nancy was right. Like her, he didn't quit before the race was over, and if his health was another enemy he had to contend with, then so be it.

It was during the following months of convalescence at

Cliveden and in Scotland – the Astor family had now been increased by a second child, a daughter, Nancy Phyllis Louise, known from the day of her birth as 'Wissie' – that Waldorf re-established his friendship with a fellow graduate from Oxford, Robert Brand. Brand had just returned from South Africa where he had been a member of 'Milner's Kindergarten', a group of idealistic young men, inspired by Lord Milner, who feared the collapse of the British Empire and sought to unite the Commonwealth into a single unit under the aegis of Parliament and the Crown. But their ambitions lay not only in the strengthening of the past but in using that structure to form something new: a unity of all nations, an Empire of the World. Idle dreams, perhaps, in 1910, when the major powers were concerned only with their own imperialism, and aggression and revolution were the order of the day. But the devotees of Milner were optimists who saw unity among all nations as the only answer to world war; they believed themselves to be knights of a new Arthurian age and, in deference to that, founded a magazine to voice their views which they called *The Round Table*. And if Robert Brand was the Galahad of that table, then the Lancelot was surely another contemporary of Waldorf Astor – a young, handsome, passionately religious and equally intense man, a Scottish aristocrat of the Lothian family: his name was Philip Kerr.

He was introduced to Nancy in 1909 and immediately, on that very first encounter, a mutual bond grew between them. It seemed to Nancy that Kerr shared her restless search for religious satisfaction – he was a Roman Catholic by birth, but had grown discontented and sought the answers for that discontent in Buddhism and Eastern mysticism; he was an adventurer, an ascetic who, like the Arthurian knight, put the spirit above the body, preferring courtly love to sexual conquest. He was a man with a quest who fought the dragons of his idealism and sought only a lady that he could champion. He found her in Nancy Astor; quite simply, he adored her. And Nancy rejoiced in that adoration in all its purity. She was his lady of the lake, even if, later, he wished her to be his Guinevere; he was her mentor, her counsellor of the soul. At least that was how it began.

But if fate in 1910 had been laying the seeds for Nancy's happiness, it had not overlooked Waldorf. Before the year was out Asquith had been obliged to call another election; in December the Astors were once more in Plymouth, and were welcomed not as strangers but as friends. When the votes were counted and the green lights illuminated the Devon sky, Waldorf Astor, at the age of thirty-one, was elected the new Conservative Member of Parliament for Plymouth. It was appropriate as well as prophetic that, as the torchlight procession of victory moved through the Plymouth streets, the crowd cheered equally for Nancy as for her husband, and Waldorf would not have wished it otherwise.

'I owe all this to you, Nancy,' he said as they returned to Elliott Terrace. 'Plymouth belongs to you as much as to me.'

'No, Waldorf. *We* belong to Plymouth. And by heaven, we're going to stay.'

Two years later a third Astor child, David, was born. Waldorf's health improved and he was accepted with respect by his fellow Members of Parliament, who saw that he was not just another Tory, content to remain a backbencher all his life. He was already setting his sights on a Cabinet position and the future for the Astors seemed enviable.

But, of course, it was not to be. In 1914 Nancy received a letter from Chillie informing her that her sister Lizzie had died. Her grief was uncontrollable and she retreated to the darkness of her room. In the night her screams were heard, and Waldorf found her in agony on the floor, clutching her stomach. She was taken by ambulance to hospital and operated on immediately. Afterwards, the surgeon told Waldorf that during the operation Nancy had almost died. The phrase he used was that Nancy had 'touched death by the hand'.

SIXTEEN

·

The Secret Way

The operation, fortuitous as it was, had not been a complete success. An internal abscess was diagnosed and a second operation was required. Refusing to wait in hospital, Nancy demanded that she be taken to the Astor House at Rest Harrow in Sandwich, on the Kent coast, where she sat alone, wrapped in a blanket, staring at the winter sea. In a letter to Philip Kerr, now in India, she wrote that she had never felt so wretched or in such despair in all her life. She feared submitting to the surgeon's knife yet again.

'This is not what God wants,' she wrote. 'It is not what He meant to happen. It can't be that God made sickness. It turns people into useless, self-centred beings who become a burden to themselves and everyone else. I lie for hours questioning why this should be. I feel there is an answer to this dilemma but, like you, I have no idea what the answer is.'

The answer arrived in the most unexpected way. Many visitors came to see her at Rest Harrow, offering consolation, bringing the gifts of their company and their conversation. Waldorf often travelled overnight from Plymouth, but his visits were regrettably brief since, in this spring of 1914, he was obliged to remain longer than anticipated at the Devon port that was his constituency, devoting most of his time in discussions with the Navy – routine matters regarding defence, he explained without elaboration.

In March Nancy's sister Phyllis came to stay, accompanied by a handsome young Guards officer, Henry Douglas Pennant. Both were clearly in love and for a while life at Rest Harrow was happy, echoing to the sound of laughter as Nancy shared Phyllis's love and watched her walk, hand in hand along the beach, with the man she planned to marry as soon as she divorced Reggie Brooks. A date had been agreed for the wedding: January 1915. 'Ten months, Nannie,' Phyllis would repeat excitedly, 'and I will be Henry's wife.' In April Douglas Pennant was unexpectedly ordered to return to his regiment, leaving the two sisters alone. They would talk late into the night, and although Nancy never referred to the forthcoming operation, Phyllis could see the fear in her eyes when the conversation stopped and she saw her reach for her Bible, reading and re-reading passages she had marked. Finally, Phyllis said:

'Nannie, I hate seeing you like this. Me being so happy and ... well, I just hate it.'

'I hate it myself. I just keep thinking that, if I go back to hospital, I'm never going to come out alive.'

'Now don't talk like that. You might as well give up now. You were never one to quit.'

'That's what terrifies me.'

Once, in a moment of desperation, she showed Phyllis a letter she was writing to Kerr, explaining how she felt, and adding helplessly: 'It doesn't make sense, does it?'

Phyllis was silent for a long time, then said quietly: 'Yes, it does. At least, there are people who think the way you do – only they claim to have found the answer. They believe that sickness exists only in the mind and that if the mind is strong enough by prayer, then the sickness doesn't exist any more. No more pain. No more medicine.'

Nancy looked at her but said nothing.

'Well,' Phyllis continued dismissively, 'I don't know whether it's true or not. I'm just repeating what someone told me. That's all.'

Nancy still remained silent and Phyllis left her alone and went to bed. In the night, Nancy appeared at her door and asked:

'What else did that person tell you?'

'Well, I confess I wasn't really interested. But it was a woman I knew in New York. She did tell me about a book she used to read with the Bible. Something like that ... it certainly didn't do *her* any harm. Eighty years old and as healthy as milk.'

At breakfast, Nancy said suddenly: 'Could you find out what book it was?'

The book was *Science and Health* by Mary Baker Eddy, the founder of Christian Science. On reading it, even before finishing the first chapter, on Prayer, Nancy knew finally that she had found what she was seeking. 'It was', she wrote, 'like the conversion of St Paul. My life really was made over. Fear went out of it. I was no longer frightened of anything.'

As if to demonstrate this revelation, and in keeping with the beliefs of Christian Science that the body could be cured by prayer alone, that the mind was mightier than the scalpel, she planned to abandon the second operation altogether. It was performed only at Waldorf's insistence, putting caution before divine inspiration. Nevertheless, Nancy refused any drugs and felt no pain. The operation was a success, and from that moment Christian Science became as much a part of Nancy's life as the Bible. She believed she could never be ill again; she was reborn.

Not unnaturally, like all converts, she wanted to spread the word, to shout it from the rooftops. However, if her friends and relatives were impressed, they were not yet convinced. She found only one disciple, only one person prepared to share 'the secret way'; he was, of course, Philip Kerr. They were united now, completely and unequivocally, in spirit. 'Sorrow is turned into joy when the body is controlled by spiritual life,' wrote Mary Baker Eddy, 'Truth and Love.' The conversion of Nancy and Kerr took place in July 1914, in that last warm summer of peace.

On 4 August, after the invasion of Belgium by Germany, Britain issued an ultimatum that was to be resolved at eleven o'clock that night. While awaiting the decision – Waldorf had left a message that he would telephone from the House of Commons – Nancy, without a word to her children, who were blissfully unaware that a golden era was about to end, entered the deserted indoor tennis court at Cliveden in order to be alone. Switching on all the lights, she attempted to distract her attention from the telephone, silent in the corner, by picking up a racket and serving ball after ball across the net until sweat poured from her; still she continued. In the drawing-room of the house Bobbie, now sixteen, was having a party with some friends, including his neighbour Billy Grenfell, the closest friend of all. Music was played on a phonograph and the sound of a tango drifted through the corridors of Cliveden. At twenty minutes past eleven the telephone rang. Nancy picked it up immediately, listened to Waldorf's voice and then closed her eyes in anguish.

'God help us all' were the only words she could say.

SEVENTEEN

·

Love and Death

If the declaration of war brought despair to every citizen and shattered the ideals of brotherhood of Kerr and Robert Brand, the war itself not only produced outrage in Nancy but also brought back the bitter memories of her childhood in Virginia when she saw the results of war long after the dead were buried. Now it was beginning again. Young men who had not yet learned to shave were volunteering in their hundreds and being transported to the trenches of France – young men whom she knew like Julian Grenfell, Billy's older brother, and Henry Douglas Pennant; and, in time, she knew, it could be the turn of her own son, Bobbie Shaw. But outrage was soon replaced by a desire to help, not only financially and spiritually, but in practical terms. Denied active service because of his ill-health, Waldorf nevertheless refused to be idle or accept a desk job; he insisted on being in uniform, to contribute in some physical way, and was put in charge of 'army waste'. To any average man, let alone an Astor whose influence and money could grant him a peaceful sinecure, it would have been a humiliating task inspecting canteens and latrines, but Waldorf accepted it without complaint. It was a job that had to be done by someone, and he saw no reason why it should not be performed by him.

As for Nancy, she decided that if she could not fight the enemy, then she would make sure that those who did were cared for and would be given the best possible treatment if they were wounded. Consequently, after repeated requests to the War Office, permission was finally granted for the covered tennis court to be converted into a hospital for the Canadian Army. It was named after the Duchess of Connaught, the wife of the Governor-General of Canada, and within six months of the outbreak of war it had beds for over a hundred men. The chief surgeon was Colonel Newbourne, a Canadian, but the guiding light, the Florence Nightingale who visited every patient day and night, listening, praying and giving strength, was Nancy herself. It was a role she was born for and she knew it; and if her bedside tactics were somewhat unorthodox, few complained.

Reluctantly leaving the medical attention to the qualified doctors and nurses – common sense prevailing over Christian Science – Nancy would move from bed to bed, knowing each patient by name, refusing to allow them to despair even though she knew many would be maimed or blinded for life or would die before another sunrise.

'Charlie,' she would say to one soldier, his sightless eyes bandaged, 'are you still here? You promised to escort me to a moving-picture show and I'm counting on it. You and I are going to be watching Chaplin before the week is out. You hear me?'

She would see the man smile and wave his hand in acknowledgment.

'Good,' she would add. 'I thought you were pretending to be *deaf*, too.'

Once, on seeing another soldier hugging the wall in self-pity, wishing to die as he waited for his legs to be amputated, she strode to his bed and shouted: 'Hey, you! Where you from?' Receiving no answer, she shouted louder: 'Did you hear me? I'm talking to you. Now – where you from?'

A voice finally murmured: 'Yorkshire....'

'Where?'

'Yorkshire.'

'Yorkshire! No wonder you don't want to live if you come from *Yorkshire*.'

There was a silence and Nancy watched as the man slowly forgot his self-pity and rose to the defence: 'What did you say, ma'am?'

'I said anyone who comes from Yorkshire ought not to be born in the first place. Now isn't that so?'

The Yorkshireman was now looking at her with defiant pride. 'You ever *been* to Yorkshire?'

'I would never dream of it.'

'Well, let me tell you that it's the finest place in the world. I might not live in a palace like you but what I own you could never buy. Because it's in *Yorkshire*.'

'Then why don't you go back there instead of taking up space here?'

'I bloody well will as soon as this bloody war is over!'

Nancy looked at him, took his hand and smiled. 'Then, take it from me, we'll make sure you'll get there. It must be a beautiful county if it produces pride like yours. God bless you now.'

And then with a flirtatious wink, she walked away.

In 1915 Billy Grenfell volunteered for the Army and went to France to join his brother. At the station Nancy said goodbye to him; she saw his mother, Ettie Desborough, watching but ignored her as if she didn't exist. Even in war, personal feuds remained.

'I think what you have achieved is remarkable, Nancy,' Philip Kerr said as he walked beside Nancy across the parterre at Cliveden. On a far lawn, a concert stage had been erected and George Robey was on the platform leading the audience as they sang *If You Were the Only Girl in the World*. The voices drifted towards them through the afternoon light.

'The credit goes to Waldorf as well,' Nancy replied. 'His idea and his money.'

'Yes, of course,' Kerr said quickly. 'Of course.'

They were now walking towards the flower beds laid out originally by the Duke of Buckingham.

'What about your mother?' Nancy asked after a moment. 'How did she react when you told her?'

'About being a Christian Scientist?'

'Yes. What else?'

'It destroyed her. The Lothians have been Catholics for generations and there are no Catholics more narrow-minded and snobbish than Scottish Catholics. She thinks CS is some kind of voodoo. She even said that the death of my brother caused her far less pain.'

'That's her religion speaking. Not her. She's just another bigoted Papist. You must realize that.'

'I do, but – '

'Philip – *everybody* disapproves. But it's just plain ignorance. Even my sister Phyll doesn't understand and she introduced me to it. But *you* have no doubts, do you?'

'None whatsoever, Nancy.'

They were now standing before a flower bed shaped like a sword. Beneath it was the date 1668.

'What happened then?' Kerr asked.

'When?'

'In 1668?'

'Oh. There was a duel.'

'A duel? For what reason?'

'The Earl of Shrewsbury discovered that the Duke of Buckingham was making love to Shrewsbury's wife.'

'And what happened?'

Nancy turned and slowly looked up at Kerr, her right hand casually curling a lock of her blonde hair between finger and thumb. 'The first owner of Cliveden killed him,' she said quietly, staring directly into Kerr's eyes. Then she suddenly smiled: 'Isn't that history for you?'

But Kerr didn't return the smile as Nancy walked on.

Then she stopped and asked, almost as an afterthought: 'Do you love me?'

'Yes.'

'I knew that. I just wanted to know whether you'd lie to me or not.'

And then Nancy was gone, running back towards the concert stage, joining in the singing, leaving Kerr standing alone, abandoned.

Darling Nance,

A million thanks for your letter and all your love. How could a man end his life better than in the full tide of strength and glory – Julian has outsoared the darkness of our night and passed on to a wider life. I feel no shadow of grief for him, only thankfulness for his bright and brave example. We are just off to the trenches, looking like Iron Pirates, so no more now except all my love.

    Yours ever,

      Billy Grenfell

Nancy read the letter twice, then put it aside on the table next to her bed. Too many deaths of young men. Like so many others of her generation, she had ceased reading the obituary columns and the cards on the mantel were now bordered in black.

'Emma?' Nancy called to her maid. 'I'd like to wear something bright today or I'll go crazy. Something colourful. Something pretty. . . .'

Dressed in yellow and white lace, Nancy toured the hospital beds accompanied by Robert Brand. She had grown to like the tall, intellectual Brand, the Fellow of All Souls who now worked for Lazard's Bank; she liked his dry wit, his charm and his calm manner in contrast to the erratic behaviour of Kerr. She also liked him because she knew that secretly he was in love with Phyllis, although he never admitted it nor attempted to win her from Douglas Pennant when he was in England.

As they walked towards the covered tennis court, past the ambulances and the canteen wagons, Brand talked of America from where he had just returned from a business trip, of how he had spent a week at Bar Harbor with Dana and Irene Gibson listening to scandalous anecdotes concerning the youngest sister Nora; Nora, like Nancy, had married an Englishman, Paul Phipps, but that had failed to halt her amorous escapades. And he told stories of Chillie, now the grand patriarch of Mirador, surrounded by his grandchildren but still mourning the death of his wife. To Nancy it was as if she was listening to a brother talking, and she loved Brand for that.

Nearing the hospital, she saw Colonel Newbourne waiting for her, and even though he was still fifty yards away she sensed something was wrong.

'Wait there a minute, Bob,' she said quietly to Brand, and hurried towards Newbourne. In his hand was a telegram.

'It arrived just now for Mrs Brooks. Would that be your sister?'

Nancy nodded, took the telegram and turned away without opening it. She could see Phyllis standing on the terrace, laughing with two Red Cross nurses.

'What is it?' Brand asked, approaching her.

Nancy didn't reply, staring at the telegram; then she tore it open. 'I shouldn't do this but I have to,' she said, and read the official message inside.

From a bench, a soldier called out: 'Mrs Astor, you look very pretty today. I'd like to take you home to be my wife.'

'Give me time to think about it,' she replied with a smile. And then she said to Brand: 'Henry Douglas Pennant was killed at the Battle of the Somme.' She turned away again, not knowing where to look and then, almost in agony, said: 'Oh, darling Phyllis – how can I tell her?'

Brand watched as Nancy suddenly hurried towards the terrace, saw Phyllis wave excitedly, smiling, the sun highlighting her hair. Then Nancy was by her side, putting her arms around her, holding her close.

'Oh God,' Nancy said later, as she listened to Phyllis weeping, 'let there never be another war like this again.'

Later that same year Bobbie Shaw enlisted in the Royal Horse Guards and was sent with his regiment to see active service in France.

It was the custom, each and every day, for Nancy to gather her children into her boudoir for readings from the Bible and *Science and Health*. It was a duty they accepted with reluctance, too nervous or too young to resist, stoically enduring the ritual before Nancy dismissed them in order to devote herself to an hour of physical exercises – a healthy mind in a healthy body, mind over matter.

The war had not changed the daily routine, and in the first week of January 1916 the three Astor children, Bill, Wissie and David (Bobbie was the only one to defy his mother and Nancy had long since given up the battle), stood impatiently as usual as Nancy paced up and down, the Bible in her hand. However, it was to be an exceptional occasion, during which something took place that was not only catastrophic but would also alter the lives of them all in a manner none could foresee. The meeting began in the traditional manner with Nancy and God fighting equally for the children's attention.

'And I will show wonders in heaven above,' Nancy declaimed, Bible held aloft, 'and signs in the earth beneath; blood and fire and vapour – stop fidgeting, Wissie – of smoke. The sun shall be turned into darkness – '

It was then that the telephone began to ring.

'Leave it,' Nancy ordered without breaking her stride – 'into darkness and the moon into blood before that great and notable day of the Lord.'

The telephone persisted.

'And it shall come to pass that whatsoever – back, children – shall be saved. Ye men of Israel hear these words: Jesus of Nazareth – stop that yawning, Billy Astor – a man approved of God among you by miracles and wonders and signs.'

And persisted.

'And the Lord added to the church daily such as should be saved.'

The telephone suddenly stopped. Then after a momentary silence it began again as the butler, Parr, attempted to draw the caller to Nancy's attention. Refusing to interrupt the lesson, Nancy continued for a further twenty minutes before dismissing the children and preparing to begin her exercises. At thirty-seven she still had the young, thin, supple body of a teenager, kept in superb health not only by exercise and the absence of alcohol and tobacco, but also by daily cold baths, swimming in the Thames, golf, tennis, and the guidance of Mary Baker Eddy. Nancy looked and would always look half her age, not out of vanity – although she was beautiful enough to be vain – but simply out of self-discipline. The portrait by Sargent painted when she was twenty-eight would remain a facsimile of her appearance for most of her life. It was no surprise that men wanted to make love to her. It was only a surprise that she didn't love love. On the boudoir table the telephone continued to disturb the silence of the room with its urgency, like a hungry dog whining to be fed. Finally, in exasperation, Nancy snatched up the receiver:

'Parr! Didn't I tell you I didn't want any calls put through to me during – '

The voice that interrupted her was not the butler but her husband, his voice loud and angry: 'Nancy! I've been trying to talk to you for half an hour! Why didn't you answer?'

'Why? Where's the fire?'

'The fire,' Waldorf snapped, 'is at Hever Castle. Didn't you see the New Year's Honours list?'

'I have better things to read – '

'Well, if you had, you'd discover that my beloved father has just bought himself a peerage.'

'Well, he's bought everything else,' Nancy replied flippantly, but the tone of Waldorf's voice suddenly alarmed her:

'Nancy – don't you realize what it means! He's now Viscount Astor and the title's hereditary. *Now* do you understand?'

Nancy was silent, confused as she attempted to interpret the true cause of Waldorf's concern. Her father-in-law was now a peer of the realm, which meant that on his death her husband would inherit the title and be –

'Oh, my God!' she screamed into the telephone. 'How *could* he do this to you?'

Waldorf's voice was trembling as he replied: 'I'm in Plymouth now. Meet me at Hever Castle tomorrow. I've got to make him understand.'

The telephone went dead. Nancy replaced the receiver and walked slowly to the window as the full impact of the news sunk in. By buying a peerage William Waldorf Astor had, for the sake of vanity, successfully destroyed his own son's future.

'That's gratitude indeed! I've made the Astors respectable for ever and you throw it back at me.'

The squat, florid face of William Waldorf Astor glared across the table at Hever Castle, his eyes darting from Waldorf to Nancy. Neither father nor son had seen each other for several years and it was clear that this lack of filial affection was not a mistake.

'You could have at least bought a *life* title,' Waldorf replied, attempting to keep his voice under control. He had travelled all night, still in uniform, and looked tired and pale, but the appearance belied his mood. 'Because I don't want that title when you die –'

'I didn't buy it. I *earned* it.'

'Bought and paid for!' Nancy remarked.

'Keep out of this,' William Waldorf shouted back. 'You haven't exactly suffered from my money.'

'Then you can have it back any time you like. I'll put the Sanci diamond in the mail tomorrow.'

Waldorf gestured to Nancy to calm down and turned back towards his father: 'Sir – I'm a Member of the House of Commons. It's what I fought for and what I won. I can't be in the Commons as a peer and you're well aware of that.'

'I'm not going to refuse a title just for you. This is for eternity. So that your children and your grandchildren can hold their heads up high.'

'You're a fool, sir, if you think that. And I say that to your face.'

Nancy glanced up at Waldorf in admiration. Why, she thought, my husband's behaving almost like a Virginian.

'Then let me tell you this,' the new Viscount Astor replied. 'When I'm dead, you're going to inherit the title whether you like it or not. But that's *all* you're going to inherit because you've just cut yourself out of my will. And I mean that.'

'I hope you do, sir. Then at least there'd be no fear of your money corrupting me as it did you.'

There was a sudden silence and it seemed as if William Waldorf was about to explode in fury. Instead he turned and walked across the room and opened the door. 'Don't think of staying here a minute longer. I don't want to ever see your face again.'

The door slammed shut and the noise vibrated around the building.

'Well,' Nancy said finally, 'that's the first time I've seen a bull elephant in retreat.'

'All my plans for Plymouth. Everything I wanted to achieve. . . .'

'Now listen! Your father's got to *die* first before you get that title. And he's not going to do that without a fight. He'll hang on to his coronet and ermine until he's ninety.'

Waldorf slowly turned his head towards Nancy and said, his voice touched now with bitterness: 'And how are you going to guarantee that? Send him a copy of *Science and Health*?'

Without waiting for or expecting a reply, Waldorf walked out of the room, out of Hever Castle, and returned on the next train to his beloved Plymouth.

If Waldorf's future career seemed in jeopardy, it was compensated by a fortuitous turn of events. At the end of 1916 Asquith was defeated and David Lloyd George entered Number Ten Downing Street. He was a man who wanted change, to bring new, younger men into power and look beyond the War towards a united Europe. Not unnaturally, he turned towards Milner's associates, and within weeks Philip Kerr became a close adviser, preparing for the peace that surely must come one day. And as his Parliamentary Private Secretary Lloyd George appointed Waldorf Astor; it was a worthy reward for Waldorf's unceasing endeavours in Plymouth and there was no one more delighted than Nancy herself. She wrote to Chillie immediately, telling him that the reluctant politician they had met on the ocean liner was now on course to be in the Cabinet itself. She also mentioned, almost with a sigh, that she had given birth to another son whom she named Michael Langhorne Astor.

Only one event clouded that year. News reached Cliveden that Billy Grenfell, the happiest and the most loyal of friends, had been killed at Ypres, just a mile away from where his brother Julian had died. Without a moment's hesitation Nancy visited Taplow to offer consolation to Ettie Desborough; in mourning, the two women finally became friends.

In 1917 America entered the War and the end seemed near. Soldiers from Virginia would arrive at Cliveden or at the Astors' house in St James's Square, and *Dixie* was played on the lawns. The Anglo-American alliance even became personal when Robert Brand finally found his own happiness and took Phyllis as his wife. The love between them was almost tangible and was to remain for the rest of their lives. The two Langhorne sisters of Mirador appeared to be sharing the same destiny: replacing one disastrous marriage to a Boston rake by another to a rich English gentleman and future peer.

In 1918 the fifth and final Astor child was born – another son, John Jacob, forever known as 'Jakie'. As Phyllis remarked, for a woman who loathed sex Nancy was demonstrating that loathing in the most extraordinary way. Finally, on 11 November, there was heard the most important news of all as Lloyd George announced to the world: 'The Armistice was signed at 5 a.m. this morning. Hostilities are to cease on all fronts at 11 a.m. today.' The worst of all possible wars was over.

In 1919, in Paris, the terms of the Treaty of Versailles were spelt out to a defeated Germany. The plans were to realize those distant dreams of a brotherhood of nations, but there was one specific article that outlined how the Allies felt about the four years of war and death:

The Allied and Associated Governments affirm ... the responsibility of Germany and her allies for causing all the loss and damage to which the Allied and Associated Governments and their nationals have been subjected, as a consequence of the war imposed upon them by the aggression of Germany and her allies.

It went on to blame not only the German government but the people of Germany themselves, and imposed on each and every one of them retribution whose aim was not only to cripple the German economy but also to humiliate German pride. It was an act of revenge whose consequences were to prove more horrifying than anyone could realize. The man who drafted this Article 231 of the Treaty was that same man who had dreamed of a world united for ever in peace and love: Philip Kerr.

EIGHTEEN

·

The Liberated Woman

War between nations had ceased and so, to a degree, had a more domestic war that had been fought for far longer and with equal pain. The suffragettes had finally won the first round of their battle for women's rights; they not only could vote, they could also be elected into Parliament. After the Bill was passed seventeen women candidates stood for candidature, including Christabel Pankhurst. They were all defeated except the Irish Nationalist, Countess Markievicz, who refused to take the oath of loyalty to the King and was thus disqualified. It was a Pyrrhic victory that remained merely a piece of paper, proving to the women that they would always remain unequal to men no matter what was written in the statute books. The prejudice was too deep.

For the Astors, however, the immediate task was the forthcoming Plymouth election. Waldorf was well aware that re-election would not be easy. The Labour Party had grown in strength and popularity as the working man, supported by the trade unions, became a voice in the land that could no longer be ignored; he had fought for his country and now he would fight for his rights. Moreover, the Liberal

Party had chosen as its candidate Isaac Foot, a man who was as popular and respected in Plymouth as Waldorf himself. Furthermore, unlike in 1910, Plymouth was no longer a single constituency but had been divided into three divisions, Waldorf being allotted the Sutton division in the east and thus losing many of his most loyal supporters. 'It's going to be a close run thing, Nancy,' Waldorf said grimly as they arrived at the Devonshire port. 'I have little faith in being re-elected.'

As it happened he was right, but for a reason far removed from politics. The spectre that had haunted him since that day in Hever Castle finally took shape. On 18 October 1919, just three weeks before the day of the election, Waldorf's father, William Waldorf, First Viscount Astor, took it upon himself to drop dead while sitting on the lavatory. He left not only an ignoble corpse but also the unwanted peerage for his eldest son. Waldorf's active political career, his ambitions, his seat in the House of Commons, were no more.

'On the lavatory!' Nancy cried in disgust as she walked along the Plymouth beach with the Conservative agent, Albert Webb. 'That man certainly died in the style he deserved, didn't he?'

In the autumn light she could see her husband, wrapped in a fur coat, standing twenty yards away on a promontory, staring out towards the grey sea. He had spoken hardly a word since hearing the news and seemed to be lost in introspective thought.

'Can't anything be done?' Nancy asked Webb. 'Representing this city is Waldorf's life.'

'Not unless we can change the law.'

'But the Astors belong here!'

Webb hesitated, avoiding her eye, as if withholding information he was reluctant as yet to share.

'Well, don't they?' Nancy demanded.

'More than that. Plymouth *wants* the Astors to belong here.'

'If Waldorf's father wasn't dead, I'd wring his neck.'

There was a crunch of feet on pebbles and Nancy turned to see that Waldorf was walking towards them, hands in pockets. He still seemed preoccupied, but where she expected to see melancholy or even bitterness in his eyes Nancy saw instead a look of determination, even excitement, that startled her. He seemed unaware of her presence and walked directly to Webb, who could only murmur apologetically:

'Do you mind if I don't call you Lord Astor immediately, sir? It's going to take some time to get used to it.'

Waldorf didn't react. Then, as if resolving a decision, suddenly put his arms on Webb's shoulder and drew him away along the edge of the tide. Even more curious, Nancy watched them, straining to hear what was being said – but the voices were lost against the sound of the sea.

'Now then, Albert,' Waldorf said, glancing back to see that he was not overheard. 'Let's go over this again. Since I have the right to nominate my successor, that should present no problem.'

'None at all.'

'Of course, Isaac Foot might object, but that's to be expected since he might consider it an unfair advantage. Have you any idea if he has any prejudices? Was he anti-suffragette? Something like that?'

'Not exactly, sir. He's played a safe wicket.'

'No matter. What about Central Office?'

'The usual doubts, but in the main they support your decision.'

Waldorf nodded and pulled up the collar of his coat. 'And you're sure there's no problem about the title?'

'Only for you. But not if it's by marriage.'

Behind them Nancy frowned as she saw the two men stop, stare back at her, then continue walking like conspirators.

'It'll also mean,' Waldorf said, 'that we won't have to change our plans at all. And there couldn't be a better candidate.'

'Sir?' Webb suddenly asked cautiously.

'What?'

'What if Lady Astor doesn't agree?'

Waldorf suddenly stopped and looked at Webb as if the thought had never occurred to him. 'But of course she'll agree. She has to.'

In the car, Nancy stared at the smiling faces of the two men beside her with a mixture of amazement, flattery and doubt.

'Are you two *insane*?'

'Perfectly sane.'

'You want *me* to stand for Parliament instead?'

'Yes. And it's not nepotism, Nancy. You're more popular here than I am. You've campaigned here by my side, know the problems, know the people. If they could have done, they would have elected *you* in 1910, not me. Plymouth has always belonged to both of us, Nancy. "The Astors here for ever." Remember that?'

Nancy looked at her husband, then out at the familiar streets that she had walked so many times in the past. A woman carrying a baby waved to her. 'How long have you been planning this?' she asked finally, narrowing her eyes in suspicion.

'Since the day my father accepted a peerage. Three years, two months.'

'Why, Waldorf Astor, you're as devious as a jack rabbit.'

'Perhaps. But do you accept?'

Nancy suddenly turned away nervously. In her mind came the image of Aunt Lewis standing before her after the funeral of her mother. She could hear her saying: 'Get in the front line. Don't hesitate a tick!' As the car approached the town hall, past the election posters of Isaac Foot and William Gay, she answered, her voice barely audible: 'I accept.'

The true significance of that 'acceptance' did not become apparent to Nancy until the day when Waldorf formally proposed her as the candidate for Plymouth Sutton. She realized then that she had to win over not only the electorate but also the Conservative committee itself. As she sat on the stage of the hall, before her prospective fellow workers, the full enormity of her decision suddenly unnerved her: she was not only seeking to be a Member of Parliament, but seeking it as the first woman in the history of the British Constitution. Moreover, she wasn't even English but a Virginian, a native of a country that had gone to war in order to rid itself of the very Parliament that she wanted to enter. Destiny for Nancy Langhorne of Danville, now Lady Astor, was playing a very bizarre game.

'And I want to tell you straight away,' she heard Waldorf address the audience, standing on the dais before a giant photograph of his wife, 'that if anybody thinks that the candidate I am proposing is going into this contest in any light-hearted spirit, not realizing the responsibilities which will be hers, that person is mistaken.'

There were scattered shouts of 'Hear! Hear!' but Nancy saw that most of the hall was silent, cautious, studying her with uncertainty. She had to admit that she couldn't blame them.

'Your worship, lords, ladies and gentlemen,' Waldorf concluded, 'I would like to nominate the Coalition candidate for the Sutton Division – Lady Astor.'

A sudden silence descended as all eyes turned towards Nancy. She saw Waldorf gesture to her to step forward.

'Just be yourself,' he whispered as she stepped into the light. 'These are our friends.'

'Then I can't wait to face the enemy. . . .' She was now standing before the lectern, looking at the rows of faces. Chairs creaked, someone tiptoed along an aisle and sat down, a door banged irritatingly in an adjacent room.

'Well now, I . . .' she began then stopped and glanced at her notes. Below her, in the front row, she saw the reporters, pencils poised over notebooks. One man was trying to light a cigarette, another was turning, talking to another and suddenly laughing.

'I have heard it said,' Nancy began again, her voice louder but still hesitant, 'that a woman who's got children shouldn't go into the House of Commons.'

There was a sudden *pop* and a flash as a photograph was taken.

'She ought to be home looking after these children.'

A male voice suddenly shouted: 'I agree, madam. She *should*!'

Nancy stared into the pit of the hall, startled. 'Well, I'm fortunate enough to have people looking after my children.

But maybe, sir, *your* wife hasn't, and if that is the case, she's not alone. I want to fight for the *unfortunate* children.' Nancy paused a moment and then added: 'Even yours.'

For the first time she heard murmurs of approval, not overwhelming, not in any great numbers, but she sensed, like an actress, that she was making a breakthrough, that the curtain would not fall yet. And then, from the back of the hall, she heard a woman's voice:

'Why don't you do that in America where you belong?'

It was a question she had anticipated. In preparing her campaign Waldorf, now acting the role of the stage manager, proud, encouraging, foreseeing every pitfall, had pinpointed this as the inevitable question. An answer had been prepared, but Nancy now abandoned it. She couldn't rely on a prepared formula; she had to be accepted for what she was or not at all.

'I already *have* fought for unfortunate children in America,' Nancy replied, 'but I'm in England now. Virginian by birth, but British by marriage, so what do you want me to do? Get in the House and sit holding hands and not work for other women? You've been fighting for equality since Eve was in Eden and you haven't got it yet. But by heaven, if you want a chance of getting it, then help me try because we've got a lot of pig-faced opposition sitting in this hall between you and I.'

There was an immediate gasp and then the woman suddenly cheered. The cheering was taken up not only by other women but by some of the men. 'I'm getting to them,' Nancy said to herself, and picking up her notes she hurled them aside, strode to the edge of the stage, and stared defiantly around her. If there had been any doubt in her mind before, it was rapidly disappearing. She now spoke, her voice strong and passionate, as if she had been rehearsing the speech all her life, and not a single man or woman in the audience missed a syllable.

'If you want an MP who will be a repetition of the six hundred other MPs, don't vote for me. If you want a lawyer or if you want a pacifist, don't elect me. If you can't get a fighting man, take a fighting woman. If you want a Bolshevist or a follower of Mr Asquith – don't elect me. If you want a party hack, don't elect me. Surely we have outgrown party ties. *I* have. The War has taught us that there is a greater thing than parties, and that is the State.'

No one could stop her now, nor did any want to. They had come to ridicule and were now ready to cheer.

'And let me tell you this, too, and I'll speak it clear so that you reporters down there can write it all down. Don't ever forget that I'm a woman. Maybe not as pretty as Gladys Cooper, and it's Mary Pickford, not me, who's America's Sweetheart – but I'm still a woman and I'm going to fight for the rights of women.' Nancy stopped for a moment, looked up into the spotlight and suddenly smiled: 'And now I'm going to shut up before I'm accused of *talking* like a woman.'

The applause was immediate, as the whole of the audience stood up and cheered. She felt Waldorf stand beside her and take her hand.

'You've won them over, Nancy.'

But she wasn't listening as she stood, head high, exulting in the praise and the applause like a prima donna before the footlights, roses scattered at her feet. 'Now,' she said finally, her voice loud enough for only Waldorf to hear, 'now for what really matters. Now we conquer the people.'

★

It was in her campaign in the streets that Nancy's true skill came to the fore. Even her opponents had to admit that. She revelled in the spontaneous interchange between herself and the crowds, encouraged hecklers, employed her natural wit to its advantage, and if some of the people were not prepared to vote for her policies, they went out of their way to listen to her views. The open car became a landmark, dominated by the figure of the beautiful, fair-haired candidate, hat tilted on her head, leaning towards the crowd, flirting, teasing, but never yielding under attack. And if the attack failed to materialize, she would provoke it. 'Come on!' she would shout, arms aloft. 'Who'll take me on? I'm ready for you!'

'Go back to America!'

'Go back to Lancashire.'

'I'm an Irishman!'

'I knew it. An imported interrupter.'

And when the attention was hers, she would say: 'Some people tell me I have a pleasing face and no policy. But I *have* a policy. I'm for the working classes, not the *shirking* classes.'

'That's easy for a capitalist to say.'

'It's easy for *anyone* to say, but I aim to do something about it.'

'Do what? If there were no capitalists, there'd be no slums.'

'If there were no *greed*,' Nancy countered, 'there would be no slums. You cannot make men economically equal, but I would be willing to throw every capitalist off the Plymouth Hoe tomorrow if you could prove to me that under Mr Gay's government or Mr Foot's government – and Isaac, I adore you dearly – this would be a better world.'

Nor was Nancy's delight in street banter too all-consuming that she failed to recognize that, as a politician, she was still a novice. If she couldn't answer a question, no matter how important the issue, she would say so: 'I do not pretend to know everything and I have the courage to say so.' Often this would alarm her committee, but Nancy, like more experienced politicians, knew that the public welcomed honesty, especially the honesty of a candidate who admitted he or she wasn't yet omniscient. Nor did she attempt to curry favour with the working man by hiding her own personal prejudices. Once, outside a public house near the port, a man shouted out:

'What do you think of drink, Lady Astor?'

'I don't touch the vile stuff,' Nancy replied immediately and then added, leaning towards him, hand extended: 'And if I'm elected, nor will you.'

If this threat of prohibition alienated a third of her voters, Nancy was unrepentant. If elected, Nancy would repeat, the question of the sale of alcohol would be the subject of her maiden speech and she was not going to pretend otherwise. It was perhaps her own personal revenge for the unhappiness while married to Robert Gould Shaw.

'That's because you're a bloody bitch of a Yank,' a drunk yelled at her when she voiced yet another unpopular opinion. Turning towards the drunk, Nancy raised her hand and pointed at him, saying:

'I want every woman in this street to see that that man does not vote for me. I don't want the vote of a man who uses language like that to a woman, even when he's drunk.' There was a silence and then immediate cheering until Nancy, with the timing of Bernhardt and the calculated mischief of George Robey, suddenly smiled and announced to the crowd: 'And now, my dears, I'm going back to one of my beautiful palaces to sit down in my tiara and do nothing. And when I roll out in my car I will splash you all with mud and look the other way.'

The effect of such an unorthodox campaign was, not surprisingly, headline news all over the country and almost overnight Nancy became a public figure, quoted and mis-quoted. But winning the attention of the press was one thing; winning an election, when the jesting and the parade were over, when each man and woman privately decided their own, not Lady Astor's, future, was another matter entirely. And Nancy, more than anyone else, including Wal-dorf, knew it.

On the eve of the election day of 15 November 1919 she remained in her room at Elliott Terrace, physically sick with nerves and exhaustion. She refused to talk to anyone – not her children, not her relatives, not Kerr nor Brand. Not even Waldorf himself. She wanted only the companionship of her Bible.

Early the next morning Waldorf entered her room to see that she was already dressed, sitting alone, gazing out to-wards the horizon in the west, the dark sea that flowed all the way to the shores of Virginia. In her hand was a silver-framed photograph of her father, Chillie, standing thumbs in waistcoat pockets, cigar in mouth, looking affluent and proud before the steps of Mirador. Waldorf didn't speak because he knew what Nancy was thinking. Ten months earlier, not in his beloved home but in an apartment in Richmond, Chillie had died on St Valentine's Day, never knowing the fame that would come so quickly to his daugh-ter, his own, true, kindred spirit.

'If only you were here, Poppa,' Waldorf heard her

whisper, her face wet with tears, 'I wouldn't be so scared.'

The next day, at three in the afternoon, on the steps of the Guildhall, the Town Clerk as recording officer announced that Lady Astor, with 14,495 votes, had been duly elected Member of Parliament for the Sutton division of Plymouth.

Nancy Astor, in her fortieth year, had become the first woman in the history of Great Britain to take her place in the House of Commons.

Sixteen days later, on 1 December, dressed in a black suit, black tricorn hat and white blouse, and accompanied by Arthur Balfour and Lloyd George, Nancy officially entered Parliament and took the oath. After the brief ceremony was over she took her place on the back bench surrounded by over six hundred men – many, including Winston Churchill, clearly resenting the presence of a woman in this most hallowed of institutions. Perhaps they foresaw that in this once all-male bastion of politics, where only men had the right to govern the country, there would come a time, sixty years almost to the day, when a woman would not only be a Member of Parliament but Prime Minister as well. Certainly Nancy envisaged that day in replying to a greeting from a neighbouring backbencher.

'Welcome to the best and most exclusive club in Europe, Lady Astor,' the man called out.

Without a moment's hesitation, Nancy answered with a smile: 'Not exclusive any more. I left the door open.'

NINETEEN

·

The First Lady

For her maiden speech in Parliament, scheduled for 24 February 1920, Nancy was true to the promise she had given the voters of Plymouth: she would speak against drink reform. During the war the licensing hours for selling and serving alcohol had been restricted to a few hours a day, so that public houses had been open for only eight of the twenty-four hours. It was now proposed by Sir John Rees, and seconded by Colonel Ashley, that all restrictions should be abolished completely; the motion had been put before the House and Nancy had chosen to be its principal opponent. She did not, contrary to press opinion, want to advocate prohibition, as was happening in America, but merely to continue the restrictions already established. To her, drink led to alcoholism and alcoholism destroyed not only the individual but also the home and, indirectly, the economy of the country. It was an unpopular proposal since the public house and inn in England were not solely places for drinking, but meeting-places, social havens where the working man could meet his friends and neighbours, could escape from the tenement and slum for a few hours. Nancy knew she would make enemies, but as she announced: 'I'm not in

Parliament to be popular but to say and do what I think is right.'

Like an actress rehearsing her role, and guided by Waldorf, she went over her speech time and again in the days before the motion was to be debated, although her impatience to enter the fray made her forget that she was not going to talk on a street corner but in the House of Commons, with all its traditions and protocol that even Lady Astor would have to obey.

'The convictions of drunkenness among women during the war,' Nancy declaimed, pacing up and down in the main hall of Cliveden as Waldorf listened attentively, 'were reduced to one-fifth after restrictions were brought in.'

'Is that figure correct?' Waldorf asked.

'Course it is. Wouldn't say so, would I? Now – I take women as an example because most of the men were away fighting. Do you realize what that means? The – '

'No, Nancy. Does the *House* realize what that means? You are addressing the whole House – '

'Yes. Yes. I know – '

'But it's important that you recognize the proper procedure – '

'Waldorf, stop being so petty. The convictions of drunkenness were reduced to one-fifth at a time when many women were earning more than they had ever dreamed of earning in their lives.'

'Now that's a good point. Emphasize it.'

' – which generally means that more is spent on drink.'

'Doesn't quite follow.'

'Course it does. Now here – ' Nancy shuffled through her notes. 'Here, I'll talk about delirium tremens. Is that with one "l"?'

'I think so. Yes. Yes, it is. But it's too specific. Talk about the general rather than the extreme.'

Nancy suddenly sighed in exasperation, hands on hips before the Sargent portrait behind her, and glared at her husband: 'Waldorf – are you with me or not?'

'Naturally I'm with you. But as a maiden speech the drink question is not going to be popular and – '

'That's exactly why I'm fighting it – but I didn't think I'd have to start in my own home.'

Waldorf looked at her, then suddenly smiled as Nancy narrowed her eyes and pointed up at him: 'You Astors haven't got shares in the breweries, have you?'

Waldorf laughed and shook his head.

'All right, then. Now *I'm* giving this speech, not you, and I'm not going to let John Rees get away with it. If he thinks that just because I'm a woman I'm not going to stand up to him, he'd better think again.'

It was then, almost imperceptibly, that a voice behind her said, with a hint of mockery: 'And Amen to that.'

Turning round quickly, Nancy found herself face to face with her eldest son. He had entered the hall during the conversation and was leaning idly against the back of an arm-chair, dressed in a grey flannel suit, a cigarette in his hand.

'Good morning, Mama,' Bobbie said in his slow, languorous voice. 'Has Ruth Draper learnt her little monologue yet?'

'If you've just come in here to be facetious,' Nancy snapped, 'I suggest you turn right round and go out again.'

Bobbie smiled but did not move, inhaling on his cigarette. He was now twenty-two years of age, as handsome as his father and, much to Nancy's concern, he had inherited many of Robert Gould Shaw's mannerisms: the lazy charm that could entrance all who met him, the elegant features, the sense of adventure allied with an air of mystery of someone who appears to remain detached from the world. These were not faults as such; they simply reminded Nancy of a husband she wanted to forget. That she loved Bobbie nevertheless was undeniable; that she would ever admit it was inconceivable. Moreover, Bobbie had also inherited the Langhorne wit, which, coupled with his courage, gave him an enviable advantage over the Astor children; he, and he alone, was not afraid of his mother, could match her line for line, barb for barb, *bon mot* for *bon mot*. He was not impressed by her nor humiliated by her, nor did he guide his life by the way she wanted him to live. He cared not a fig for Christian Science or Bible-reading, smoked when he wished and drank alcohol, not furtively like his eldest half-brother, but openly, almost defiantly, enraging Nancy even more. It is possibly superfluous to add that, despite all this, he loved Nancy, even adored her, more than any other person in the world. He would die for her.

Stubbing out his cigarette, Bobbie walked to the drinks table and poured himself a large measure of whisky.

'What are you doing with that?' Nancy demanded automatically.

'I'm going to drink it,' Bobbie replied, reaching for the soda siphon.

His accent was English, fashioned in the public school. Unlike the Astors, whose tradition was to go to Eton, Nancy, for inexplicable reasons of her own, had sent Bobbie to Shrewsbury. His life there had been considered reckless and undisciplined by the tutors, although he had been idolized by his fellow students. He had excelled, like his father, in horsemanship, a sport that had been tragically curtailed for him after a fall while steeplechasing at Sandhurst. His skull had been fractured and yet, although he could no longer compete, he continued to ride after redesigning his riding hat, reinforcing it with a protective shield – an innovation now adopted universally. If credit for this safety measure was owed to Bobbie Shaw, he never sought it or even cared less either way.

Sandhurst was followed by a commission in the Royal Horse Guards, 'The Blues', where he saw active service in France and returned to England as a subaltern to continue his career in the Guards. Though not strictly a playboy or a man about town – he was too much of a loner and a rebel – he was adored by the women he escorted, even if he treated them with indifference, for his laconic wit. He was admired because of his bravery, his loyalty and the spirit of danger that seemed to be under the surface of everything he did. And yet he remained an enigma, surrounding himself with a mist of secrecy that not even his most intimate friends could penetrate, especially his own mother.

'Now, Bobbie,' Nancy repeated, 'you put that drink back.'

'Mama, I'm twenty-two years of age. And you haven't brought in prohibition yet.'

'I said put that back.'

Bobbie splashed the soda into his glass and raised the whisky to his lips but did not drink, almost as a challenge. 'Just think of me as another Member of the Opposition.'

'Bobbie,' Waldorf interceded, attempting to play the mediator, 'tomorrow is an important day for your mother.'

'So I have been reading.'

'You just take one sip,' Nancy called out across the hall, 'and that money your father left you – '

'I know, mother, it will never be mine. Even though it belongs to me.'

The money was Bobbie's allowance after his father's divorce. It had been entrusted to Nancy, who, fearing that her son would squander it like Robert Gould Shaw, had refused to grant him anything more than a meagre stipend. Her decision merely aggravated their relationship and, although she knew she was wrong, her pride refused to admit it. By blindly trying to create a son to be the antithesis of his own father – a man he had never met – Nancy was laying the seeds for something far worse.

'That belongs to you when you reach maturity,' she replied, her voice cold. 'And by the way you're behaving, that's a long way off.'

Bobbie looked at her for a long time, then suddenly smiled: 'Good luck with drink reform, Mama,' he said, swallowing the glass of whisky and walking out of the hall.

The public and press reception outside the House of Commons as Nancy arrived was ecstatic. She was greeted with cheering that she could hear from Whitehall, saw the crowds straining past the police cordons to look at her, the banners of praise and welcome held high in the sky. It was as if she was attending a première, which, in truth, she was. Descending from the car she was immediately surrounded by reporters as she made her way towards the main door of the building.

'Lady Astor – is it true that you are in favour of prohibition?'

'If you're talking about liquor,' Nancy replied, acknowledging the crowd and her supporters, 'the answer is no. I'd never go that far. Why, if you come to my house – '

'Which one?'

'Any one. You'll find that if you want a drink you can have it. If that's the way you want to kill yourself.'

'But your country's introducing prohibition,' another reporter insisted.

'As a politician, *this* is my country. Didn't they teach you in school that Plymouth is in England?'

In the archway of the door she could see Robert Brand smiling at her in admiration. She glanced at him and winked as a female reporter pushed towards her: 'Lady Astor – may I ask who designs your clothes?'

'If I told you that, honey, they'd put the price up.'

Then, turning to the photographers, she posed, smiling, tilting her chin: 'Make me look pretty, now. I'm the only woman they've got.'

The tide of people engulfed her, wanted to touch her, to share this moment of history, and Nancy was overwhelmed. The warmth and excitement of the reception were more than she had dreamed was possible. The people loved her and that, to Nancy, was enough. But of course it wasn't. Her fight was not with the citizens of Britain but with those men who represented the citizens in Parliament. Moreover, although she was unaware of it, she had already made one implacable enemy before she had even begun. He was watching her now, standing on the edge of the crowd, a short, porcine, bibulous man of ruthless ambition whose sole aim in life was power. His name was Horatio Bottomley, and he was Member of Parliament for South Hackney.

Like many vain and self-opinionated men, Bottomley's ego was as sensitive as the surface of a lake. The slightest breeze disturbed it, no matter whether that breeze was temperate or hostile. Nancy had inadvertently disturbed that surface, distorting its image, so that the ripples became waves and, to a man like Bottomley, there was only one solution: revenge. The cause seemed trivial. He had always boasted that he was 'the Soldiers' Friend'; it was the symbolic banner that he carried. But during the Plymouth campaign he had seen Nancy identified with the same attributes, had read of her endeavours at the Cliveden hospital and he felt that he had been cheated of his rightful claim to fame. It was irrational thinking: the paranoia of a petty man who now watched the supporters he wanted praising not him, but a beautiful woman at a moment of glory.

If Bottomley had been only a Member of Parliament he could have attempted to upstage Nancy in the House, to belittle her achievements before her fellow politicians, if that was at all possible. But Bottomley's plan of action was far more dangerous. To seek retribution before a mere six hundred was not enough; he wanted to shame Nancy before every man, woman and child in the country and, as editor of *John Bull*, one of the most popular magazines in Britain, he had the means to do it. His only problem was that at present there was nothing about Nancy, both public and private, that he could use against her. He needed a scandal and, like all those who make their living out of the frailties of others, he knew that everyone, man or woman, has something in their life they wish to hide. To Horatio Bottomley Nancy was no exception; before the day was out he would begin delving into her past. He would find something to contaminate her. And when he did, and the time was right, he would cover every billboard in the country with it. Such was the nature of the man whom Nancy passed without a second glance as she entered the House of Commons for her first day as an active Member of Parliament.

★

'I will not enter into the question whether it is good or bad, but if my Honourable Friends opposite who are so keen on individual liberty ...'

From her seat in the Chamber of the House Nancy listened to Colonel Ashley, eager to reply, but found her attention drawn to the visitors' gallery above her head where she could see Waldorf, her sister Phyllis and her husband, and her son Bill. She smiled at them and began to wave until, catching the eye of the Speaker, she stage-managed a frown and stared back at Ashley as he finished his speech.

'... and on doing away with war regulations in time of peace, speak during this debate, I hope that they will say what they think about the Liquor Control Board and the present regulations.'

Nancy saw Ashley glance at her in defiance, then he sat down. It was now her turn to reply. Cautiously she stood up, noticed a smile of encouragement from Waldorf, and began.

'I shall not begin by craving the indulgence of the *House*' – a glance at Waldorf; a nod of approval in return – 'I am only too conscious of the indulgence and the courtesy of the House. I know that it was very difficult for some Honourable Members to receive the first lady MP into the House. It was almost as difficult for some of them as it was for the lady MP herself to come in. Honourable Members, however, should not be frightened of what Plymouth sends out into the world.'

There was a quiet crescendo of polite laughter and Nancy smiled and looked up towards the gallery. It was then that she realized that Philip Kerr was not among the spectators, nor had she seen him among the welcoming committee outside. In fact, although she knew he was in London, he had not visited Cliveden for over a week nor even communicated with her. It had not concerned her then, since she had been too preoccupied preparing for this particular day. But she expected him, of all people, to be there for her maiden speech. He was not, and it puzzled her. Instead she saw someone else arriving late and joining the Cliveden party. It was Bobbie, who looked at her and winked. Drawn back to the House by the coughs and murmurs around her, Nancy glanced quickly at her notes and continued:

'Now, as the West Country people are a courageous lot, it is only right that one of their representatives should show some courage and I am perfectly aware that it does take a bit of courage to address the House on that vexed question: drink. However, I *dare* do it.'

Two floors above where Nancy was speaking, Horatio Bottomley was talking on the telephone in his private office overlooking the Thames. On the walls were framed covers of *John Bull* and photographs of himself posing with reluctant former prime ministers, celebrities and members of the royal family. At a desk nearby his private secretary was typing out reports. The subject of Bottomley's telephone conversation was Lady Astor, which was not unusual for a magazine editor on that particular day. However, Bottomley's interest was more concerned with Nancy's past, the years in England before she met Waldorf Astor. He was making notes quickly, writing down everything he heard. The name 'Revelstoke' could be seen; then 'Desborough' followed by a question mark. There were paragraphs scribbled down, much of it unearthed from an ex-reporter on the *Daily Mail* named Mackenzie. But none of it satisfied Bottomley. It was not enough; nor was it what he was looking for.

He replaced the telephone and dialled again, seeking another informant. After a preliminary dialogue Bottomley suddenly said: 'Wait a minute. Let's go back before the lady arrived in England. What about this man Shaw that she married? What do you know about him?'

He listened for a moment, his pig-like eyes narrowing, before shouting into the telephone: 'Well, if you have to go to Boston to find out, go to bloody Boston. I want *facts*, not brochures. Is the first husband still alive?'

The answer was affirmative.

'Then *talk* to him. And if *he* won't talk, find someone who will. . . . Then *bribe* the man, for God's sake. Do I have to spell it out to you?'

It was at this moment that the secretary looked up in surprise and attempted to attract Bottomley's attention.

'Mr Bottomley?'

'Not now.'

'But, Mr Bottomley – did I hear you say that Lady Astor's first husband was still alive?'

'Yes. Yes. What of it?'

The secretary hesitated, then reached behind him and took a copy of *Who's Who* from a shelf. Opening it, he placed it before his employer. 'Then read that. I think it will interest you.'

'I want you to think of the effect of these restrictions in terms of women and babies.'

Nancy's voice sounded clear and confident across the floor of the House. She felt excited, sensing that she had overcome the cynics and that she was about to win her first *coup* of success.

'Think of the thousands of children whose fathers had to

put up with more than these vexatious restrictions, who laid down their lives. Think of their fatherless children. Supposing they were your children or my children, would you want them to grow up with the liquor trade flourishing? I do not believe the House would. I do not want you to look on your lady Member as a fanatic or a lunatic. I am simply trying to speak for hundreds of women and children throughout the country who cannot speak for themselves. I want to tell you that I *do* know the working man. I know that, if you do not try to fool him, if you tell him the truth about drink, he would be as willing as anybody else to put up with so-called "vexatious restrictions".'

Nancy stopped and looked around as her first speech in Parliament ended. There was a momentary silence then suddenly the shouts of 'Hear! Hear!' were heard from both sides of the House, more as a sign of welcome than as an endorsement to what she had said. It didn't matter for, at that moment, Nancy knew she had been finally accepted, not only as a woman, but as a politician.

Raising her eyes towards the gallery she saw Waldorf and then, to her surprise, the face of Philip Kerr. His unexpected arrival startled her, not only because she thought he had snubbed her, but because he was accompanied by someone she had never seen before: an attractive, dark-haired young woman whose right hand rested on Kerr's arm. Nancy looked directly into Kerr's eyes, but he was suddenly hidden from sight as her fellow politicians rose to congratulate her.

'How do you feel, Lady Astor?' she heard a neighbour ask.

'Right now,' Nancy replied, 'I feel like a drink.' Then suddenly she laughed and sat down, hand within hand on her lap, a solitary woman in black on a green leather bench. She suddenly looked very alone.

The next morning Waldorf confirmed the success of that day. While Nancy was preparing for her daily exercises he hurried excitedly into her boudoir clutching a pile of newspapers. 'Nancy? Have you seen these? "Lady Astor triumphant at Westminster." "In debate she proves herself equal to any man" – '

'Only equal?' Nancy asked dismissively, reluctant to disrupt her routine.

'Here's another: "Lady Astor may look like a flyweight but she fights drink reform with the punch of Jack Dempsey "'

'That sounds like Northcliffe's prose. Let me see.'

Waldorf held up the newspaper, whose front page was dominated by a photograph of Nancy.

'That makes me look more like a waxwork than a flyweight.'

'Nancy – one of these days, you're going to learn how to accept a compliment.'

'Best compliment would be when the Bill goes to Committee.'

Nevertheless she stopped and stared at the telegrams, letters and newspapers.

'I'd sure like to see the faces in Virginia now,' she smiled wistfully. 'I bet I know what Poppa would have said if he'd been alive. "Can't even scratch your backside, girl, without some damn fool reporter writing about it." He used to say that all the time to Irene.'

'He'd have been proud of you, Nancy. *I* am.'

Nancy gazed up at her husband, then gently took his hand. 'Thank you. Not only for what you just said, but I know that it should have been *you* in the House yesterday. . . .'

'No, Nancy. I never thought I would thank my father for

what he did. But I do. Because I know now that Plymouth chose the best candidate of them all. And it doesn't need these newspapers and telegrams to prove it.'

Nancy looked away, then glanced back at Waldorf. 'Bob Brand once said to me that you were a saint. Well, you're not, Waldorf Astor, but this woman is certainly glad she married you. Now shoo! Before you disrupt my whole day.'

Waldorf smiled, and then said quietly: 'Those faces in Virginia you were talking about. Well, I think we should both take a look at them very soon.'

In a corridor of the offices of *John Bull* a man stopped Horatio Bottomley and handed him a file of papers. Bottomley glanced at them and then asked: 'Are you sure these were the grounds for the divorce?'

'I'm sure.'

Bottomley had closed the file and begun to walk away when the man asked: 'What are you going to do about it?'

'Nothing,' Bottomley replied. Then he added: 'At least, not at the moment. We will wait until the time is right.'

TWENTY

·

The Sins of the Father

As Bobbie Shaw entered the officers' mess he could hear laughter from two young men sprawled in armchairs, their feet up on a table before a portrait of their commander-in-chief.

'But then what woman *wouldn't* adore being alone in a room with six hundred men?' one of them was saying, a lean, athletic junior officer with the dark, romantic features of a matinée idol. His name was Naish. 'There she is in a place where not only the King is banned from entering, but so is her own *husband*!'

His companion, a thin, red-haired junior officer, christened James but known by his nursery name of Truffles, laughed, then suddenly saw Bobbie calmly watching him. Truffles began to redden but Bobbie merely smiled and said:

'Very amusing. I assume you are talking about my mother?'

'I'm sorry, old chap,' Naish replied. 'Didn't mean to be offensive.'

'Quite right.'

Turning away, Bobbie slumped into an armchair next to a third officer, a year older than himself, who had known him since they were at Shrewsbury. The two men had remained the closest of friends ever since, although their public behaviour often betrayed this fact. Whereas Bobbie was publicly more extrovert and self-confident, masking his private instability, the other, Edward Hartford-Jones, was quiet, intellectual, almost shy; yet he presented an air of calm authority that Bobbie admired, even to the extent of belittling it.

Throwing Edward a cigarette, Bobbie called out to the waiter: 'The usual all round, Harris. And put it on Ashwood's slate.'

'Now hold horses,' Truffles protested. 'That's not on.'

'My dear Truffles, you know mother only gives me enough pocket money for sweets and a comic.' Lighting a cigarette, he turned to Edward: 'How are you?'

'Tolerable.' Then: 'How did the big event go yesterday?'

'Not a dry eye in the House. And not a dry throat afterwards either. Harris! Hurry it up with those drinks. If Lady Astor has her way, you'll be one of the unemployed.'

Immediately there were good-natured jeers from around the room.

Raising his hand in defence, Bobbie announced: 'Now. Now. I represent the sins of the father, not of the mother.' And then, looking directly at Edward, he said quietly: 'I telephoned you *twice* last night. I thought you might want to join the celebration.'

'Sorry. I was dragged off to some beastly play. Couldn't get out of it.'

A hesitation, then: 'Well,' Bobbie shrugged, 'you would have hated it. Barley water and Virginia ham. What was the play?'

'Oh ... one of those tiresome socialist things. Long

monologues, heavy symbolism and no scenery. You know the kind I mean?'

But Bobbie pretended not to listen, stage-managing an attitude of indifference as he flicked through a copy of *Country Life* and studied a photograph of the jockey Steve Donoghue. As the drinks arrived, Naish called across to him and asked if he was going to the 45 Club, but Bobbie remained silent and introspective. It was a mood Edward knew well; a quiet rebuff to him for preferring a stage play to Bobbie's company. He said nothing and sipped a gin and tonic. A group of officers in evening dress crossed the floor of the mess on their way to supper at the Savoy, dancing at the Embassy or the Kit Kat.

'I wish I hadn't cracked my skull,' Bobbie said finally, hurling the magazine aside. 'I'd have been riding at Cheltenham this weekend.'

'Then come to Arundel instead. I'll be motoring down on Friday.'

'On your own?'

'At the moment,' Edward replied, remaining in profile.

'I'll think about it.' Abandoning him, Bobbie sat next to Naish and asked: 'What was that about the 45?'

'I thought you were on duty tonight?' he heard Truffles ask. Ignoring him, Bobbie leaned closer towards Naish. Opposite, Edward watched.

'And who are we going to astonish with our company, Naish?'

'How about Venetia Thingummy?'

'Not *the* Venetia Thingummy?' Bobbie laughed. 'The one who always enjoys herself by being blissfully sick? Usually in a pink napkin while they play *Bye Bye, Blackbird*?'

'That's the one.'

'Right. And how about Jennifer Fenton?'

'Ratty's sister?'

'No. Is she? Good God. Did *you* know that, Edward?'

Edward said nothing.

'But surely you must know Jennifer Fenton,' Bobbie persisted. 'Adores being seduced. Especially in the Cavendish after *Pêches Rose de mai*.'

'Don't know her,' Edward replied flatly.

'No? Then obviously she's not someone who enjoys going to the theatre.'

'I wouldn't know.'

There was a silence as Bobbie studied Edward, then suddenly he stood up and said to Naish: 'All right, then. Let us go.'

At the door, Edward said: 'You *are* on duty tonight, aren't you?'

'Now, Edward, would I be going to the 45 if I was?'

'Yes.'

Bobbie smiled, thrust a cigarette into his mouth and walked out into the street. Edward watched as Bobbie sauntered towards a green Vauxhall saloon in which sat Naish, Truffles and two débutantes with shiny, expectant faces. He saw him enter the car and put his arms around the two girls and then the Vauxhall was moving fast along the street in the direction of Mayfair. At the corner, just before he was out of sight, Bobbie glanced back through the rear window as if to establish that his actions had been observed.

Although Nancy was an early riser ('Someone's got to wake up God around here'), she was nonetheless surprised to be disturbed, while still in bed, by the arrival of Bobbie Shaw at Cliveden. It was the following morning, and Bobbie, after spending the night at the 45 Club, had decided to drive back to Buckinghamshire. Mislaying his keys, he had been obliged to wake up Lee, who had replaced Parr as butler, and consequently his mother. She appeared on the stairs, a robe over her nightdress, to encounter her eldest son leaning against the main door, his tie loose and clearly drunk.

'Good morning, Mama. I was hoping the early bird wouldn't catch the worm.'

It was the image that startled her, a horrifying sense of *déjà vu*, suddenly recalling an earlier dawn incident, another Gould Shaw returning home after a night of drinking. At first she couldn't speak, but simply watched as Bobbie slumped in a chair, not even giving her the benefit of appearing guilty but assuming the air of a bored schoolboy waiting to be chastised by a teacher for discovered pranks.

'What are you doing back here?' Nancy demanded finally. 'You're supposed to be at the barracks.'

Bobbie lifted his head wearily.

'True. True. But I tossed a coin to decide whom I could bear to face least at this fragile hour. You or my commanding officer. The commanding officer lost.'

'How *dare* you talk to me like that.'

'Experience, Mother.'

'Stand up.'

'Impossible – '

'I said stand up. Not only are you drunk, but you've got no respect either. Not for me, not for anyone. Now stand up.'

Turning towards a statue behind him, Bobbie said: 'Mr Speaker, the Honourable Member for Plymouth Sutton – '

'I said stand up,' Nancy repeated, her eyes blazing, 'or I'll whip you here and now. It's something I ought to have done a long time ago.'

For a moment Bobbie hesitated, then slowly stood up. 'Do you want me at ease or at attention, Mother?'

'Bobbie Shaw, you were born with the devil in you. I've spent half my life trying to get rid of it. And I'll spend the rest of it if I have to.'

'And you'll enjoy every minute of it, won't you?' Bobbie countered, looking directly at her for the first time. 'Lady Astor, the saviour of souls, the Joan of Arc of noble causes. There's nothing you like better than playing the Good Samaritan, picking up a tramp in the street and saying: "Now come along, honey chile. I'm going to give you a home, you hear? I declare, I'm going to feed you with grits until you bust" – '

It was then that Nancy hit him, striking him hard across the face and seeing him recoil in surprise. 'At least they're grateful, which is more than I can say for you. You've been more spoilt than anyone alive. You've had everything. There hasn't been a thing that's been denied you – '

'Except my father's money! All your other children are going to be millionaires at twenty-one because their name is Astor, not Shaw – and there isn't a bloody thing you can do about it – '

'Don't bring your barrack-room language back here – '

'Then for God's sake, allow me what I'm entitled to. That's all I ask.'

Mother and son were now screaming at each other across the main hall and Nancy wanted to stop before the knives were drawn, as they inevitably would be. She wanted to walk out of the room to avoid the pain that would be inflicted, but the stubborn Langhorne pride stopped her. She could only continue, her body tense, her mind recalling all the bitter moments of a marriage that she knew she should forget.

'No! No, I won't. You pay for your own ticket to the gutter. I'm not going to let you squander it on women and liquor like your father did.'

'Like my father did?' Bobbie asked quietly, moving closer, his voice cutting deep. 'I wonder *why*, Mother?' He watched Nancy gasp and turn away and then suddenly he was smiling and kissing her gently on the cheek. 'Goodbye, Mama. I'll go back to the regiment now. Under the carpet and out of your sight.'

He was walking steadily to the door, adjusting his tie before Nancy realized what had happened. She had lost the fight, defeated by a reversal of tactics that confused her.

'Now, Bobbie, we haven't finished yet – '

But it was too late and she knew it.

'But of course we have, Mother,' Bobbie replied, his voice calm, almost affectionate. 'You just won't admit it, that's all.' Opening the door, he added: 'Perhaps you could write to me now and again. A postcard would do.' And the door was closed, leaving Nancy alone in the half-light as she heard a car start outside, then roar away along the driveway, the sound decreasing until there was silence.

That morning Nancy read the Bible alone and remained in her boudoir, not wanting to be disturbed. She wrote several letters to friends and admirers, including her former opponent, Isaac Foot, who was to revere her all his life, as well as such diverse personalities as Hilaire Belloc, T.E. Lawrence and Lloyd George; she also wrote to her sister Phyllis, now living with her husband, Robert, in the north of England. In that particular letter she talked ultimately of

her life, her love for Waldorf, her concern for her children.
Not once, however, did she mention the one person who
was uppermost in her mind. Not a single line referred to
Bobbie Shaw.

TWENTY-ONE

·

A Scandal in Public

If Nancy believed that she could hide her private strife from the world, she was to discover all too soon that the spectre of her first marriage was to become very public indeed. In April 1920 a Bill for divorce reform, introduced by Lord Buckmaster, passed its Second Reading in the House of Lords. It was therefore, according to the Constitution, required to be introduced and debated in the House of Commons where Nancy, as the only woman, could not avoid speaking for or against.

The principal recommendations for reform were that, apart from adultery, divorce should be granted for desertion, insanity, criminal conviction and habitual drunkenness. Her own tragic marriage to Shaw made it seem predictable that Nancy would support the resolution; instead she chose, surprisingly, to oppose it and oppose it as vehemently as she could. Perhaps she believed that the details of her past life in Boston were known only to herself and were of no concern to anyone else. As a private citizen, she was right; but Nancy was not a private citizen any more. She was opposing divorce reform as a public figure and a Member of Parliament who had been divorced from a man for the very same reasons she refused to accept as legal causes for marital separation. Perhaps Nancy felt safe knowing that the official grounds for her own divorce were adultery and that no one would know otherwise. But someone else did, and that someone was Horatio Bottomley. Unaware of this fact, she spoke to the House, using religion as the basis for her argument:

'In the Christian world, it is the spiritual aspect of marriage that the law attempts to protect, and it is the spiritual element that makes marriages happy. Most Honourable Members have said that. They all know it, and we women particularly know it. The spiritual idea of marriage, though started in the East, has been more highly developed in the West, and it is that that has elevated the Western women a little above their Eastern sisters. That is the difference between the East and the West. However, I am not convinced that making divorce very easy really makes marriages more happy or makes marriages more possible.'

The words had been said and Bottomley, sitting directly in front of her, knew that at last he had the fuel for his personal revenge. He was not going to hesitate in using it. Within days every billboard, every advertising space in the country acquired by *John Bull* announced in three bold words 'LADY ASTOR'S DIVORCE!' The magazine was sold out overnight.

It was inevitable that the public would think that the divorce referred to one between Nancy and Waldorf, not to a previous marriage of which few of them were aware. However, Bottomley's calculated publicity had caught their attention and the article itself did not disappoint the less prurient readers, especially those, in this era of depression, who considered the rich and the aristocracy to be nothing more than spoilt, idle classes living within their own set of rules.

'Lady Astor, A Hypocrite of the First Water', Bottomley trumpeted. 'The Poor and the Rich.' Seeking to embarrass and scandalize Nancy, he played on the contrast between Nancy's private life and public views: 'Lady Astor divorced her first husband Robert Shaw seventeen years ago. The divorce was granted on the grounds of desertion which Lady Astor now objects to becoming legal in Britain. In other words, Lady Astor took advantage of a divorce law which she herself does not wish to grant to others.'

Apart from the fact that the records stated that Nancy's divorce was on the grounds of adultery, not desertion, the article was damaging since it alluded to a conspiracy of secrecy, implying that details of the Shaw–Langhorne marriage were deliberately suppressed and that Nancy, like all 'privileged beings', had one law for herself and another for those less fortunate. It was compulsive reading, written with the right degree of spice, moral outrage and malice.

Typically, Nancy's initial reaction was to ignore it, dismissing Bottomley as just another street-corner heckler. She could answer that, as a divorced woman, she knew enough about the subject to speak from experience; that what she said in England in 1920 was, right or wrong, the views of a mature, experienced woman who had learnt that a marriage *could* succeed, as opposed to the attitudes of a young girl in turn-of-the-century Boston. She could also have said that, unlike most Christians and all Catholics, she was not against divorce *per se* but merely attempting to stop it becoming so readily available that marriage would have no value whatsoever. She could have said all that and more except for the fact that Bottomley held one trump card that, like the master tactician he was, he reserved for the climax of his tirade. He declared that Nancy, on marrying Waldorf Astor, had made a false allegation about her first marriage. And in this respect he was absolutely right.

Adding weight to his argument that Nancy was attempting to disguise the true facts of her divorce, he quoted from printed evidence in *Who's Who* and *Burke's Peerage* that in 1906, when Nancy had married Waldorf, she had referred to herself as 'a widow', when she knew full well that Robert Gould Shaw was alive, as, indeed, he still was. The implication, to Bottomley, was obvious: if Nancy had nothing to hide, why then did she pretend – and *still* pretend – that her first husband was dead?

It was a damaging question that Nancy found impossible to answer. Whatever her motives for this 'misrepresentation', she knew that to involve herself personally with Bottomley's allegations could only result in unearthing the more salacious aspects of the Shaw marriage and even the possibility of Robert Shaw himself being produced to give evidence against her. On the advice of Waldorf and encouraged by the sympathy of the House, who despised Bottomley's gutter press tactics, Nancy decided that she would allow herself to be judged by her own constituents in Plymouth. It was they who elected her; it would be they who would decide her political future.

Before that event, however, Nancy was to be confronted by someone who took the article even more personally than she did, someone whom she had overlooked, the one human being in her life who saw denial of Robert Gould Shaw's existence as nothing more than the most heinous form of betrayal: Robert Gould Shaw's son and heir, Bobbie. On reading the article he drove directly to Cliveden, burst into

Nancy's room and with uncontrollable fury hurled the magazine into Nancy's face.

'Is this true? Is it? That when you married Waldorf you said you were a *widow*!'

Taken aback, Nancy found it impossible to reply.

'Is it? Is it?' Bobbie repeated.

'Now, Bobbie – '

'*Is it?* For Godsakes, answer me.'

'Not if you – '

'Mother – you are calling yourself a widow. You are saying my father is *dead*.'

'But of course he's not dead – '

'Then why did you say it? *Why?*'

'It was – '

'*Why* did you say it? Is it because you wish he was dead?'

'Of course not . . .' Nancy began, but she couldn't continue nor could she lie as she saw Bobbie almost in tears of pain. She attempted to touch him: 'Bobbie, it was foolish of me – '

'Foolish! Is that all you can say? Oh, my God, you really *do* wish he was dead, don't you? You wished he'd never appeared in your life. And that's why you hate me. Because every time you look at me, I remind you of him. Robert Gould Shaw the Third.'

'I don't hate you, Bobbie . . .'

But her words were too late.

'I'm glad Bottomley wrote this,' Bobbie said coldly, 'because now the whole world knows what kind of mother I have. You always accused me of inheriting the bad side of me from my father. Well, dear Mama, I don't think that's quite so true any more.'

There was nothing more to be said. Nancy couldn't

defend her action, an act of petty spite against her first husband that had tragically rebounded to hurt not only herself but the son she loved more than any other. But if such private wounds could be healed in time, the more immediate question of her political future was still to be reconciled. The following week, Nancy stood on the platform in Plymouth and nervously addressed the leading members of her constituency.

'Ladies and gentlemen of Plymouth,' she began, holding a speech in her hands. Behind her Waldorf sat, listening anxiously. 'I've come to speak to you about the past events because you are the people who elected me, you put your faith in me and I owe it to you to be honest. If after what I have said to you you seek to choose another candidate to represent you, I will understand. Let me say first that the grounds of my divorce was adultery on the part of my husband and adultery alone. There was only one petition. There was none claiming divorce on the grounds of desertion or anything else.'

Nancy hesitated, assessing the mood of the hall, but there was only silence.

'But I would like to say that when I claimed to be a widow, I was ...'

She hesitated again. What could she say?

'I was ...'

And then suddenly a voice called out: 'We don't need to hear any more, Lady Astor. Tear it up!'

Nancy stared confused at the faces before her, as other voices joined in with the same enthusiastic shout. 'Tear it up! Throw the speech away!'

And then she heard Waldorf say: 'Do as they say, Nancy. Tear the speech up. They want you to stay.'

The voices were now singing *For She's a Jolly Good Fellow* in a jubilant demonstration of loyalty.

Almost in tears, Nancy tore up the speech and stood with her head bowed in gratitude. On the public stage she was triumphant once more; it was, in the final analysis, all she really wanted. As the applause and the cheering continued, nothing else seemed to matter.

Nancy returned to Westminster exonerated and was applauded as she entered the House. Her attacker, Bottomley, attempted to continue the fight but he knew he had lost. Two years later he himself became the victim of his own publicity and was charged with fraud. He was sentenced to seven years' imprisonment, thus destroying his own political career for ever. The House of Commons had no regrets.

TWENTY-TWO

·

America's Heroine

In 1922 the youngest Langhorne daughter and the most tempestuous and high-spirited of all the 'Mirador girls', Nora, arrived in England to visit her elder sisters. After marrying Paul Phipps – her daughter from this marriage was the actress Joyce Grenfell – she ran away with a reckless ex-baseball player called 'Lefty' Flynn who took her to Hollywood where he pursued a career as a cowboy star and stuntman. Brought back to Virginia by one of her brothers, Nora immediately ran back to 'Lefty' Flynn and hid out in the California hills. She was later to marry her cowboy hero and continue a life of uninhibited pleasure in the company of another, more notorious Southern belle, Zelda Fitzgerald, whose husband, Scott, openly adored Nora, seeking consolation from her during his bouts of depression. But all this was in the future. In the early 1920s Nora was still attempting to lead a reasonably conventional life, bringing her children to Cliveden and joining in the family games, the charades that had become a tradition in the Astor household.

It was during such an occasion that an unexpected visitor arrived – unexpected because Philip Kerr had been conspicuously absent from Nancy's life since her election, although he had continued to write to her. He had explained that his work with Lloyd George, the necessity to travel throughout Europe and the colonies had, regrettably, prevented him from meeting Nancy as often as he wished. Nancy, however, knew there was another, more personal reason. After all, she had seen the woman leaning on Kerr's shoulder in the gallery of the House of Commons. Consequently, on the first evening of Kerr's visit to Cliveden she ignored him and talked to Nora and her other guests, glancing up at him only when she heard him tell Waldorf that he had resigned as Lloyd George's adviser. However, Nancy made no comment, waited until the meal was over and everyone began to adjourn to the main hall for the evening's entertainment, and then said:

'Don't go, Philip. Stay here a moment.'

Her voice was almost a command as Nancy leaned back in her chair, pushed her tiara to the back of her head and began to fan herself with a side plate. It was an absurd but not untypical pose that made Kerr nervous as Nancy gazed along the empty table as if she had suddenly forgotten that he was there. He found himself standing helplessly in the middle of the room, stepping aside as footmen began to clear the table, then breaking the silence by talking once again about his resignation.

'Of course, Lloyd George tried to dissuade me, but in the end I had no alternative but to resign. After Russia and America withdrew from the League, there seemed no point any more.'

Nancy pretended not to hear, turning to the footmen and saying: 'Leave that. Come back later. I said leave that.' After the footmen had left, she finally turned, still fanning herself with the plate, and said with undisguised criticism: 'So you *quit*?'

'Nancy,' Kerr replied, moving towards her. 'Lloyd George is not going to win the next election. That isn't speculation. That's fact. And without him – '

'You gave up the ghost. All your talk about a brother-hood of nations is just that. Talk. You're the last person I thought would give in.'

'I haven't abandoned the ideal – '

'You *resigned*, didn't you? Even Waldorf didn't do that without a fight.'

Kerr looked at her but said nothing.

'So what are you going to do now?'

'Think about my future. . . .'

'Your future with *who*?' Nancy asked pointedly, and for the first time Kerr realized the cause of her mood. He glanced away guiltily and murmured:

'Oh, I see. . . .'

'Yes!' The word scythed through the air.

'Of course,' Nancy continued, 'it's none of my business. What's her name?'

'Victoria Netherton.'

'Sounds dreadfully middle-class. Where does she come from? Uxbridge?'

'Now, Nancy, she's only an acquaintance. Nothing more.'

'Then you sure blush easy over "nothing more". But then, as I said, it's none of my business. It's your affair. *Is* it an affair?'

Regaining his composure, Kerr sat down on a chair beside her and said quietly: 'Nancy, listen to me. I'm not going to marry Victoria. I admit I thought about it – '

'You did more than that.'

'I considered it on rational grounds and realized I was seeking happiness for the wrong reasons. Physical passion alone is not important. Is it?'

'Are you expecting an answer to that?'

'No. I realize it's spiritual love that unites two people. Nothing else. And I have already found that. It was what you described once as "the secret way". . . .'

Outside the room laughter could be heard – someone, a child, was running along the passageway.

'It would be impossible for me to marry anyone,' Kerr said quietly. 'Ever.'

There was a silence as Nancy studied him. Finally she said: 'You're getting fat, Philip Kerr. . . .'

Later, when she was alone, Kerr having rejoined the others at Nancy's request, she walked around the room, studying the paintings, the bust of Madame de Pompadour on the mantel. The door suddenly opened and Waldorf entered:

'Nancy – we're all missing you. Bobbie's about to do his Negro preacher act.' And then: 'Are you all right?'

Turning towards him, Nancy smiled and took his arm. 'Yes. Everything's fine now.'

In April Waldorf fulfilled his promise and accompanied Nancy to America. After she had arranged leave of absence from Parliament and the American press learnt of her visit, she was surprised and flattered by the countless invitations, both public and private, that she received from every state of her native country. Although she knew that her political success had been acclaimed abroad, that her comments had been widely reported, the more quotable ones having been dubbed 'Astorisms', she was unaware of the extent of her fame. She was returning to the United States not only as a favourite daughter but as a celebrity. Before the ship docked in New York, the news media had anticipated that she would dazzle them with her beauty, amuse them with her witticisms and provoke them with her comments. Naturally, being a born trouper, she did not let them down.

Before leaving England Nancy had been advised to avoid any political argument, especially the sensitive issue of the League of Nations. It was a subject that was out of favour with America and consequently ought to be avoided, especially by a visiting backbencher. Nancy's reaction to this advice was demonstrated at her first public meeting:

'I was told not to talk about the League. And so, of course, I am. That misrepresented and much despised League has already prevented three small wars, it has registered over one hundred treaties, has repatriated nearly four hundred thousand prisoners – not a bad record for only half a League. But if it *is* only half a League, at least it's half a league onward.'

Across the United States, travelling by train from city to city, Nancy's theme was the same. As an American, riding in triumph, she was greeted by crowds lining the platforms and the streets; as a politician, she couldn't resist declaiming her views, 'speaking from the heart, since it has been a safer guide to me than my head'. In Chicago she said, 'I think the world's gone mad about the common man. It isn't the common man at all who is important. It is the *uncommon* man. You Americans like to quote Abraham Lincoln as a great "common man" – but you've only had one Lincoln. And he wanted peace. He wanted unity. And so do I.' In Washington she declared, 'I, and many others, believe that until the British Empire and America get together and lead the world in peace – peace will be a long time coming. We feel too, that in fighting for understanding between these two countries, we are fighting for something far greater than any one country – for a civilization based on Christianity.'

But if her public self enjoyed the attention and the controversy, privately Nancy saw the true purpose of her visit as a pilgrimage, a return to her roots, to the state where she was born. In May Waldorf and Nancy arrived in Danville, Virginia, to be welcomed by bands and crowds and schoolchildren carrying flags. They were made honorary councillors and presented with golden keys, and a plaque was unveiled outside the Langhornes' old house on Broad Street. Later, alone, the Astors travelled to Mirador where Nancy paid homage to her dead parents, standing before the graves of Chillie and Nanaire. She offered gratitude to them, refusing to leave the graveyard, remaining in the darkness in tears.

Bobbie Shaw was drunk. He sat in the officers' mess, now deserted, with only the waiter as a reluctant companion. He had been there three hours, oblivious of the time, and had no intention of leaving.

'So ever since I cracked my skull, Harris,' he said, after ordering another brandy, 'ever since I cracked my skull – can you see the scar? – ever since then I have to drink in moderation. Which pleases my dear mother no end. And shall I tell you why? Because two of these is enough. Any more brandies and I behave just as I am now.'

The waiter attempted to move away, but Bobbie seized his arm:

'Now, Harris, I've always considered you the indispensable kingpin of the Royal Horse Guards. I really have. When I think of dear old King George sitting at Windsor right now with only his stamp collection as company, I think "Thank God for Harris who gives us the strength to guard his sovereign, keeps him from mortal dangers, protects him from the Hun and the Bolshie and the tsetse fly – "'

'Sir, I really think that you – '

'Now my grandfather used to make a mint julep. Do you know what that is, Harris? Of course you jolly well do. Well, I want you to make me one now in honour of my poor late grand-daddy – '

'Mr Shaw!'

The voice, loud and authoritative, came from the far end of the room. Turning his head, Bobbie saw an adjutant striding towards him.

'Mr Shaw – aren't you supposed to be on duty?'

Blearily, Bobbie looked down at his uniform, then slowly stood and smiled: 'Don't worry. His Majesty is safe. My horse is absolutely stone sober.'

The adjutant, however, was not amused. 'Return immediately to your room, Mr Shaw. And report to the commanding officer in the morning.'

'Well, if that means I'm no longer on duty, I'll have another drink.'

'Mr Shaw! I *order* you to go back to your room. Immediately.'

It would be, as Bobbie knew, the last order he would receive as an officer. The next morning he was asked to send in his papers and then resigned his commission. When Nancy returned from America she discovered all too soon that her eldest son had failed her yet again.

'It was the least I could do,' Bobbie told her, 'to save you the embarrassment of a court martial.'

But there was little remorse in those words. Like his father, Bobbie had chosen to live his life by his own rules, and, like his father also, authority had caused him to be an outcast. Without a career, Bobbie now seemed destined to drift into idleness; he was popular, had many friends, including his half-sister Wissie, but his natural melancholy made him an outsider. Moreover, he refused to face the daily recriminations from Nancy, the constant reminders of his fall from grace, and consequently it was only a matter of time before he left Cliveden altogether and rented rooms in London. Bobbie was not happier there, but at least he believed that the umbilical cord had been severed for ever.

In 1929 Nancy sought re-election for Plymouth Sutton, aware that it was to be the most difficult campaign of her career. She no longer had the advantage of being the only woman in Parliament, since within less than two years of her triumphant entry into Westminster another woman, Mrs Wintringham, was returned as a Member, and in 1923 no fewer than eight more women, three of them Labour, became Members of Parliament; one of them, Margaret Bondfield, would eventually become a Cabinet Minister. The door to the most exclusive club in Europe had indeed been left open. Moreover, since the General Strike of 1926, the strength of the Labour Party had increased, and issues, not personalities, were what mattered.

No one could deny that Nancy had not devoted herself to the problems of her constituency, especially regarding the welfare of women and children. The Lady Astor Housing Trust had been established to provide houses for the working mother and her children at reduced rents. The Astors also set up two recreational centres, the Astor Institute and the Virginia House Settlement, that included cinemas, libraries and gymnasiums as well as facilities for outdoor sports. Inspired and guided by the educational reformer Margaret McMillan, nursery schools became a priority in the poorer areas of Plymouth, but nevertheless this benevolence, as Nancy knew, was not enough to secure her re-election. The major problem, common to every town and city in England, was not houses and schools but unemployment. Fathers and sons needed jobs; the dole queues were everywhere. And with a majority of only 211 Nancy's political future was in the balance.

Even to the most casual observer Nancy's campaign in Plymouth seemed to be fuelled by an almost obsessive desire to win, as if the very idea that anyone would vote her out of office was not only unthinkable but bordered on treason. Shunning, as always, the formal halls and meeting-places, she took to the rain-swept streets, striding into the heart of her Labour opponent's territory, standing in tenement squares beneath the lines of washing. Dressed in furs and pearls amid the squalor, it was an act of defiance that almost led to a riot. Accompanied only by her agent, Albert Webb, increasingly nervous as he saw the faces at the curtainless windows, Nancy began, in traditional manner, by attacking Parliament itself.

'What I notice in the House of Commons is that the men who want to run the business of the country are never men who run any business of their own.'

'They'll never do worse than you!' a voice shouted from above.

'Never mind,' Nancy replied immediately. 'Let them do

as well. Now I'm a Tory, but I don't think that there are no hypocrites in my party. There are. But unlike the Socialists, our policy is not a *policy* of hypocrisy.'

'It's a policy of lies.'

'I heard someone calling me a liar. Well, I don't mind that – because I'm not. But if he said I was a nuisance, I'd hate it. Because I am.'

It was then that derisive laughter was heard, windows were opened and tin cups were banged against the wall to drown her voice. Undeterred, Nancy continued until suddenly a bottle was hurled in her direction. It struck her open umbrella, bounced and smashed into pieces on the ground.

'I think we'd better leave,' Webb urged, as voices began to chant *The Red Flag*.

'We'll do no such thing!' Nancy snapped, suddenly closing the umbrella and walking out into the centre of the square, unprotected. She shouted up through the rain: 'Am I a better target now? Come on – you pack of Bolshies. Here I am!'

'Go back to your mansion.'

'Don't you wish *you* had one to go back to? Is this how you want to live? Is this the best Socialism can offer you?'

In reply, a tin can sailed past her head, followed by another.

Without flinching, Nancy raised her head towards her assailant: 'Better learn to throw better than that if you want a revolution.'

'If there is, you'll be the first to go.'

'If there is, I'd accept. But until then, I intend to fight for every one of you whether you like it or not. I don't want to represent a city that has buildings like this. You there! How many children have you got?'

At a window, a woman replied that she had five.

'Five!' Nancy repeated. 'Well, do you want them to grow up in a slum like this? Do you?'

'No. . . .'

'Well then, let me make you a proposition. Vote for your Socialist friends. Go on. We're still a free country. Vote for them. But when the next election comes around and you're still living here, I suggest you think again. Because *I* won't forget you and I won't bear no malice.' There was a momentary silence and Nancy smiled. 'Thank you for listening,' she said, as if taking her leave of a polite charity dinner. Splashing through the puddles and the rain, she shouted across to Webb: 'Come along, Albert! The day's just begun!'

It was to be a long and bitter campaign that left Nancy exhausted. But in the end she won by the narrowest of margins, defeating the Labour candidate, Westwood, by little more than two hundred votes. It could have been worse. If there had not been a Liberal candidate, she most certainly would have lost.

Nancy now believed that the enemy was not just the traditional and recognizable division of parties, but an ideology that was taking control not only of the working classes but of the country itself. That ideology was Communism and its leader was Stalin. True to her nature of confronting danger face to face, Nancy, with the encouragement of Waldorf, decided to visit the Russian dictator personally, to find out for herself what kind of man he was. She would do it with the utmost publicity, encouraging interviews with the press for weeks before the visit. Moreover, in order to ensure that the spotlight was firmly upon her, she planned to be accompanied not only by Waldorf, her son David and Philip Kerr, now Lord Lothian, but also by the most celebrated playwright in Britain, her friend and fellow pub-licity-seeker, George Bernard Shaw. She believed it would be the highlight of her career. However, before the visit even began it was almost destroyed by a scandal that left its scar on Nancy's life until the day she died. The figure in the centre of this scandal was, of course, her son Bobbie Shaw.

TWENTY-THREE

•

A Clandestine World

From the day that he resigned his commission Bobbie's life took on a course that was reckless and uncontrollable. Resentful about being denied his father's money, he lived in a secret world in London, a cynic and a rake. He was now thirty and still handsome, even though alcohol was taking its toll on his health and his weight, and still popular among his few chosen friends. And yet he remained a creature of melancholy and despair, suffering from depression and loneliness and feeling more and more estranged from life at Cliveden. He still loved his mother more than anyone, but refused to see her; Nancy on her part stubbornly resisted any demonstration of her own, unqualified love for him. And so they lived as distant strangers and that was the heart of the tragedy.

His closest friend remained Edward Hartford-Jones, now a captain in the Guards, but even that relationship was threatened. Bobbie suspected that Edward had found affection elsewhere, although that was denied. Once Edward invited Bobbie to be his guest at the officers' mess, but it was a mistake. Bobbie was depressed by the reminders of his past, the equine trophies that he had won for the regiment had remained on display long after the winner himself had been dismissed. Edward seemed unable to relax with Bobbie, as if he were guarding a guilty secret; he made embarrassed excuses when Bobbie proposed a weekend in the country or a visit to a theatre. Finally Bobbie no longer cared. He simply lost all hope in himself and rarely smiled. He believed he had been cursed with the bad blood of the Gould Shaws, that he was born a Cain and there was nothing he could do about it.

Then, quite unexpectedly, a telegram was forwarded to him from Cliveden. The message inside was an invitation to meet a man he had never seen and yet had haunted his whole life. It suggested a rendezvous in Claridge's Hotel where the man was staying during his brief visit to England. Without telling anyone Bobbie accepted and, in February 1930, he went to a second-floor suite overlooking Brook Street, knocked nervously on the door and waited until it was opened by an undistinguished middle-aged American, who looked and dressed like a banker, his grey hair thinning, his skin the colour of porcelain. When he offered his hand, it trembled. He seemed self-conscious, shy, as if regretting the meeting, and Bobbie could only stare silently at this nondescript figure before him who seemed as volatile and demonic as a curtsy. He thought he had come to the wrong suite, but there was no mistake. The man he was meeting for the first time was his own father.

'Robert?' Shaw asked, as if equally unsure.

'Yes. . . .'

'I'm sorry. I don't know what to say. I rehearsed some things and even wrote them down. Forgive me, but what *does* a father say to a son whom he's never seen before?'

In the suite, Bobbie stood quietly in the centre of the

room, aware of the other man's nervousness and yet unable to accept him as a father. He could not believe that all the bitter stories that Nancy had told him, all the hatred, the tales of violence and rebellion could have been perpetrated by this mild, almost absurdly conventional American, fumbling for glasses, removing a suitcase from a chair so that Bobbie could sit down. Was this paunchy man in bi-focals the wild animal who had seduced and betrayed his mother and then abandoned her with a son and a lifetime of hatred? Bobbie almost felt sorry for the poor man and, perversely, resented the fact that he was not sharing a drink with the devil incarnate.

'How is your mother?' Shaw asked, emptying an ashtray and replacing it neatly on the arm of a chair. On a dresser was a framed photograph of a pleasant-looking woman standing beside a younger Shaw and before four children, all boys. Bobbie assumed that the woman was his father's second wife and that the boys were his half-brothers, but he hardly gave them a second glance.

'She's well, sir,' Bobbie replied.

'You don't have to call me "sir", Robert. You can call me....'

Shaw suddenly blushed and looked away, concentrating on refilling a glass. Finally he said: 'I've read a great deal about Nancy. She has certainly made a success of her life....'

'Yes. And success hasn't changed her at all. Unfortunately.'

He wanted to leave, to get out of this claustrophobic suite, away from this dull, pathetic old man in his shapeless suit and vulgar tie.

'Is it true that she's planning to visit Russia with Bernard Shaw?'

'Well, it's certainly not with *Bobbie* Shaw.'

His father looked at him directly for the first time. 'Why are you so bitter, Robert?'

'I'm not, sir. I just say things like that. It's expected of me.' Bobbie suddenly smiled and lit a cigarette, flicking the match on to the floor. 'Are you staying in London long, sir?'

'What? Oh. No. Only a few days. Business. But I did have time to see Buckingham Palace and Trafalgar Square. And where else? . . .'

Hands in pockets, Bobbie sauntered to the window and looked out at the traffic as if forgetting that his father was there.

'The Tower of London,' he heard him say. 'Have you ever seen the Tower of London?'

'I drove past it once,' Bobbie replied, without looking around. He was admiring a green Bentley being driven towards Grosvenor Square. He then turned to see Shaw quickly swallow a drink, the bottle in his hand ready to refill the glass. Ignoring this, Bobbie said directly, his voice steady: 'Sir? Forgive me for asking this, but my mother once said that there was insanity in the family.'

Shaw laughed nervously: 'Nancy always exaggerated – '

'You mean, there *is* some truth in what she said?'

'Of course not,' Shaw said unconvincingly. 'What people called insanity then is not how we would describe it today. We're more knowledgeable about . . . about these things. My mother suffered from illnesses but . . . Why do you want to know?'

'In case I have inherited it.'

This was said so simply and matter-of-factly that it startled Shaw. 'No, Robert. . . .'

'Pity. Then I have only myself to blame.' Walking to the

241

door, he asked: 'On what grounds were you divorced? You and my mother?'

'Robert – that's all in the past.'

'I'd like to know, sir. Just for myself.'

'Well . . . the grounds initially were incompatibility. But then your mother insisted that it was based on my adultery.'

'With *her*?'

Bobbie pointed at the photograph.

'Yes. With Mary.' And then, 'It was for the best, Robert. . . .'

Bobbie didn't speak, but remained staring at Shaw.

'We were both very young – '

'Did you love my mother, sir?'

Shaw hesitated and then nodded. 'Very much. I never loved anyone as much as I loved Nancy. But I could never make her happy.'

'No *one* person can. Mother needs a crowd. If she had her way there would be a sign on the wall of Cliveden reading "Stage Door".' Bobbie smiled, then added wistfully: 'And I'd be the first in the queue.' And then: 'Goodbye, sir.'

Shaw didn't move, as if surprised that Bobbie was leaving so soon. He suddenly wanted to hug him, to put his arms around him just once in his lifetime, but Bobbie had gone and the door was closed. From the window he watched the son he never knew cross the street and get into a taxi, and then he was gone. Shaw remained with his face against the glass for a long time, until it grew dark and the lamps came on outside. He felt an unbearable loneliness and was frightened to move.

Robert Shaw never saw Bobbie again. He returned to America the following week and, less than a month after meeting his estranged son, he collapsed in the Plaza Hotel in

New York and died at the age of fifty-nine. A single para-
graph in a Boston newspaper announced his death.

Immediately after leaving Claridge's, Bobbie took a taxi to
his flat and telephoned Edward. There was no reply at his
home and the surly voice of a junior officer at the barracks
informed Bobbie that Captain Hartford-Jones was on short
leave. Partly because of the meeting with his father and
partly out of loneliness Bobbie decided to get drunk. He
remained in that condition for a week, seeing no one, not
caring what was happening to himself and especially what
was happening in the outside world. If he had, he would
have been aware that the newspapers and magazines were
dominated by photographs of Nancy and Waldorf as they
prepared to leave for Moscow, together with the Irish
cynosure, George Bernard Shaw.

The playwright had been a friend of the Astors, and
Nancy in particular, for almost a decade. He and his wife
Charlotte had visited Cliveden often and GBS had even
gained the privilege of being an informal guest in the house
whenever he wished. The familiar tall, white-bearded figure
became part of the family, accompanying Nancy on her
walks, spending long evenings by the fire, talking incessantly
and charming everyone he met. At Christmas he put a red
cloak over his tweeds and played Santa Claus to the children.
Unquestionably he adored Nancy. It might even be said that
she was a living creation of his heroines – a Major Barbara
or a Candida, though Nancy might have preferred to be
identified as his St Joan. They shared the same irreverent
humour, the same intolerance of bureaucracy and fools, and,
needless to say, the same disinterest in sex, which might have
complicated the relationship. Nancy considered that GBS

was her personal sage but never took him seriously, while GBS saw Nancy as his muse and never took her seriously either.

There had, of course, been other intellectuals at Cliveden who had been seduced by Nancy's personality and beauty, drawn to her like moths to the flame. Philip (Kerr) Lothian led the field but was obliged to acknowledge the presence of other rivals, notably Hilaire Belloc, Lionel Curtis and, the most remarkable of them all, T.E. Lawrence, late of Arabia and now masquerading under the name of Shaw. It was ironic that Nancy's life should be influenced by so many men with the name of Shaw. Due to the respective natures of the two protagonists, the liaison with Lawrence/Shaw was pure and ascetic. They were both unconventional romantics, both public figures who guarded their private emotions and who shared a love of excitement and speed. Nancy would ride Lawrence's Brough Superior motorcycle at high speed along the country lanes near Cattewater, Plymouth, where Lawrence was stationed as an aircraftman in the RAF. She would visit him in his cottage and listen to him talk, even if at times she objected to his self-pity. But she enjoyed playing the role of confidante to a legend, even if she knew less about Lawrence than she admitted. But the relationship never equalled that between Nancy and GBS. Lawrence was too much of a recluse, and it is impossible to say whether Nancy's influence would ever have changed that, since the relationship ended all too soon when Lawrence was killed while riding the very motorcycle he had lent to Nancy.

GBS, then, remained the major luminary in Nancy's social set and Fleet Street's favourite eccentric. The combination of him and Nancy Astor travelling together to confront Stalin was irresistible, and on the eve of their departure the press gathered in their legions outside the Astors' house in St James's Square.

'And what are you going to say to Stalin, Lady Astor?' a reporter asked.

'I'm going to be very polite as always and ask him when he's going to stop killing people.'

In the laughter GBS stepped forward into the flashlights, refusing to be upstaged: 'And I'm going there simply to attend the opening of a very great play, *The Apple Cart*, which Lady Astor will no doubt upset.'

Less than a mile from this press conference, in the dark shadows of St James's Park, two policemen were watching a man walking somewhat unsteadily along a dimly lit path. They saw a youth appear, glance around furtively, then say something to the man. It was clear that an assignation was being suggested but, for the moment, the man was unsure. He walked on, then stopped, walked a few steps further, then suddenly turned and approached the youth. Without a further word the youth led the man into some bushes, hidden from view.

'Give the bastards a couple of minutes,' one of the policemen said.

The telephone in the Astor house was answered by Lee. He listened for a moment, then put the receiver down and stared through the window at the crowds outside. For once he was unsure what to do, anxious not to create cause for alarm before the world press. He did not know the reason for the telephone call except that it was serious and that it was from the police. Lord and Lady Astor had to be contacted immediately. Seeing Philip Lothian on the main steps, Lee drew him aside and related what had happened.

'Tell my driver to bring my car to the corner of the square,' Lothian said quietly. 'And say not a word to anyone.'

Pushing through the crowd, Lothian managed to reach Nancy and stood beside her as the reporters moved nearer. His voice barely above a whisper, he said to Nancy with controlled urgency: 'Try to keep smiling and act as if nothing is wrong and make your way back to the house.'

He could see Nancy frown in reaction, but otherwise her expression gave nothing away.

'The police are waiting on the telephone.' Lothian added. 'I believe Bobbie is in trouble.'

He heard Nancy gasp, saw a photographer thrust a camera into her face, and then Nancy was grinning, apologizing, and waving to the crowd as she retreated as casually as she could to the door of the house. Five minutes after answering the telephone call she was sitting in an almost catatonic trance in the back of Lothian's car as it hurried through the evening traffic.

'Don't worry,' Lothian reassured her. 'It won't get to the press. Waldorf and I will make sure of that.'

But Nancy wasn't listening. Convinced that it was a mistake, she couldn't believe what she had been told by the police. Such things did not happen. Indeed, to Nancy, such things did not exist. It couldn't be true and yet she knew that there was no other answer.

'We can't possibly cancel the Russian trip,' Lothian continued. 'That would arouse too many questions. But we can certainly postpone it for a few days.'

'What have I done?' Nancy suddenly cried, her voice distorted in anguish.

'It isn't your fault, Nancy.'

'Oh, but it is. It *is* my fault. It is. It is. . . .'

At the police station Nancy asked to see Bobbie alone, and was taken to a small, dark cell where her eldest son sat, arms folded, staring into space. His face was expressionless.

Sitting next to him, Nancy asked: 'Is it true?'

'Yes, Mama. It's true.'

It was then that Nancy felt herself about to break down and looked away, seizing the bars of the cell tightly. She wanted to scream, to shatter this nightmare. Her own son arrested for a crime that she couldn't even envisage without disgust. She believed such creatures were animals, perverted beings practising base acts that she was incapable of describing. She was not to know that Bobbie had been seduced as a child by a priest, and later, it was claimed, by Lord Kitchener himself. Nor was she to know that he had had male lovers at Shrewsbury and in the Guards – Edward being his favourite – and that, even though he had deflowered many a débutante, his sexual preference was for men. But he was not an exhibitionist and none could have detected his homosexuality by his outward appearance and manner. His was a clandestine world and even the incident in the park had been an exception.

Attempting to regain control of her emotions, Nancy turned back towards Bobbie and said quietly: 'The police say that they will delay issuing a warrant of arrest. Do you understand what that means?'

'Yes. It means that, if I leave the country, it'll all be carefully pushed under the carpet, glossed over, whitewashed. Forgotten.'

'It'll also mean you won't go to prison.'

There was silence.

'Bobbie – did you hear what I said?'

Slowly turning his head, Bobbie looked at his mother. 'Would *you* run away? If you were guilty of a crime – what would *you* do?'

'Bobbie, I realize what you are saying, but sometimes – '

'Sometimes we can twist the rules to suit ourselves? No, Mother. I'm not going to run away. You see, I'm not ashamed of what I did. It just happens to be a crime and so I'll go to prison.'

Nancy gasped, finding it hard to breathe. 'Not ashamed? Bobbie, just tell me. What can a man . . . a stranger . . . I just don't understand. Just tell me *why*. What do you do it for?'

Bobbie looked at his mother for a long time, studying her face that comprehended nothing. And then finally he answered her question with a single word: 'Love.'

He watched Nancy recoil in pain as if he had driven a knife into her heart. And then she was weeping, clinging to him, kissing him as if releasing every emotion in her body. A week later, found guilty of the crime of homosexuality, Bobbie Shaw was sent to Wormwood Scrubs where he was to be confined for not less than six months.

TWENTY-FOUR

·

Rebellious Children

The arrest and imprisonment of Bobbie Shaw in 1931 heralded a decade of personal and public tragedy not only for Nancy but also for Waldorf. Neither of them could foresee the events that were to take place in the next ten years, events that would place them in the centre of a controversy that remains to this day. But the portents were already there.

The visit to Moscow had demonstrated that even though Nancy was far from being a diplomat in her conversations with Stalin, she was not a woman who was afraid of being forthright with the enemies of democracy. Whereas Waldorf and Lothian were content to observe and learn, and GBS was happy being flattered and amused, Nancy treated the ruler of the Soviet Union as a pest she had discovered in her drawing-room and from whom she was determined to find the causes for his misbehaviour.

'I asked him when he would stop killing people,' she told a reporter on her return to England. 'And he wouldn't answer. So I asked him again. Finally he replied that slaughter was inevitable. Would you believe that? He said that it was necessary to kill in order to establish the Communist State. Well, that's Communism for you. Obey or die.'

Such an orthodox and somewhat facile appreciation of foreign policy was, not surprisingly, very good copy for the more sensational newspapers and Nancy was delighted by the attention. Ignoring the warnings of her more responsible colleagues, especially Churchill who classified Nancy as a naïve and rather silly political soubrette, Nancy flirted with the press, feeding them material to suit her mood:

'I told him that the children I'd seen in Russia were just too *clean*. They weren't like children at all. Why, children should be allowed to run wild and get muddy. Well, let me tell you what Mr Stalin said to that. He said that in England we *eat* our children! So I told him that I knew all about children. I'd not only founded nursery schools, I'd given birth to six children of my own. And I certainly haven't *eaten* them yet.'

If Nancy had not gone so far as eating her children, she could not deny, privately, that she had rejected them. She almost totally ignored the eldest Astor son, Bill, making it quite clear that she had little affection for him. Lacking self-confidence and charm, he could not counter Nancy's apathy and lived a wretched and lonely life seeking comfort wherever he could find it. One day he would inherit Cliveden; and one day a notorious sexual scandal would commit him to a premature grave. But if Bill Astor lacked mother love, Bobbie was now smothered by it. Haunted by guilt, Nancy would visit him in Wormwood Scrubs almost daily, often dressed in formal evening dress, a tiara on her head, as if she was just stopping by *en route* to a ball or an elegant dinner party. Bobbie recognized her courage in seeing him, openly and without recrimination, but he was nevertheless embarrassed by her visits and found little to talk to her about, though he never denied her the right to see him. After all, out of all his friends, none came or even wrote a letter. Outside his family he was *persona non grata*. When finally he was released he refused to return to Cliveden, because that would have been the easiest and most secure path to take. Instead, he asked Nancy to stop the car and leave him 'somewhere in London'. He assured her he would be all right; he simply wanted to face the world on his own. His last words to her as the car drew away were '*Tout lasse, tout casse, tout passe. . . .*' And then, in a note he wrote her three days later, he said: 'Don't ever die, Mother. Not before me.'

But if Nancy believed that her home life would now be free of drama, she was to be disappointed. An incident now took place that threatened not only her role as a mother but also her religion itself. Her only daughter, Wissie, had always been an independent and headstrong girl, who, though resisting being classified as 'a bright young thing', certainly was beautiful and admired. She had been christened 'Phyllis' and, like her namesake, Wissie's dominating passion was riding; she was skilful, tireless and sometimes reckless. However none who witnessed the accident while Wissie was riding to hounds with the Pytchley Hunt could fault her horsemanship. It was true that the ground was dangerous since a thaw had followed a hard December frost, but Wissie's horse was running well and responded immediately to Wissie's instructions. But then, quite suddenly, the horse lost its grip on the slope before a fence, stumbled, crashed through the fence and, after throwing its rider, rolled over on to Wissie, crushing her underneath its weight and forcing the pommel of the saddle deep into her back.

Other riders, including Henry Tiarks and Ronald Tree, fearing that Wissie's back was broken, carried her to their

house and then she was taken by ambulance to a hospital in
Kelmarsh. A doctor and a radiologist were sent for and it
was only then that someone telephoned Nancy in London
to tell her what had happened. She and Waldorf arrived on
the first train, accompanied by a Christian Science practitioner, to discover that Wissie, semi-conscious, was already
being attended by doctors. It was this defiance of her beliefs,
more than the accident itself, that induced the outrage that
was to follow. Her actions were predictable.

Striding into the hospital room, she screamed: 'Why is
my daughter in hospital? Do you want to kill her?'

The radiologist, Harold Hodgson, stared at her in alarm
as Nancy moved to the bed and pulled aside the blankets.

'Wissie, you get out of there. Where are your clothes?'

'Lady Astor,' Hodgson interrupted, 'we had to bring her
in here – '

'Falling off a horse, Wissie. You've done that a dozen
times. You must be getting lazy to want to end up like this.'

Wissie didn't react, being unable to move.

'Lady Astor,' Hodgson insisted, 'it's more serious than
that – '

'Course it's not. Now outside is my CS practitioner.
My very own. He'll get rid of those bruises before you
know it.'

'Lady Astor – may I talk to you?'

'Why? Who are *you*?'

'My name is Hodgson. I'm a radiologist. Your daughter's
friend, Mr Tiarks, sent for me.'

'He had no right to do that. I said no doctor – '

'May we talk somewhere else?'

'No, we may not. Wissie! You get out of that bed and
show me there's nothing wrong with you.'

Fear could be seen now in Wissie's eyes, a fear that had replaced the pain.

'Wissie?' Nancy repeated. 'Did you hear what I said?'

'Lady Astor,' Hodgson urged, 'she can't move. That would be impossible. Her spine has been damaged. The X-rays I took leave no doubt that she needs – '

'Don't you tell me what she needs. No doctor is going to touch her except my own practitioner and that's final. I'm taking her out of here.'

'If you move her, you could cripple her for life.'

Nancy hesitated, glanced at Hodgson, then knelt beside her daughter. 'Wissie, you believe in me, don't you? It's all right, Wissie. They're just making you afraid. You just fell off a horse, that's all. You put your faith in the Bible and everything will be all right. Isn't that what I've always taught you?'

Nancy attempted to smile and took Wissie's hand, but there was no reaction. The hand was almost lifeless and Wissie's eyes stared into space seeing nothing. For a long time Nancy didn't speak, then she slowly stood up and walked out of the room to the corridor where Waldorf and Lothian were waiting.

'She'll be fine,' she said quietly, closing the door. 'God's already taking care of her.' But she could look at neither of the men and remained with her face pressed against the wall.

Waldorf hesitated, then said cautiously: 'Dr Fairbank said that Wissie would have to be in plaster for no more than a month. Then she would be all right.'

Raising her eyes, Nancy snapped: 'Your conversion was certainly short-lived, wasn't it?'

'Nancy,' Lothian said, stepping forward, 'the doctor *was* assisted by a Christian Scientist.'

'Compromises. That's all it is.'

'Wissie is old enough to choose – ' Waldorf began.

'And you allowed her to.'

'She's my daughter.'

'*Our* daughter.' Nancy stared at the two men as if she had been betrayed. 'Both of you are getting old,' she said dismissively.

'Nancy,' Waldorf smiled. 'I'm the same age as you.'

But Nancy wasn't listening, turning her attention towards Lothian: 'Compromises! If it was a question of life and death, would *you* compromise?'

'No.'

'Life and *death*?'

'No,' Lothian repeated.

'I don't believe you.'

Then she was gone, returning alone to the house where she was staying, finding comfort in the Bible: 'Woe to the rebellious children, saith the Lord, that take counsel but not of me. And that cover with a covering but not of my spirit, that they may add sin to sin.' She read the passage over again: 'rebellious children'. In her eyes she believed that she was plagued by them. Nor could she accept that Wissie was seriously ill. To her, the power of prayer was stronger than any medicine, so that when Waldorf finally allowed the doctors to reset her daughter's damaged spine, Nancy considered him nothing less than a Judas.

At Wissie's bedside, after the operation, Nancy remained unrepentant. 'It was your strength and my prayers that pulled you through,' she said. 'That's what it was. Not the scalpel. It was prayer that made your body well again.'

But Wissie's body was not completely well; she suffered from the back injury for the rest of her life. Whether matters would have been different if she had received orthodox medical treatment immediately is debatable. Certainly her relationship with her mother was never as close after the accident. Within months of leaving hospital, and without consulting Nancy, Wissie became engaged to Lord Willoughby D'Eresby and left Cliveden for ever. At the wedding reception Nancy, in a petty show of pique, allowed only barley water to be served. By this time, however, Nancy was becoming involved in a far larger arena of discontent, an arena that seemed a long way from the family home; and yet the family home was to become synonymous with the most unpopular period in Nancy's life. In 1933 Adolf Hitler became Chancellor of Germany, and Cliveden gained a sinister notoriety that it was never to lose.

TWENTY-FIVE

·

Guests for the Weekend

It began slowly. Cliveden was now the home of three politicians, since Bill Astor had become Member of Parliament for Fulham, and the Astors owned the more influential newspapers in the country, so it was not unnatural that the majority of guests who visited the house were Members of Parliament, many from the front bench, as well as journalists and political commentators. Nor was it unnatural that the conversation over dinner or before the fire in the great hall often concerned the rise of the leader of the Third Reich, the man who had united England's enemy into a strong and united Germany. Few considered Hitler a threat to peace, since his ambitions, as he repeatedly declared, were purely national and it seemed unthinkable, a mere fifteen years after the most barbaric war in history, that anyone should contemplate waging such a war again.

But Hitler could not be ignored. To Nancy he was just another Fascist dictator whose policies, like those of Stalin, she abhorred but which had to remain, for the sake of peace, unchallenged. It was intolerable to live side by side with tyranny, but the alternative was too horrendous to consider. Nancy, it must be said, was far from being alone in thinking thus; it was the opinion of the majority. Moreover Hitler as yet had threatened no frontier, nor even intimated that he would. His sole aim, he decreed, was the stabilization of Germany and nothing more, and some degree of comfort could be found in that. But if democracy was prepared to survive alongside Fascism - and a Fascism that also included Mussolini's Italy - there was always the question whether Hitler himself might not be so content with such an enforced isolation. The stronger his country became, the more demands he might make - demands that might, in time, be impossible to accept. Moreover, as Philip Lothian was well aware, the Treaty of Versailles had made punitive and humiliating demands on Germany. As he voiced to Nancy: 'Some people think that we didn't lay the seeds for peace - but for revenge.'

It was imperative, therefore, that approaches should be made to Hitler, that some form of rapport be established in order to effect a peaceful understanding. It seemed to those at Cliveden, and many in Westminster, the most sensible path to take. In fact it seemed the *only* path to take - accept Fascism or fight it, and the latter had to be avoided at all costs.

Waldorf was the first to leave Cliveden and visit Hitler, under the aegis of a Christian Science delegation. Surprisingly, Nancy refused to accompany him, declaring that she had met one dictator and was not prepared to meet another. It was irrational thinking, since Stalin and Hitler were as dissimilar as Churchill and Chamberlain. Whereas Stalin, as leader of a massive, disunited country, realized he had to concentrate on the internal problems of Russia and resist any entanglement with the West, Hitler had no such qualms. His country was economically and militarily strong, his people were loyal – and if they weren't they were either dead or in labour camps – and Germany was a *part* of the West, even if that part was significantly smaller than during the days of the Kaiser. Moreover, if Nancy had been with Waldorf in Munich, she would have met a man who had no remorse over his treatment of Jews, nor any inhibitions about reclaiming land that once belonged to his country. More significantly, she would have met a man who, unlike the cautious, patient Stalin, was quite clearly not only irrational in his desire for more power, but was also mad. Even a fool would have realized that peaceful negotiations with such a man were absurd.

Philip Lothian was not a fool, but he was an idealist. After twenty years he still dreamed the same dream of a league of nations. It obsessed him and distorted his vision, so that on his own visit to Germany he believed everything Hitler said and was even charmed by the Führer. And without doubt Hitler himself was amused to see the very man who had helped to draft the treaty that had maimed his country, the man who was unofficial adviser to Cabinet members and a close friend of the British aristocracy, listening to his every lie, his avowals of peace, and believing them because he wanted to believe. No, Lothian was not a fool, but he was misguided. In a letter to Nancy he described Hitler as 'surprisingly tame'. Before Lothian had even set foot back on English soil, that surprisingly tame man he had just visited had marched into the Rhineland.

Even in Cliveden, standing before Nancy, Waldorf and Robert Brand, Lothian sought to defend Hitler. His idealism made it impossible for him to think otherwise. Peace at any cost must be maintained, and Hitler's actions must therefore be justifiable.

'He believes he was right in entering the Rhineland. After all, we took it away from him. It *is* his own back garden.'

'Right in breaking a treaty?' Brand asked coldly.

'Bob, I am not Hitler's advocate, but he does see Germany threatened by the Communists on one side and the French on the other.'

'That sounds like hell on earth,' Nancy remarked, toying with her pearls, but no one listened.

'And so he's determined to unite the whole of Germany,' Lothian continued, 'simply as a security for peace.'

'And you believe him?'

'Yes, I do.'

'I'm afraid I don't,' Brand replied, moving towards the door.

'Bob, if we don't allow ourselves to trust him, he won't trust us. And next time it won't be the Rhineland, it will be Austria. Then after that, somewhere else. The government's got to recognize that fact. Stop talking amongst themselves, and talk to *him*.'

'The man's insane,' Brand answered. 'What is there to say to him?'

'You sound like Churchill.'

'Maybe so.'

Brand walked out of the room, refusing to stay with Lothian any longer. Their friendship was coming to an end.

'Well, no one listens to Churchill any more,' Nancy smiled, looking up at Lothian. 'Thank God.'

Sitting in an armchair Waldorf said nothing. He had been silent throughout the evening, listening to the discussion. When he finally spoke Nancy and Lothian looked at him in surprise, as if they had forgotten that he was there.

'*I* believe Hitler wants to avoid war at all costs. But not for reasons of altruism or because he wants to be on good terms with us. That's why you're wrong, Philip. Hitler hates Britain, probably more than any other country in Europe. But I don't think he wants the German people involved in another war any more than we do. At least not yet.'

'That shouldn't stop us talking to him.'

'No, it shouldn't, but I don't think it would make the slightest difference to his plans. Like all lunatics, he'd be flattered by the attention. But that's all.'

'Then what *are* his plans?' Nancy asked.

Waldorf hesitated, then said: 'I've listened to Garvin talk. And Halifax. And Dawson and Cranborne. We all have. And I still haven't the slightest idea.'

'Then you haven't listened to the right man.'

'Who?'

'Ribbentrop.'

'God help us, no – '

'Waldorf,' Lothian insisted, 'he's the ambassador here.'

'I *know* who he is.'

'But you don't know *him*. He's very forthright and there is no one who understands Hitler better.'

'I doubt that, and I have no intention of finding out. Now I think I'll go and find Bob. I hate to abandon my guests.'

'He's probably with Phyllis in the library,' Nancy said.

'Then let us go and see them.'

Nancy looked at Waldorf, then at Lothian, then shook her head. 'No, I'll stay here. I'm too comfortable to move.'

Waldorf stared at her, then nodded and walked away.

When the door closed, Lothian was alone with Nancy. Sitting beside her, resisting an impulse to take her hand, he said: 'We've known each other a long time, for which I'll always be grateful. You've allowed me to be as close a friend as I could ever be.'

Nancy remained in profile, her face impassive.

'Nancy – I know that I am right. And you do too. I can see that. If you met the German ambassador – '

'No – '

'Talk to him. He's not an ogre. I could arrange for him to visit you.'

'I said no. I refuse to entertain a Nazi in this house.'

'But you agree that we must keep open negotiations with Germany at the highest level. You've said that often.'

'I know, but – '

'Then in London. You'll find Ribbentrop a charming man. And I know he's anxious to meet you. Will you agree?'

There was a long silence, and then Nancy replied, in a voice barely above a whisper: 'Yes.'

It was the first mistake. Although her intentions were honourable, she failed to realize that entertaining the German ambassador at a private dinner party in her own house, whether in London or at Cliveden, could easily be interpreted as an act of fraternization with Hitler himself. Even though Nancy considered Ribbentrop a buffoon, attacked Fascism across the table and ridiculed Hitler by comparing him to Chaplin, all that could be seen by the prying outsider was a clandestine meeting between a rich and powerful family and the enemy of democracy. It needed little encouragement for someone with a political axe to grind to talk of conspiracies in higher places, of 'deals' being made between prominent politicians and Hitler in a joint attack against Communism. The country was becoming nervous of Hitler and it seemed that nothing was being done to check his territorial ambitions. A scapegoat was needed and the

Astors and their friends at Cliveden now seemed to supply it.

On 17 November 1937 Claud Cockburn, a Communist journalist, seized the opportunity in his magazine *The Week* and declared that Lord Halifax had gone to Germany to propose an Anglo-German truce wherein Great Britain would agree not to interfere in any German expansion in the east. The statement, if true, was sensational enough. It was made even more sensational when Cockburn linked Lord Halifax with the Astors and their associates and thus invented a generic term for such 'high-ranking conspirators'; it was the 'Cliveden Set'.

It was an astute piece of journalism to fan the prejudices and fears of the ordinary people by implying that a rich, aristocratic clique meeting in secret in a grand house were selling the country out to Germany. Though the article was clearly biased and inaccurate – it claimed that Halifax's visit to Cliveden had been arranged without the knowledge of the Foreign Secretary, Anthony Eden, when the truth was that it was Eden who had been at Cliveden, not Halifax – the charges in *The Week* were sufficient, at a nervous time, to cause consternation and single out Cliveden as a seat of pro-Nazi prejudice. Needless to say, Waldorf was astounded by this personal attack on his character and name; he wanted, like every sane man, to avoid war, but would never stoop to allying himself with a madman's tyranny.

'This man is trying to make us a scapegoat, Nancy,' Waldorf declared as he stormed into his wife's boudoir.

'Scapegoat for what?' Nancy inquired casually. She was writing a letter to Phyllis and that was all that mattered to her.

'He accuses us of being pro-Nazi, of using this house to dictate to the government.'

'Has he only just realized that?' Nancy laughed. 'I thought we'd been doing that for thirty years.'

'Nancy – this is serious.'

'It is if you make it so.'

She glanced at the paper, then threw it aside. 'I never realized we were so important.'

'But, Nancy, can't you see what the man is doing?'

'Of course I can. He's just like Dawson or Garvin. He's trying to sell a newspaper. Now throw it on the fire and see if there's any smoke.'

But Waldorf didn't move. He was breathing hard and Nancy glanced at him anxiously. Taking his hand, she said quietly: 'If that man Cockburn sees fit to criticize us because we want to avoid conflict with Germany, then let him find an alternative. Because unless he wants war, I can't see that there is one.'

But Waldorf was not to be consoled. He could ride out any attack on the Astor family because he knew the charges were without foundation. But the problem of Hitler's imperialism still existed and the portents of war were getting nearer. Nancy's inability to recognize the gravity of the situation alarmed him; she was not qualified in foreign affairs and naive in her attempts at diplomacy, as the Ribbentrop incident had demonstrated. He feared that one day, without realizing it, she would go too far. Already she was wasting no time in criticizing her old enemy, Churchill, who saw Hitler for what he was and was urging for rearmament. But Churchill was in the wilderness and Nancy was only one of many who berated him, calling him a warmonger. Moreover, when Chamberlain returned from Munich waving the historic piece of paper declaring 'Peace in our time', she felt herself vindicated. Did this not prove that she had been right all the time? And that those who saw Hitler as a blood-seeking monster without principles were now the misguided fools, not her? She could hold her head up high and let Cockburn go to the devil.

But the 'Cliveden Set' affair had hurt Nancy deeply, as she confided to GBS, among others. Her popular image had been tarnished; she had been linked with people she loathed, tyrants and heathens, and her reputation in Parliament had suffered, as well as the trust given to her by the people of Plymouth, those citizens of a major naval port who would be in the front line of battle as they had been for generations. They, like their Member of Parliament, did not want war, but, unlike her, they were prepared to fight for democracy and not be dictated to by the jackals of Fascism. Even after Chamberlain's return from Munich, Nancy failed to convince them that she too thought like them. The gutter press had worked their mischief too well. Moreover, Nancy's depression was compounded by one of the great tragedies of her life, as if fate had refused to allow her any quarter.

Early in 1937 Phyllis's son fell from a window in New York, although it was more probable that he had jumped and killed himself. Not long afterwards her favourite brother, Buck, died in Virginia just before his fiftieth birthday. Nancy had barely recovered from this when she had to face the most grievous heartbreak of all. Phyllis, her adored sister Phyllis, caught pneumonia while riding in the rain and death seemed inevitable. She was taken to her room in Eyden Hall where Nancy hurried to her bedside.

Kneeling beside her sister, Nancy said: 'Don't you die on me, Phyll. I'll kill you if you do.'

But the words were never heard. As Nancy held Phyllis in her arms she saw her die, taken away from her without a word. The shock was so immense that for a time Nancy was deranged. Her maid, Rose, saw her mistress hysterical for the first time since she had been in her employ, saw her scream in agony before breaking down, sobbing uncontrollably. The hysteria after Phyllis's unexpected death lasted for days, but the mourning lasted Nancy's lifetime. She rarely wrote a letter without mentioning her; she prayed for her day and night, but nothing could make up for the immeasurable loss that equalled the death of her mother.

She felt totally alone and all the comfort from Waldorf and Bob Brand seemed inadequate. Without Phyllis, in this darkest hour of her life, Nancy needed to turn to someone she could love and trust, someone who would understand her – someone, in fact, just like herself. There was only one person like that now. A week after the funeral Nancy left Cliveden early, before anyone was awake, and drove south across the Thames to Wrotham in Kent to visit for the first time the new home of her son, Bobbie Shaw.

TWENTY-SIX

·

The Eve of Destruction

It was an elegant house, close enough to a main road to ease Bobbie's fear of solitude, yet set within sufficient acreage to ensure his privacy and allow room for his innumerable dogs and seventeen peacocks. Nancy arrived just before noon, having lost her way twice, driving the car in her erratic fashion, oblivious of the speed limit. Entering the driveway she saw Bobbie, who was walking with two Irish wolfhounds, stop and look first at the car, then at the driver, in surprise. He was now in his fortieth year and had put on weight, and his face was rounder and pinker from alcohol. From within the house music could be heard, a record playing Big Band jazz. Stepping out of the car, Nancy slowly looked around her as if passing judgment on the garden, the lawns and finally on her son.

'You really found a nest in the wilds, didn't you?'

Bobbie gave a brief smile and walked towards her. He was delighted to see her, but he neither said it nor showed it in his manner. 'I'm impressed that you found it.'

'Well, since you don't come to visit *me*, I have to make the effort myself.'

'Mother, I'd hate to add fire to the Cliveden Set. You've got enough trouble as it is.'

Nancy pulled a face: 'You been believing that nonsense too?' And then: 'You've got greenfly.'

Bobbie laughed and watched as Nancy peered at a row of rose bushes, flicking the leaves aside as if inspecting for dust. A door opened at the side of the house and a young man in an open-neck shirt and corduroy trousers appeared, began to walk out into the daylight, then suddenly retreated.

'I assume,' Bobbie said quietly, 'you don't want to be introduced.'

'No, thank you.'

The young man watched from the shadows for a moment, then closed the door. The music suddenly stopped and there was silence. Immediately Nancy appeared to regret that she was there, walking away from Bobbie, not looking at him, and glaring at the peacocks that wandered aimlessly around her feet, trailing their tails on the grass.

'If you don't like it here,' Bobbie suggested, recognizing the mood, 'we could go to the village. There's a rather *louche* olde worlde pub – no, on second thoughts, perhaps not.'

'I won't stay long,' Nancy remarked dismissively. The encounter was not what she had anticipated. She wanted to relax, to find comfort, but she was incapable of it. 'I was just passing by.'

'Passing by?' Bobbie said, startled. 'But nobody passes by in Kent, unless they're leaving the country. You're not leaving the country, are you?'

'Bobbie, can we stop this?'

'But, Mama, you've won. "Peace with honour. Peace for our time." Isn't that what Chamberlain said?'

'Then why are you so cynical about it?'

267

Bobbie looked at her, suddenly saw the pain in her eyes and kissed her on the cheek. 'Come and sit down.'

'What have you done to your hair?'

'Just sit down.'

'You been *dyeing* it?'

Without comment, Bobbie gently led Nancy to a bench set against a stone wall covered in clematis. 'Sit down for a while. We'll have some tea in a moment.'

Nancy hesitated, stared at Bobbie's hair, now stained with a reddish dye, then shrugged and reluctantly sat down. She made no attempt to talk, being unable to think of anything to say. A face appeared at a window of the house, then ducked quickly away.

'David was down here last week,' Bobbie said, making conversation. 'He gave me that plum tree. At least, I *think* it's a plum tree. Certainly not a *palm* tree....'

Silence.

Then quietly, changing the mood, he said: 'The press have been treating you pretty badly, haven't they?'

'I've never worried about that.'

'You look as though you do.'

'I've lost a sister and a brother in one year,' Nancy replied sharply. 'That's why I look like this.'

'I'm sorry. That was unfair of me.' Bobbie leaned over and took her hand: 'Well, you still have me. We'll survive them all. That's if there's no war.'

'Of course there'll be no war. Why do you say a thing like that? You're just thinking like the others. Are you sure you haven't got Churchill hiding in that house as well?'

Bobbie immediately laughed and lit a cigarette, studying his mother's face. He was always surprised at how young she

268

still looked. The walls of his room were dominated by photographs of her.

'Mother, I've always said I know you better than anyone else. We're almost like husband and wife.'

'Perish the thought!'

'But you're a fool to trust Hitler. Even more of a fool to listen to Philip.'

'Now Bobbie, don't *you* tell me what to think – '

'No one could do that. I just – '

'Just what?'

Bobbie hesitated, not wanting to provoke an argument, but Nancy was already on her feet and striding across the lawn.

'I must have been mad to come down here.' Then, turning around, she shouted back: 'I've always stood by you, Bobbie Shaw. No matter what you did. I thought you might have done the same for me!'

Bobbie said nothing. He could only watch as Nancy got in her car and reversed wildly along the drive, the tyres sliding on the gravel.

At the gate, she thrust her head out of the car window and yelled: 'It's a *cherry* tree! And you planted it in the wrong place.'

And then the car was hurtling away towards the main road and northwards back to London. Bobbie didn't move until the noise of the engine had faded into the distance, then he whistled to the dogs and walked to the village to drink alone.

On 5 October 1938, in a speech to the House of Commons, Winston Churchill gave his opinion of Chamberlain's appeasement policy with Hitler that had now found the approval of the majority of the country, including the royal family. Churchill's words from the backbenches were typically direct:

'I will begin by saying the most unpopular and most unwelcome thing. I will begin by saying what everybody would like to ignore or forget, but which must nevertheless be stated, namely, that we have sustained a total and unmitigated defeat and that France has suffered even more than we have.'

The reaction was immediate, none more so than from Nancy, who sat directly behind Churchill and whose shout of 'Nonsense!' was heard on all sides of the House. Her voice against him came as no surprise to Churchill; he had been hearing it for over a quarter of a century. As early as 1912, as a fellow guest with the Astors at Blenheim Palace, he had spent the weekend embroiled in a violent argument with Nancy until it reached a stage of such intensity that Nancy declared:

'Winston, if I was married to you I'd put poison in your coffee.'

Churchill had replied immediately: 'Nancy, if I was married to you, I'd drink it.'

Twenty-six years later, their mutual animosity was more public, if less eloquent.

'When the noble lady cried "Nonsense!" ' Churchill continued with only the briefest nod in Nancy's direction, 'she could not have heard the Chancellor of the Exchequer admit in his illuminating and comprehensive speech just now that Herr Hitler had gained in this particular leap forward in substance all he set out to gain – '

'Which is *peace*!' Nancy interrupted.

'I thought I might be allowed to make that point in its

due place, and I propose to deal with it. The Chancellor of the Exchequer said it was the first time Herr Hitler had been made to retract – I think that was the word – in any degree. We really must not waste time upon the difference between the positions reached at Berchtesgaden, at Godesberg and at Munich. They can be very simply epitomized, if the House will permit me to vary the metaphor. One pound was demanded at the pistol's point. When it was given, *two* pounds were demanded at the pistol's point. Finally, the dictator consented to take one pound, seventeen and sixpence and the rest as promises of good will for the future.'

Nancy continued to heckle Churchill, but now she was a lone voice, though she was unaware of it. The speech had deflated much of the false optimism in the House and even the most ardent Chamberlainites were subdued. But not so Nancy Astor. To her, appeasement had been achieved and that was all that mattered. She had no doubts, no fears, and refused to believe that Hitler would or could renege on an agreement with the Prime Minister of Great Britain. It was a time of personal rejoicing that at times reached absurd heights. She began to ridicule the press, little realizing that she was being seen as a figure of mockery, something to be jeered at. Cartoons were drawn of her dancing like an obedient chorus girl to Goebbels' tune; she became a target for jokes and socialist propaganda. That she was premature in her behaviour, and misguided in the manner of it, was undeniably clear. But she had never learned to be objective about herself, to see herself as others saw her, and it was impossible to change her now, although her own husband, in exasperation, tried.

'Nancy, aren't you aware of what is happening?' Waldorf

asked her one morning after photographs of her dancing a jig of defiance were circulated. 'I no longer open any letters any more because I know what they will say. They're beginning to hate us.'

'I pay no attention to that kind of poison,' Nancy replied.

'Then it's about time you did. Look at these photographs. How can you behave like this? If only there was an excuse. You were drunk and didn't know what you were doing. But you did. Do you know what you look like? An overage soubrette grasping for publicity.'

'How *dare* you say that to me? How dare you behave like a *viper*? You've been bitter against me for ten years or more now. Because you hate me being in the limelight and you're not. You never did want me to be MP for Plymouth.'

It was a cruel and thoughtless attack on the only man who had stood by her, selflessly and without complaint, even at the bitterest of times. It was an attack of stubborn pride without logic to it or an awareness of what she was doing. And Waldorf knew it and despaired for her.

'Nancy, you know that's not true. I've been proud of you. During the War I saw you work day and night caring for the wounded and never once complaining. You gave men who had given up hope a reason to live. I saw you in Plymouth working in ghettoes in rain and snow. Those people there would have died for you. That's why I was proud. You achieved so much for so many people. Is that how you want to be remembered? Or like this – an easy joke for the comedians, a caricature to be jeered at?'

Without waiting for an answer, Waldorf continued as diplomatically as possible:

'Despite what Chamberlain said, everyone is still frightened, Nancy. Frightened of another war. They need reassurance from someone they respect. For them, it's not a game any more.'

If these words had any effect on Nancy, she didn't show it. She still felt betrayed by Waldorf's scepticism regarding the Chamberlain appeasement; only Philip Lothian remained a personal ally. But soon even that alliance was broken, not by the individuals themselves, but by events that were far beyond their control. Defying Chamberlain, defying Britain, defying democracy itself, Hitler sent German troops into Bohemia and Moravia and then into the city of Prague. In a proclamation Hitler announced with cold defiance to the world that 'Czechoslovakia now ceases to exist.'

It was the end of appeasement, the end of all the dreams. Naturally there was still some hope that war could be avoided, but not for Nancy any more. Philip Lothian, a broken and disillusioned man, left England as the British ambassador for Washington, from where, as he confided in Waldorf, he believed he would never return. Nancy avoided saying goodbye. Like a woman scorned, her hatred for Hitler was of such intensity that she was put on his blacklist, side by side with Churchill. She now saw war as inevitable and turned her energy towards fighting it.

There was no room for regret in her character now, nor did she feel any shame for wanting peace at any cost. All frivolity was abandoned and she became the politician, the representative of the people. The country was about to fight for its survival once again, and personal sentiments and prejudices were no longer important. In time she would defy the majority of her own party, cast aside her pride, and vote for Churchill as Prime Minister because she believed him to be the only man who could save Britain. But before that, in the summer of 1939, as Hitler continued his invasion of Europe, Nancy travelled to where she was needed most and where she belonged. When the siren of war was finally sounded, she would begin her fight overlooking the English Channel, in Plymouth.

TWENTY-SEVEN

.

The Burning of Plymouth

Since it was a naval port, there were no illusions that Plymouth would not be one of the first casualties of the war. Despite every precaution and defence the bombing started in earnest in March 1941. By good fortune the King and Queen had just left when the bombers started to arrive, coming in from the east by night. One of the first hits was on the Astor home in Elliott Terrace while Nancy was relaxing after dinner, waiting for Waldorf, now the Lord Mayor, to return from a tour of the city.

As the bombing increased Nancy, still in evening dress and anxious for Waldorf's safety, went searching the streets for him, defying the warnings of the ARP wardens and oblivious to her own danger as buildings began to burn and houses collapsed. She found Waldorf in a tenement square of smoke and rubble, carrying buckets from a pump as a chain of men vainly attempted to put out a fire. This primitive method of firefighting horrified Nancy; but when the dawn light revealed the extent of the devastation, her horror turned to anger.

'There goes thirty years of our life,' she said bitterly to Waldorf as they stood amid the smouldering ruins of

Plymouth. More than a square mile of the city had been bombed and the onslaught had only just begun.

'We'll build it again.'

But Nancy wasn't listening: 'Half of this could have been saved. We've been at war for two years and we're still fighting fire with *buckets*!'

'Nancy – I've been warning the Town Hall for months that this would happen, but they wouldn't listen.'

'Wouldn't listen! Well, by heaven, if *they* won't listen, I'll make sure Westminster does. I'm not going to let this city die for nothing.'

In the House of Commons her anger had far from abated, and her attack drew blood from the opening salvo: 'The very fact that the government are bringing in a Bill like this after we have had six months of fire blitz and bomb blitz shows that there is something wrong with the Home Front.'

The murmurs of disapproval began to be heard, a sound that was now familiar to Nancy. She was no longer the popular lady politician of twenty years before; her behaviour during the Munich crisis, her increasing refusal to toe the party line and her flaunting of protocol had brought disfavour. She had made too many enemies on her own side of the House, either through personal criticism or simply because she no longer attempted to court them with her charm. Her American birthright was suddenly used against her when America hesitated for too long before entering the war; her sex was no longer an advantage or even an excuse for her erratic behaviour, since there were now many women in Parliament who were far more worthy than Nancy. She may have been the first, but that was twenty-two years and another generation ago, a long time for someone who was still a backbencher. Moreover, her age had begun to show – not in her physical appearance, but at the times when she would ramble during a speech, losing the thread of her argument, and would digress on to trivial matters as if she was standing before the hearth in her own home. In short it was becoming clear that, as a member of His Majesty's government in a time of world crisis, Nancy was becoming an embarrassment, even to her own party. The tragedy was that she did not know it. Or if she did, she refused to admit it.

'I put this to the House,' Nancy continued, ignoring the comments around her. 'Supposing you had a general who had lost twelve battles, would you not begin to wonder whether you ought to get rid of him?'

Next to her Mavis Tate, one of the few friends she had left in Parliament, looked up at her anxiously.

'The Home Secretary has lost twelve battles because there have been twelve towns blitzed, bombed and burnt. I do not only blame him – I blame the whole government.'

The uproar was immediate despite the Speaker's demands for order. Nancy was now openly making herself an enemy of the very party to which she belonged. It was tantamount to political suicide.

But still she ignored the warnings, and continued: 'I knew, when the battle came to Plymouth, that I had no respect for the feelings of the local authorities. But I was not thinking of them. I was thinking of the people. Everyone knows in these blitzed towns, and in the House of Commons, that the first thing a local authority wants to do when a town is blitzed is to cover up its mistakes. I was not going to have mistakes covered up in Plymouth. When I was in Virginia – '

'You're not in Virginia now!' a voice called out. 'Keep to the point. If you have one.'

'All right. I'll keep to the point by saying this to the Home Secretary. Let him make his speeches, let him rouse the country, but for Heaven's sake, get someone else to do the job!'

As Nancy sat down the jeering began again, even louder.

'Mavis,' Nancy said, turning to her neighbour, 'I'm beginning to understand what it was like at Gettysburg.'

'Has the Honourable Member for Plymouth Sutton finished speaking?' another voice called out. 'Because if she has – '

'Yes!' Nancy stood up and shouted back. 'She has.'

Waldorf, as always, was the first one to be aware of what was happening to Nancy, not only from his associates in Westminster but also from what he observed himself in the privacy of his own home. It was no secret, even to the children, that Nancy had begun to turn against her husband, using him as a scapegoat for the faults of others, either in the House of Commons or in her own family. She rarely consulted him now about anything and, although they were the same age, Waldorf's continued ill-health had aged him beyond his years. He had neither Nancy's strength nor her energy, and avoided arguments at all costs. Moreover, he knew that Nancy's outbursts were a way of masking a private anguish that she would never reveal to anyone, except perhaps to her God. The anguish was a mixture of loneliness and depression brought about by the fear that her political career had been a failure and that it might be too late to do anything about it. She had clung to the hope that Philip Lothian, who had remained loyal in his love and admiration for her, would be her saviour. But now even that dream was cruelly denied her. In the winter of 1940, while in America, Lothian became gravely ill and died during the night of 12 December. He refused any medical help except for a Christian Science practitioner, thus keeping his promise to Nancy. But his death brought only more grief as Nancy realized she would never see him again. Cliveden was now like a mausoleum, with her children living elsewhere and only Waldorf sharing the same roof. The emotional estrangement between them caused Nancy to turn her depression into action either in Plymouth or in Westminster. Only these two avenues mattered to her now.

All this Waldorf knew and understood, while attempting to disguise his concern regarding Nancy's undisciplined behaviour in Parliament. As he remarked to Bobbie, now in the Civil Defence after being turned down by the Scots Greys:

'We've all got to be a little more patient with Nancy. Even though she looks half her age, she can't continue for ever.'

'But of *course* she can,' Bobbie had replied in her defence, misunderstanding Waldorf's words. To Bobbie, the idea of his mother no longer existing was impossible to contemplate. 'She'll outlive us all.'

'Yes,' Waldorf said finally, 'she'll outlive us all.'

But if Westminster had turned against Nancy, the citizens of Plymouth considered her nothing less than a heroine. Their admiration for her was limitless as she risked her life in the bombed streets, visiting shelters at night to comfort the children, and organizing hospitals, food wagons and temporary homes. By day she raised their morale by instructing a band to play on the Hoe, encouraging everyone

to dance as if the war didn't exist. If anyone was reluctant to
join in, she would seize his arm and spin him round in a
hornpipe, saying: 'Come on, now! We're not going to let
Hitler get us down, are we?'

The image of Nancy, now in her sixties, head thrown
back in laughter as she skipped along the shoreline while the
band played yet again, was never forgotten. She was a min-
istering angel and inspiration to the city she loved above all
others and never wanted to leave; and if she was looked on
with disfavour by her fellow MPs, none of her constituents
in Plymouth, in a time of battle, would want her to be
otherwise.

The time of battle, however, would one day be over, and
Waldorf on his part turned his attention towards the future.
His first objective was the replanning and eventual rebuild-
ing of Plymouth, to which aim he persuaded his colleagues
to hire the architect Patrick Abercombie. Both men shared
the same vision of a new, modern Plymouth when peace
finally came, but for Waldorf it would be a Plymouth where
he would no longer have any power. After suffering a mild
heart attack he had decided to resign as Lord Mayor at the
end of the war, and his resignation was accepted. But, as he
feared, it was not only *his* resignation that was demanded.

Nancy's unpopularity in Westminster was now echoed
by the local Conservatives in Plymouth. They believed that
she ought not to stand again, that her political instability
could only do the city harm, and that a post-war Plymouth
needed someone younger and more in touch with contemporary issues. They believed this, but none dared tell Nancy
to her face; that unwelcome task was placed in the hands of
Waldorf, and it was to prove one of the most painful decisions he ever agreed to. By 1944 he could see that the tide

of political opinion was turning and, that even if Nancy was willing or capable of adhering to Conservative policy, the chances of her winning the next election were doubtful. Moreover, Waldorf feared that she was no longer fit enough, mentally and physically, to survive another general election. Nancy's personality and charm would no longer be enough; post-war Britain would be demanding a new government, new faces in power, with none of the reminders of the past. Waldorf chose to tell Nancy himself that her political career had to end. He did it not only because he thought it was right, but more importantly because he loved her. On the beach in Plymouth where twenty-five years earlier he had offered her the key to Parliament, he now took it away. For a year Nancy had resisted, but surrender was inevitable.

'Is it true that even Churchill could lose the election when the war's over?' she asked, refusing to look at her husband but staring out at the sea.

'It's not as insane as it sounds. The country will want a change. It's human nature. They don't want to be reminded of war any more or anything associated with it. Churchill could well go the way of Lloyd George.'

'And you think *I* will, too?'

'Yes,' Waldorf replied quietly. 'The Tories may not even adopt you as a candidate. I'm sorry, Nancy, but that's the truth.'

Nancy slowly turned and looked at him: 'You all want me out, don't you? You. Bill. The Whips. Everyone.'

'No one's denying you what you have achieved in Plymouth. I'm not talking to you as a politician but as a husband. Leave Westminster with honour. Resign undefeated.'

'Where I was born, resignation *is* a defeat.'

Waldorf hesitated, knowing what he had to say and wishing it could be otherwise. 'Nancy, I have to tell you this. If you insist on standing for the next election, I won't support you.'

'You would go as far as that?' she screamed in horror.

'Yes, I would. Because I love you too much – '

But Nancy was no longer listening. Brushing past him, she strode up the beach towards the waiting car, on the road, then she drove away fast, leaving Waldorf alone.

The next day, in Plymouth Town Hall, she publicly revealed her bitterness towards Waldorf as she offered her resignation.

'Today I have done a thing that has been terrible for me – one of the hardest things I have ever done in my life, but a thing that every man in the world will approve of. I have said that I will not fight the next election because my husband does not want me to. I have had twenty-five years in the House of Commons and I am bound to obey. Isn't that a triumph for the men?'

Nancy waited after this question, expecting a reaction from the hall as had happened so often before. She listened for voices urging her to stay, for the familiar shouts of support and encouragement. But none came. The hall was silent, and Nancy finally knew that her days in Parliament were over. Raising her head, she looked at the giant photograph of herself hanging above the stage, then said in a steady voice:

'Take it down! You won't be needing it any more.' In the wings, unseen by anyone, she collapsed. It was over.

In 1945 she left Westminster for ever, without illusions. 'I'll miss the House, but it won't miss me. It never misses anybody. I've seen them all go – Lloyd George, Asquith,

Baldwin, Chamberlain – and not one of them was missed. MPs are like ships that disappear over the horizon. Some of them carry a light. Others don't. That's the only difference.'

After twenty-five years Plymouth was no longer her home. No memorial was built for her; no statue was carved. At sixty-six Nancy was now a private citizen once more, viewing her future with despair and living with a husband she could never forgive. To her Waldorf, and Waldorf alone, was responsible for the destruction of her political life, and none could convince her otherwise.

'Answer me this,' she would say. 'What, in heaven's name, am I going to live for now?'

TWENTY-EIGHT

·

Days of Solitude

In the years after the war Nancy, almost wilfully, spent less and less time with Waldorf. Apart from Bobbie her children were now all married, and although she visited them occasionally she became more and more a recluse, rarely staying under the same roof as Waldorf. The house in St James's Square was sold and another bought in Hill Street, Mayfair, for her to live in alone. It was a demonstration of her independence and her estrangement from her husband, and the only man she allowed to remain there as a guest was her brother-in-law Robert, now Lord Brand. Losing all interest in public life, refusing to be on committees, shunning the press, Nancy rarely left the Hill Street house, returning to Cliveden only when Waldorf was not there. She never wrote to him or attempted to contact him; her resentment towards him was far too deep.

As for Waldorf, his health had declined to such an extent that even climbing stairs had become an effort. Consequently he chose to sleep in a box-room on the ground floor of Cliveden that was almost spartan in appearance – it contained only a single camp bed, a table and a blanket to keep out the draught from the window. His isolation was forced upon him, and his loneliness increased. At times he would stay with one or other of his sons but felt himself an intruder and returned to Cliveden, often without warning. He acquired an electrically driven wheelchair and would explore the house, finding rooms and places that he hadn't seen for years. It became one of his rare moments of happiness. But if his health was failing, he refused to dwell on it. It was not himself that he cared about, but Nancy. He would inquire about her every day and worry about her, constantly seeking a means to re-establish their relationship and bring Nancy out of her self-imposed seclusion. The problem was how to entice her back into public life, or, more pertinently, on to the political platform. It could not be her own platform any more, but it could be someone else's, someone close to her, such as one of her own sons. Both Bill and Jakie had refused any help from their mother, considering it more of a hindrance than an asset, and perhaps they were right. But there remained a third son who was about to enter politics and who, Waldorf believed, needed all the assistance he could get.

So, on the pretext of organizing a family reunion, Waldorf invited Michael Astor, the most cultured of all the Astors, to Cliveden, as well as Wissie and Bobbie Shaw, the latter being the only one knowing the true nature of the occasion. Waldorf also invited Nancy herself, and much to his surprise she accepted – more, it seemed, out of curiosity than for old times' sake.

Bobbie arrived at Cliveden first and found Waldorf waiting for him on the terrace. On the parterre below he noticed Nancy walking alone, stopping now and then to glance suspiciously at the house, as if she sensed a conspiracy. Both men shook hands and, as they did, they both noticed the change in each other's appearance. Waldorf's face was gaunt, the eyes sunk deep into the skull, his hair and moustache white. As for Bobbie he was now, at fifty-two, almost obese, his face permanently flushed beneath the dyed hair. Neither man, naturally, made any reference to this either by word or by look.

'Michael's here,' Bobbie said.

'And Wissie?'

'No. Just Michael.'

'Have you said anything to him?'

'No. I thought I'd leave that to you.'

Bobbie then glanced over the balustrade towards Nancy and added: 'Does Lady Bracknell know all about this?'

'No – '

'Is it still non-speaks between you two?'

'Of course not,' Waldorf replied, avoiding Bobbie's eye.

'I hope she appreciates what you've done.'

'I'm her husband.'

'Yes, sir. You are.'

It was at this moment that Michael walked quickly along the terrace from the house. He smiled as he greeted Bobbie, shook his father's hand and asked in all innocence: 'Now what exactly are we celebrating?'

No one answered.

'Well, that's why we're here, isn't it?' he asked, but he was now puzzled.

'*Courage, mon brave*,' Bobbie whispered and walked away.

'What?'

Finally Waldorf gestured to a chair and Michael sat down.

'Michael,' he heard his father say, 'I think your election campaign needs some help. Don't you?'

'Help? What kind of help, sir?'

But Waldorf didn't reply. Instead he was staring in the direction of Nancy who had stopped and was looking up at them, her hand shading her eyes. It was only then that Michael realized. But it was too late.

'So you want me to speak for you? Now you're showing more sense than any of your brothers.'

Michael stood in the boudoir, his shoulders pressed against the wall like a cornered animal. Before him Nancy strutted up and down, her whole body suddenly alive with renewed energy. Her eyes were bright and she was laughing, then frowning, pulling at her pearl necklace and pushing back her hair as if she was back on the platform once more and the spotlight was on.

'Well then, I'll talk about the humbug of the Labour Party. I *know* the Labour Party. They preach brotherly love but they're ruled by envy. They squeal like pigs too when I tell them this – but I know it's true.'

'Mama, tell them what you like,' Michael stammered nervously, 'but – could you please leave me out of this?'

'I like your cheek. I'll say what I like. You've given me an idea. I'm going to make my speech about *you*. I'll pay you out, Michael. I'll tell the meeting that politics bore you stiff and that all you really like is painting. I'll tell them you're just a lothario, an artist and not a very good husband. And that you make fun of them all behind their backs and that they shouldn't vote for you.'

Michael closed his eyes in despair as if attempting to dismiss a nightmare.

But Nancy continued regardless, almost unaware that he was there. 'How would you like that?' Her voice had now changed to a Virginian accent. 'I'll tell 'em you don't know nothin'. I'll tell 'em you're crazy. I'll tell 'em I got a son who's crazy. That ought to rouse them if nothing else will. Or – ' The accent was suddenly English again. 'I might tell them how *privileged* they are to have the opportunity to vote for my distinguished son, how *privileged* they are to be addressed by his distinguished mother. But that wouldn't rouse them. No. That would put them to sleep. Now get on with you. I must work at this.'

The door was being opened and Michael felt himself being propelled into the hall.

'Oh, dear God,' Nancy said, her hands thrust into the air. 'I never knew that I could miss anything as much as the House of Commons. Never in my life.'

The door was slammed shut and Michael, in a daze, stood staring at the grinning face of Bobbie who was holding out a glass of whisky towards him.

'I think you need this.'

Taking it, Michael slumped morosely into the nearest armchair. 'I should never have agreed to it. I'll lose the election.'

'Well, that would be a step for democracy.'

'I can't let her on to that platform. Bill and Jakie were right.'

Bobbie sighed and turned towards Michael: 'You don't understand, do you?'

'Understand what?'

'Letting mother speak is not just for *her*. It's for Waldorf. Don't you realize that? Ever since mother left Parliament – well, you know what I mean. You've seen them together.'

'I know. But you didn't hear her in there.'

'I can imagine. Now drink up. Let's celebrate.'

'Celebrate what?'

'Why, you ol' jackass,' Bobbie replied, mimicking his mother, 'you don't think Lady Astor's goin' to lose that election for you? Do you now?'

Bobbie was right. Despite her increasingly irrational behaviour, Nancy ensured Michael's entry into Parliament, short-lived though it was. Regrettably, her feelings towards Waldorf remained unchanged, and she refused even to acknowledge that he might be responsible for her brief return to the political arena.

'Your father talks people *out* of Parliament, not *into* it,' she snapped at Michael. And nothing more could be said. It was to be the last opportunity for a reconciliation between Waldorf and Nancy. In September 1952 Waldorf suffered another stroke and was confined to his box-room at Cliveden. It was clear now that he was dying and he was visited by all his family – all, that is, except his own wife. For three weeks Nancy refused to go near his room or even accept that Waldorf was ill. To her children it was the most callous act imaginable.

'Why do you hate Papa so much?' Wissie finally asked her, horrified that her own mother should deny comfort to a man who had selflessly dedicated his whole life to her.

At first Nancy had refused to answer, sitting alone in her boudoir, clutching the Bible in her hand. It was only after Wissie persisted with her questioning that she spoke, her voice quiet, almost a whisper: 'I don't hate him, Wissie. I just don't want to see him die. I sat by the bedside of the only two people I really loved and watched them being taken away from me. I hated them for that. If I didn't hate *them*, I'd have to hate God. And that's something I could never do.'

'But Papa needs you now. You just can't leave him alone as if he didn't exist. You've hurt him.'

It was then that Nancy looked up, her eyes suddenly filling with tears. 'Oh, my child, don't you think I *know* that? I've been wed to Waldorf for almost fifty years and I can't see my life without him. We were born on the same day and I always prayed we'd die on the same day. He's got no right to – ' As if in agony Nancy turned away, cursing her own stubborn pride. 'Oh my God, sometimes I think I'm going crazy. Insanity in the family, Nannie. Insanity in the family – ' And then she was running to Wissie, hugging her like a child. 'Oh, Wissie, give me strength. I'm going to need it so much.'

That evening Nancy walked alone along the corridor to Waldorf's room, entering it with stage-managed casualness as if nothing was wrong and she was just passing by. 'Everybody thinks you're dying,' she said with a smile, closing the door. 'They've already built the coffin for you. You're not dying, though, are you?'

In the bed, Waldorf smiled and shook his head, grateful to see her and aware of the role they were both playing.

'No, Nancy. Of course I'm not.'

'That's what I thought. I told them that you were just being lazy.'

'I'm ashamed to say that you're right.'

'Well, this time I'll forgive you.'

Nancy looked at him and was startled by his appearance, but she disguised her reaction and sat on the bed next to him. 'You're a very handsome man. Do you know that?'

'Thank you – '

'It's lucky I caught you when I did. I'd hate to think what hussy you might have ended up with.'

'A doe-eyed vamp after my money?'

'Something like that – '

Nancy suddenly felt her pose begin to crumble and stood up to leave, hiding her face.

'Nancy?' Waldorf asked quietly. 'Would you read to me?'

'What would you like me to read?' Nancy asked, without turning around.

'The Ninety-first Psalm. The one we used to read together.'

Slowly Nancy turned and stared at the book in Waldorf's hand, then at Waldorf himself. He was sitting up, smiling at her, looking suddenly young and relaxed like the man she had first met many years before on the ocean liner.

'I love you, Waldorf,' Nancy said. She opened the book and began to read: 'He that dwelleth in the secret place of the most High shall abide under the shadow of the Almighty. I will say of the Lord, He is my refuge and my fortress: my God, in Him I will trust.'

Waldorf Astor died on 30 September 1952. He was buried at Cliveden.

It was only after Waldorf's death that Nancy finally admitted how much she had loved him and how much she missed him. She was now seventy-three years old, a widow, with almost nothing left to live for. Although she was still physically strong, her mind was failing her and there were times when she believed she was back in her beloved Virginia, walking across the lawns of Mirador. In the tradition of the rich widow she travelled the world, visiting countries for the first and last time, but ultimately she was bored, a lonely woman living in hotel rooms and large apartments or staying with relatives in one place or another. Her closest friend remained her son, Bobbie, as he had always been, despite the fact that their quarrels increased. He despaired seeing her deteriorate mentally, but never failed to love her. 'We are like husband and wife,' he would repeat, hiding his grief in alcohol when she ridiculed him, making him a scapegoat for her own loneliness.

In 1964, when Cliveden became the centre for another scandal, Nancy suddenly collapsed while visiting her daughter in Lincolnshire. She remained in a coma for several days and then opened her eyes to see her bed surrounded by flowers.

'Is it my birthday or am I dying?' she asked Jakie.

'A bit of both,' he replied.

Her last word, screamed out into the night, was 'Waldorf!'

In death they were both finally reunited, as the ashes of Waldorf and Nancy were mingled together and placed in a vault, wrapped in a Confederate flag, at Cliveden. There was now nothing left on this earth for Bobbie Shaw, and he ended his own unhappy life by committing suicide. His grave lies alongside that of his mother.

MORE ABOUT PENGUINS
AND PELICANS

For further information about books available from Penguins please write to Dept EP, Penguin Books Ltd, Harmondsworth, Middlesex UB7 0DA.

In the U.S.A.: For a complete list of books available from Penguins in the United States write to Dept CS, Penguin Books, 625 Madison Avenue, New York, New York 10022.

In Canada: For a complete list of books available from Penguins in Canada write to Penguin Books Canada Ltd, 2801 John Street, Markham, Ontario L3R 1B4.

In Australia: For a complete list of books available from Penguins in Australia write to the Marketing Department, Penguin Books Australia Ltd, P.O. Box 257, Ringwood, Victoria 3134.

In New Zealand: For a complete list of books available from Penguins in New Zealand write to the Marketing Department, Penguin Books (N.Z.) Ltd, P.O. Box 4019, Auckland 10.

Also by Derek Marlowe in Penguins

THE DISAPPEARANCE

Jay's wife is missing. He's offered four times his usual rate to kill a man called Feather. He dithers. Goes places. Searching for Celandine, dodging his assignment, running into trouble.

A contact is killed. Friends blur into foes. More and more it looks like Jay's last job . . .

The Disappearance is a tense, close-knit triumph in which Derek Marlowe deploys highly wrought thriller tactics to X-ray the soul of a man whose cynicism has hardened into an arctic despair.

and, coming soon,

THE RICH BOY FROM CHICAGO

Freddie Geddes, born into a rich Jewish family, is a 20th-century outsider, whose life is undercut by a central irony – that he narrowly escaped death at the hands of notorious killers Leopold and Loeb. Despite an unsuccessful marriage to an English aristocrat and a doomed, passionate affair, Geddes is protected by a curious innocence. His life intertwines with a working-class Englishman, Henry Bax, an ambitious, ruthless and penniless young man who, unlike Freddie, knows exactly what he wants and who envies Freddie his success.

Derek Marlowe's skill in creating an atmosphere of sinister unrest makes this a compelling story, in which a subtle blend of fact and fiction suggests, rather than describes, fashionable society in the twentieth century.

ORIGINAL SINS
Lisa Alther
'Triumphantly surpasses her splendid novel, *Kinflicks*' –
Cosmopolitan

When Americans believed in God, Fidelity and the Flag Lisa Alther's
five 'heroes' were childhood friends in small-town Tennessee. In this
triumphant successor to *Kinflicks* she cuts their various careers through
the sixties and seventies – back to nature, on to New York, into Civil
Rights, women's liberation, the sexual revolution – and gives us a novel
that is gutsy, funny, stylish . . . a slice of American life you've never
tasted before.

A WOMAN'S AGE
Rachel Billington

Stepping into the world of country houses and nannies at the turn of
the century, we follow the life of Violet Hesketh, from childhood,
through two world wars, the roaring twenties, the depression, through
years of social and political upheaval, to the fulfilment of her ambitions,
as a leading public figure and politician in the seventies.

'A remarkable history of women over three-quarters of a century' –
Financial Times